Evie Woods is the author of *The Story Collector* and *The Lost Bookshop*, the international bestseller, which was shortlisted for a British Book Award, translated into 30 languages and sold over a million copies.

Evie lives on the West Coast of Ireland where she escapes the inclement weather by writing stories that push the boundary between what is real and what we wish were so. Drawing inspiration from the unseen forces that shape our lives and the healing power of storytelling, she invites the reader to embrace the magic that exists in our ordinary lives.

www.eviewoods.com

𝕏 x.com/evgaughan
instagram.com/eviewoods.author
tiktok.com/@eviewoods.author

Also by Evie Woods

The Lost Bookshop
The Story Collector

THE MYSTERIOUS BAKERY ON RUE DE PARIS

EVIE WOODS

One More Chapter
a division of HarperCollins*Publishers* Ltd
1 London Bridge Street
London SE1 9GF
www.harpercollins.co.uk
HarperCollins*Publishers*
Macken House, 39/40 Mayor Street Upper,
Dublin 1, D01 C9W8, Ireland

This paperback edition 2025
25 26 27 28 29 LBC 5 4 3 2 1
First published in Great Britain in ebook format
by HarperCollins*Publishers* 2025
Copyright © Evie Woods 2025
Evie Woods asserts the moral right to
be identified as the author of this work

A catalogue record of this book is available from the British Library

UK ISBN: 978-0-00-870670-8
US ISBN: 978-0-00-871322-5

Printed and bound in the United States

To all those with a taste for magic

Prologue

Nestled among the cobblestone streets of Compiègne, there existed a bakery unlike any other. When customers crossed the threshold, they found not only sustenance for the stomach, but also for the soul. In the soft light of dawn, the baker began each day in the basement with flour-dusted hands, working a secret ingredient into the dough.

Before long, rumours were whispered throughout the town of a mysterious bakery whose pastries offered a taste of magic that could chase away even the darkest of sorrows. Just one bite of a croissant might bring luck, unlock a precious memory or reveal hidden longings.

But dark clouds were looming on the horizon and when the war began, everything changed.

Chapter One

A recipe for disaster doesn't require that many ingredients. An unhealthy amount of wishful thinking, mixed with a large dollop of devil-may-care when it comes to reading maps. Add a sprinkle of desperation distilled from wanting so badly for things to change, and you had the perfect recipe for my current situation – barricaded inside a toilet cubicle at the Gare du Nord with only my shame and embarrassment for company. I wasn't sure when I would come out, if ever, and so I decided that the best thing I could do now was replay all of the events that had led up to this moment so I could make myself feel even worse.

The storm had really taken hold by the time I got to Dublin airport. A leaden sky lashed down rain onto the tarmac and buildings with a fury, as though the Gods themselves had something negative to say about my decision to leave.

'Paris? In France?'

'Yes, Dad, we've been through this a million times, and I do wish you'd stop saying it as though it's the outer reaches of Mongolia.' As I checked I had my passport for the umpteenth time, the trusty old Ford came to a halt outside Departures.

'I don't mean to, Edie, it's just...' He hesitated, rubbing his early-morning stubble and fixing his gaze on anything but me. 'Are ya sure now? Rushing off to France on a whim seems a bit drastic. Would you not consider, I dunno, getting a cat?'

Great. The only thing worse than having an identity crisis was having it confirmed by your father. I took my phone out of my purse and confirmed that the flight was still on time.

'I have to go. Listen, I'll be grand and so will you.'

'It should be me saying that to you,' he said a bit sheepishly.

It wasn't the first time our roles had been reversed. Way before my time, I'd become fluent in the world of adult emotions, and that was why I had to do something drastic. I had to strike out on my own and find out who I could be without my past weighing me down. I had felt so confident answering the ad online. I'd spotted it one night, after a couple of glasses of wine, when I indulged in my usual fantasy of moving abroad. Scrolling through the website English Jobs in France, I typed in 'Paris' and suddenly it popped up:

Assistant manager wanted for a quaint little bakery in Paris.
Accommodation provided. English required.

I'd sat up in bed and stared at the words. This was something I could actually do. It was something I knew I could be good at, despite the language barrier. All at once, my imagination was filled with visions of a chic, sophisticated *boulangerie* in one of the posh *quartiers* of Paris; modern but with a nod to vintage.

Frankly, I was surprised by how quickly I got the job, even without a proper interview. I couldn't quite believe my luck. A few quickfire questions over the phone, ensuring my fluency in English and a background in the service industry, and that was it. My career path had been something of a cul-de-sac up to that point. I never really figured out what I wanted to do, so I just ended up waitressing in a café. It was meant to be a temporary thing; an escape from the pressures at home and an easy way to earn some money while I figured things out. But over time, my future became more and more unclear and my job was the only stable thing I had to hold on to. At the age of thirty, I just couldn't see myself doing anything else. Until Paris came calling.

Once inside the airport, I tried to distract myself from the awkward goodbye with my father by trying to choose between a Mac blusher and a liquid eyeliner. I wouldn't ordinarily treat myself, but this was Paris after all. I had to up my game. Just then, I heard a breathy young woman sing the announcement:

'Final call for passenger Edith Lane, travelling to Paris on flight EI754. Please proceed to gate nine immediately, as the gate is now closing, thank you.'

I grabbed both products and practically threw money at the shop assistant, making a dash for the flight. This was my great adventure and I intended to soak up every second of it. For years I had watched old films with my mother, sighing enviously at elegant actresses like Grace Kelly or Audrey Hepburn, who embodied the kind of self-assured, fearless woman I hoped to be. Just thinking about how we used to lie on the couch together and listen to my mother's old jazz records, dreaming of the day I'd find the courage to be the star of my own movie, brought back bittersweet memories. For when the time came for me to flee the nest, she needed me to stay. Not that she would ever have asked it of me, but it was natural as breathing, caring for her. That was when those movies, *High Society*, *Breakfast at Tiffany's*, became our escape. More recently, my own additions, *Amélie* and *Moulin Rouge*, created a world of timeless fantasy where we could pretend reality didn't exist.

Ever since I could remember, I'd been obsessed with the city of love. My parents had their honeymoon in Paris and spoke about it as though it was the most magical place in the world. Whenever we needed cheering up, we'd take out their photo album and my mother would point out all of the amazing places they'd visited. I chose French as my foreign language at school and I spoke incessantly about living in Paris one day. My father, being a pastry chef, had always promised that we would go, as a family. But there are some promises you can't keep, no matter how hard you try.

As the rain lashed relentlessly against the plane's oval window, I noticed a tall, silver-haired man scanning the aisles for his seat. There was something in his piercing blue eyes that caught my attention. I tried to arrange my features into a nonchalant yet inviting look and to my great surprise, he smiled back and deftly swerved into the seat beside me.

This is it, I thought to myself, an actual meet-cute and we haven't even left the tarmac yet!

He removed his coat, revealing a distinct white dog collar and a cross pinned to the breast of his shirt. 'Do you mind if I sit here?' he asked politely.

'No, not at all, father,' I sighed, breathless with disappointment. Oh, well, at least God would be keeping an extra special eye on the plane. Which was just as well, for when we made our laboured ascent into the angry sky, I and my fellow passengers recited silent prayers several times over as our flying tin can lurched up and down in the turbulence. Babies cried, children whimpered and I anxiously chewed my nails, wondering why the universe had picked today to unleash a storm.

'Are you all right?' asked the dapper priest at my side, startling me out of my fear-induced stupor.

'Oh, me? Yes of course, I'm grand,' I assured him, decidedly pleased to have a man of the cloth at my side.

'There's no need to worry at all,' he continued, closing the Ken Bruen crime thriller he was reading. 'I've read the end of this particular story, and we all arrive safely in the end.'

This statement, coupled with a mischievous wink, made me laugh and automatically I relaxed a little.

'What takes you to Paris?' he enquired.

'I'm starting a new job: assistant manager of a little bakery.'

'Well, that's very interesting. Isn't it amazing that they

7

couldn't find someone in all of Paris to do that job?' he marvelled, shaking his head.

It struck me as most peculiar that this thought had never once entered my head, and it irritated me no end that he was the one to spot such an obvious oversight. I smiled politely in agreement, but inside felt a mountain of doubts towering over my new life. What did I really know about where I was going? And why were they so quick to offer me a job without so much as an interview?

'Do you have family in Paris?' he interjected again, not finished with his interrogation.

'No, no family. Just going on my own,' I replied in an upbeat tone that felt contrived.

'Aren't you the brave one,' he said.

I wasn't sure I liked this guy anymore. Every remark made me feel like I was being undermined. I gave a slight nod and turned my attention towards the window, unofficially ending our interaction.

A flash of lightning lit the entire inside of the plane with a blinding spotlight, silencing everyone on board for a moment and then causing the children to cry even harder.

Oh, shit, I thought, that's what you get for being mean about the priest. I kept my eyes closed and, for some reason, hugged my handbag to my chest, as if I'd need it close to hand when the plane went down. I whispered quietly, 'Help me, Mum, help me.' Eventually, the captain's voice crackled over the intercom and assured everyone that all was well and we were now beginning our descent into Charles de Gaulle airport.

~

I could still see the lovely woman's face, Julie, the proprietor of the *boulangerie* on Rue de Compiègne. I recognised the facade immediately – I'd spent long enough drooling over their pictures on Instagram. As I crossed the street, I could hear music in the air. Outside, a trio of musicians played the same classic French soundtrack of jazz music I'd saved on countless playlists. One sat squeezing an accordion, another strumming a guitar, while a tall, thin man wearing a flat cap plucked a double bass. I had arrived! But following a halting conversation of broken English and French, my stupid mistake became clear.

'*Désolée, mais je crois que vous vous trompez,*' Julie said, while placing some cups on a tray for the waitress to take to a table of four.

Tromper, I knew that word... *Se tromper* – to be mistaken. I took out my phone and pulled up the ad I had answered. Julie pulled a pair of glasses down from her head and peered at the screen.

'*Ah, voici La Boulangerie sur la Rue de Compiègne. Vous cherchez La Boulangerie sur la Rue de Paris. A Compiègne.*'

My emotions were a swirl of embarrassment and panic. Even my bum cheeks felt as though they were turning red. Despite my broken French, I knew what she was saying. I was at the wrong bakery. Worse still, I seemed to be rooted to the spot. Julie was waiting for me to leave, our business was at an end, and yet I couldn't quite move. I had simply run out of steam. And where the hell was Compiègne?

The waitress returned with an empty tray to the counter and on seeing my face, must have taken pity.

'I speak some English, may I see?'

I nearly cried at her kindness. *Keep it together, Edie,* I

warned myself. The last thing we needed was a scene! She looked at the screen and nodded affirmatively. *Thank God*, I thought to myself, *at least someone knows where I'm supposed to be.*

'You must take the train to Compiègne, is approximately one hour north of Paris.'

'Sorry, did you say one hour north of Paris? No, there must be some mistake. I'm here to take up my position in the Boulangerie et Pâtisserie de Compiègne ... in Paris,' I said, feeling a little less confident now.

'I can show you, if you like,' she said, pinching the map on the screen. 'See, it is in ze department of Oise, in ze region of Picardy, see? *Vous voyez là?*' she asked, pointing to the map.

'*Oui, je vois*, yes,' I whispered in response, with a sinking feeling in my stomach. I wasn't going to be living and working in Paris at all. And if that was true, what else had I been misled about? The helpful young woman continued and even wrote everything down, as I must have looked completely lost. And besides, what was a 'department' when it was at home?

'*Alors, nous sommes juste à côté* ... we are right beside la Gare du Nord,' she assured me, from where, apparently, I could get a train to the bakery where I actually had a job. Maybe. Did it even exist? Had I been scammed? I thanked them both and followed their directions for the train station, where I now sat, weeping in a toilet cubicle.

∾

'Right,' I said, to no one but myself. I had to do something. I couldn't spend the night in the toilet. I wanted to ring home so badly, but I couldn't let Dad know that he was right and that this had all been some foolish plan to reinvent myself (which it absolutely had). My finger hovered over my friend Gemma's number. We'd started working together at the same café on the same day and she'd become the closest thing I'd had to a best friend. But even Gemma didn't get to know the real me. I was so used to keeping the sunny side out at home, I'd begun doing it with the people around me, too. That's when I realised that I couldn't call her, either. She had been so enthusiastic about me 'finding my true self'– how could I turn around and tell her the truth? I had no clue who my true self was, and she certainly wasn't here. No. I had to make my own decisions now and stop wondering what everyone else would do in my shoes. First things first, I had to find out if the job I had applied for was real.

I found the number for Madame Moreau – my future employer at the bakery – and after several rings when my heart seemed to stop beating, she answered.

'*Âllo*?' came a croaky old voice.

I recalled the line I had been practising and responded. 'Um, *oui* … hello, eh, *bonjour* Madame Moreau … eh, *ici* Edith Lane?' I planned on ending every sentence with a question, as in 'Do you understand me?' Even though I had spent the last few weeks cramming with language apps and watching reruns of *Amélie*, my level of French felt painfully inadequate now.

'*Que voulez-vous*?'

'Yes, well, *je suis* here, in Paris, and um, you're not.'

Silence.

'*Je cherche la boulangerie…?*' My voice wavered.

'*Ah, vous êtes la fille qui va travailler dans la boulangerie, c'est ça?*'

'*Oui*, yes, the girl you hired to work at the bakery. I'm Edith from Ireland – *Irlandaise*!' I sighed with relief at her recognition of my name. I wasn't going mad. The job *was* real.

'*Vous devez aller à la Gare Du Nord, et vous prenez le train à Compiègne, d'accord? A plus tard alors.*'

'Yes, no, I know that part, it's just—'

The line went dead.

'Eh, hello? *Âllo*, Madame Moreau?'

I puffed out a sigh of indignation. 'Fine, I'll just Google it, then, shall I?' Great, now I was talking to myself out loud. The search results for the bakery's location came up and pointed to a little street with no name.

'Well, that can't be right,' I said, squinting. On top of everything else, I probably needed glasses. Yet another unwanted sign that the years were rolling by, whether I wanted them to or not. I put my phone in my bag and used my irritation as fuel to get out of the cubicle and take some action.

Looking at myself in the mirror, I saw a very sorry sight indeed. The rotund chignon I had so carefully pinned my hair into this morning had completely unravelled, my chic cream coat was creased and the Mac eyeliner I'd bought at the airport had smudged and leaked, giving me watercolour panda eyes. My chin began to wobble at the sight of my dishevelled appearance and my broken dreams.

'Look, you're a grown woman; get a hold of yourself!' I

shouted, giving myself a quick smack on the cheek. Wrong move; that just left me feeling sad and bullied.

'Right, different approach. OK, no one said this was going to be easy,' I assured myself, like an audio self-help book. 'Every heroine must face her obstacles and that's all this is: an obstacle.' Talking in such a positive tone began to calm me down and I reached for some tissue to start rebuilding my facade of confidence with make-up. 'So I won't be living a glamorous life in Paris,' I mumbled, 'but this Compiègne place can't be that far, and who knows, maybe it's the most picturesque part of France.' That was the spirit, and besides, how would it look if I gave up on my big adventure before it had even truly begun?

Just then a woman stepped out of the other cubicle, giving me a wary look.

'Oh, never mind me, just talking to myself!' I joked, and received a stony-faced glare for my troubles. I was already a major hit with the French, that much was clear.

'*Alors*, ze trains depart every fifteen minutes and *ze* ticket is twelve euros and fifty cents,' said the woman at the ticket desk, who took pity on me and switched immediately to speaking English. 'I wish you a good journey, Madame.'

'It's Mademoiselle,' I croaked, trying to focus on the map she had given me, full of odd street names and road numbers.

I boarded the train on the Paris–Saint-Quentin line to Compiègne. I found a seat by the window, though by this stage the sky was growing dark and as the train pulled away from the station, the lights of Paris blinked a luminous farewell. Monuments gilded with gold, fountains splashing generously and red-white-and-blue flags flying proudly on every building. I was already leaving Paris behind. I let my head rest against the glass and tried to find some scrap of positivity. I thought back to all of the old films I'd watched with Mum. The storyline never did run smoothly and the good people didn't always get what they deserved, at least not until the end. I had to believe that, no matter the bumps along the way, the journey would be worth it. Maybe it wasn't about dreams coming true (although that would be nice). Maybe it was about becoming the kind of person who chases them, regardless. Well, I would soon find out.

I took my phone out and called the number I reserved for very special cases – when my heart really needed a hug. It clicked straight onto answerphone and I heard my mother's voice singing.

Smile, though your heart is aching,
smile even though it's breaking,
when there are clouds in the sky, you'll get by,
if you smile through your tears and sorrow,
smile and maybe tomorrow,
you'll see the sun come shining through, for you…

Chapter Two

The sky was completely dark by the time the train pulled into Compiègne station. I felt tired and hungry as I pulled on my coat and prepared to step once more into the unknown. Alighting the train, I noticed a young boy of about fifteen sitting on one of the two benches adorning the platform. He was engrossed in some sort of video game, and only when the wheels of my case announced my presence did he look up from under his hoodie.

'*Pardon, Madame?*' he shouted.

My instincts told me to keep walking, so I pretended I hadn't heard and continued on my way.

'*Pardon, êtes-vous Madame Lane?*' he persisted, and I stopped and turned round.

'Oh, yes. I mean, *oui*. And you are?'

'*Je m'appelle Manu. Madame Moreau m'a envoyé vous chercher.*'

'*Oh, bonjour,*' I said, just about catching his rapid-fire French. His name was Manu and it sounded like Madame

Moreau had sent him to meet me. Right. Already he had taken the handle of my case and was leaving the station.

'But, wait, I…' My words bounced off his heedless back. That was it; I'd had enough. I was tired, hungry and fed up with being treated like an imbecile in this country.

'Oi, kid, you listen to me, right? I've been travelling all day to get here, nearly went down in a thunderstorm in the process, so I think the least you can do is tell me exactly where we are going, instead of herding me there like a lost sheep!' There, that felt so good and I was certain that I had left him in no doubt as to the cut of my jib.

He turned casually and simply said, '*La boulangerie*,' as if it was the most obvious thing in the world, which in fact it was. He gave a little signal with his hand that I should follow and set off once again with my brand-new suitcase rolling behind him.

'And just so you know, it's Mademoiselle!' I finished, determined to have the last word.

I finally caught up with my hooded guide as we entered an old, cobbled street. The place seemed deserted and a million miles away from my Parisian dream. Still, it did have an old-world appeal and despite the cold and the dark, I did my utmost to feel optimistic about what lay ahead. 'A hot cup of tea and everything will seem better,' I reassured myself. We walked along by a river lined with benches and manicured trees, and crossed by ornate bridges leading to who knew where. I couldn't imagine ever feeling at home or familiar with this place and if I had a dog, I would have told him we weren't in Kansas anymore. Turning a corner, I was surprised to see a street full of wooden-frame houses, like something out of Tudor

England. The old section of the town was like a fairy-tale village and I half expected the walls to be made of gingerbread. Nothing seemed to have a right angle and dormer windows peeped out of crooked roofs with pointy hats on.

'*Ici*,' my guide announced curtly. 'Here.'

Overhead, I saw a sign – La Boulangerie et Pâtisserie de Compiègne – while on the corner of the building was a small sign with the street name – Rue de Paris. Oh, how I rued my ignorance.

'Well, it's exactly what it says on the tin then; a bakery on the road to Paris.'

'*Comment*?' Manu drawled, as if the effort of speaking was too much of a drain on his time.

'Nothing, forget it, or what is it again… *peu importe*?'

Something between a grunt and a sniff was all I got in return. He had a key and opened the glass-panelled door to the bakery. I could feel my excitement return at the prospect of seeing my new 'career' in France. At first I noticed the floor tiles – exquisitely ornate and designed in peacock-blue and gold, with hints of bright orange at the centre. The counter was plain, but functional and of course empty at the end of the day. The shop was just large enough to accommodate three typically French bistro tables and chairs, all located by the large front window looking onto the street.

A large art nouveau-style mirror with a gilt gold frame took up the entirety of one wall from floor to ceiling, creating the illusion of a grander space. Sconces lit the honey-coloured walls with a dim light and as my eyes adjusted, I found myself suddenly confronted with a sturdy-looking woman dressed in a black skirt to the knee and a matching cardigan that fought admirably to contain her large bosom. Grey hair framed a sour face that held the echoes of kindness long since departed. Despite myself, I instinctively took a step back.

'Madame Lane,' she announced in a way that wasn't really a question or a statement.

'Mmhmm, *je suis*, well, it's Mademoiselle, actually,' I floundered. Her deep-set brown eyes were formidable, despite her short stature.

'*Venez, je vais vous montrer votre chambre.*'

Chambre… Oh, yes, my room. The way she'd said it made it sound like some kind of Victorian boarding house. I was entering my Jane Eyre era.

With that, she padded silently behind the counter to an open doorway and began climbing some rather steep-looking stairs. I turned around to thank Manu, but he had already left.

'Welcome to France, Edith,' I muttered, picking up my suitcase.

Following Madame Moreau up the stairs, I juggled unsuccessfully with my suitcase as it banged against the narrow walls and in the end resorted to carrying it over my head. The stairs took a dangerous ninety-degree turn and then, quite suddenly, I found myself in my studio apartment. The term attic would have been a generous one in describing my new home. At the nearest end of the oblong room a daybed sat snugly in front of an unlit stove and to my right was a kitchenette consisting of an electric hob and a sink with a tiny shelf above it. At the far end of the room stood a giant oak wardrobe taking up far more space than was practical and behind a screen was what I assumed to be the WC.

'*Voilà*,' Madame Moreau announced, evidently impressed by her own lodgings. I was literally speechless, but she took this to mean quiet bliss. With a gruff '*Bonne nuit*,' and orders to be up for seven, she took her leave and left me to my doll's house.

I flung my case on the bed and myself along with it, where I sat motionless for a long time. The wind whistled through the gaps in the eaves and I became alert to every unfamiliar sound – the gurgle of old pipes, a cat meowing on the street outside. The moon was like a fingernail hanging loose in the sky as I stared out of the little square windowpane.

My phone announced the arrival of a text message, rousing me from my mini coma. Dad, of course. Checking to see if I got to France in one piece. I texted him that I had arrived safely and was just settling into my lovely new home. Somehow, this little fib gave me strength to get back on my feet, unpack and set about making the space my own. I was used to making the most of small spaces and while I had hoped this journey was leading me to bigger and better things, I assured myself that great things start with small beginnings.

～

I had a fitful sleep that night and woke to some strange noises in the building. I put this down to the creaking timbers and fell back into strange dreams that were vivid and disturbing. My mother, as always, was there and we were on a ship trying to get somewhere. At some point I lost her and spent the dream searching frantically over all the decks. I awoke to the sound of low whimpering, then realised the strangled noise was coming from my throat. The alarm on my phone rang soon after to announce the dawn of my first morning in Paris. It was six o'clock and already I could smell the scent of warm bread wafting up the stairs. It hadn't occurred to me the night before to ask who or where the baker worked. Still, today would be my first official working day and I figured I would discover all the inner workings of the place soon enough.

The attic, or the atelier as I chose to call it, to give it a more romantic aesthetic, was bloody freezing. My nose felt as though it had spent the night at the North Pole, and my toes along with it. In fact all of my extremities were in serious danger of frostbite. Insulation was obviously a foreign concept over here, so I set to lighting the little stove with a bundle of wood stored in a basket at its side. Fifteen minutes later, after filling the room with eye-watering clouds of smoke, I admitted defeat and instead turned on the little portable electric hob to heat my coffee pot and the room. I danced briskly on the chilly floorboards as I pulled on some woolly tights and a red tartan dress. Some might say (my father being one of them) that March was perhaps not the ideal time to start a new life abroad, and feeling the chills running down my spine, I had to agree. But Madame Moreau was quite insistent that she needed an assistant manager to start immediately, which now made me wonder what had happened to the previous one.

Chapter Three

I gingerly made my way down the stairs for a quarter to seven. Madame Moreau was already piling every size and shape of baguette, loaf and roll into wicker baskets behind the counters. The smell was intoxicating. The warm loaves filled the air with a slightly sweet and robustly fragrant scent, like a warm, doughy hug. I ignored my salivating mouth and straightened my dress before I greeted Madame Moreau.

'*Tiens,*' was all she said, handing me a navy gingham apron.

'*Merci,*' I replied chirpily, ignoring her taciturn, monosyllabic style.

'Madame Moreau, I was wondering if I would be able to see the ovens at some stage … you know, see where all the magic happens?' I'm not sure why, but I used jazz hands to convey my excitement.

The look I received in return could only be described as disdain mixed with a good dollop of annoyance.

'You 'ave no business going downstairs, ever.'

I was quite shocked to hear her reply in English. I knew she spoke some English, the ad in the paper had said so, when it explained how popular Compiègne was among tourists. But choosing that statement as her first in my own language made it clear she meant it to be understood. No going downstairs.

'Of course, no problem. I just thought it might be nice to—'

'*Non!*' she bellowed, her dark eyes fixing me with a stare that turned my blood cold.

'*Non*, OK, I got it,' I said, like a sulky child.

'*Écoutez, Édith,*' she began in a more conciliatory tone, 'ze *Boulanger*, 'e is *très* particular about who is going in his kitchen, *hein*? Is better if you are 'ere to manage ze shop, *non*?' She nodded.

Unfortunately, Francophiles have no 'th' in their language and so I was still hung up on the fact that she had just pronounced me '*Édeet*'.

'*Édith, vous comprenez?*'

'Sorry? Oh, yes, right, got it. Grumpy baker, do not disturb,' I spoke slowly as I copied the words in my notebook.

'What is *zis*?' Madame Moreau asked, looking curiously at my notebook.

'Well, it's where I keep my notes. You see I like to write everything down so if I forget anything, I can refer to it, um, here.' Her bemused look was quite confusing. I mean what did the old curmudgeon want? I was being professional. 'And for orders, people will be placing orders, won't they?'

At this she began to grin, a not altogether unpleasant grin, but it held the kind of mischief that made me nervous.

'*Ma pauvre*, you will 'ave leetle time for writing notes,' she cackled and continued stacking bread into baskets.

I couldn't imagine how a little bakery in a small provincial town would be overrun with customers, but I decided to keep my thoughts to myself. Just then Manu appeared at the front door looking far more alert and groomed than he had the previous evening. After a chorus of *bonjours*, he set about loading boxes of bread on a small scooter just outside in a tower that seemed to defy gravity. Seeing my inquisitive glance, Madame Moreau informed me that Manu was in charge of deliveries to local hotels and restaurants. Despite the old-fashioned look of the place, their business seemed to be organised and profitable enough to keep at least four employees in earnings.

She gave me my first job of filling the counter window to the side of the serving counter full of mouth-watering patisseries. First I began with some classic *pains au chocolat* and croissants, which sat in large baskets on top. Then I placed two large, round flans – bright and yellow like the sun – on the bottom shelf at the front along with a *tarte Tatin*. The middle shelf was for savouries such as *croque-madame* and *croque-monsieur* and pizza cut into squares, which left the top shelf for tempting treats like eclairs filled with fresh cream, fruit tarts glazed with apricot syrup, and not forgetting those little scallop-shaped *madeleines*. Everything looked so wonderfully appealing; I could understand the old adage of eating with your eyes.

At 7am sharp, Madame Moreau turned the *Ouvert* sign

over and opened the bakery for business. To my surprise, there were a handful of customers already standing by the door and she greeted them with an easy charm I wouldn't have thought possible a moment before. I braced myself for my first French customer, mildly confident that I had enough mastery of the basics to see myself through. Wrong! The first gentleman to approach the counter gave his order so quickly that all I heard was *'Bonjour'* but nothing else.

'Um, pardonnez-moi?' was all I could manage in a voice that sounded embarrassingly pathetic to my own ears.

'Je prends deux croissants et une baguette, s'il vous plaît,' he repeated, but he may as well have not bothered. I was painfully unprepared for the speed at which the customers spoke, their regional accent or their slang. For the first time, and unfortunately with an audience, I realised that this had been a big mistake. Huge. I wanted to just run out of there and never look back.

Madame Moreau began introducing me to her patrons as *'Edeet* from England'. On any other occasion that slip-up would have warranted a very patriotic comeback, but I was floundering and she was offering me a lifeline.

The man, who wore an overcoat and a chapeau that made him look like a character from a detective movie, reached up and raised his hat a fraction.

'Very nice to meet you, Edith,' he said, pronouncing my name correctly.

He had kind and intelligent eyes and I gave him a grateful smile.

'Monsieur Legrand est un *avocat,*' Madame Moreau explained.

'*Avocat, avocat…*' I echoed, hoping that the meaning would reveal itself with repetition.

'A lawyer,' he offered helpfully.

'Oh, of course, I knew that one,' I said, as though this were a gameshow.

Another gentlemanly tip of his hat and he moved to the left, making way for the next in a line of customers that was now reaching out past the front door. Rather than helping, I seemed to be slowing everything down. In the end, we worked out that simply pointing was the best means of communication until my French improved and for the most part, it began to work out quite well.

La Boulangerie et Pâtisserie de Compiègne had a steady flow of customers all through the morning. I had not yet been entrusted with the coffee machine, but I was now making short work of the cash register that mercifully resembled a straightforward calculator. Our own lunchtime finally arrived at noon, when I was informed that the bakery closed from twelve noon to 2pm daily. It seemed a little old-fashioned, but Manu told me that it was a tradition Madame Moreau held fast to. At first I felt a little dismayed at having to spend two hours in my cramped attic alone, but on balance I figured that a snack and a little nap might just be ideal. I had lost my appetite for most things and when I was at home, I often ended up eating cereal for lunch and dinner. That was when it dawned on me that I didn't even have cereal here. My little kitchenette cupboards were almost entirely bare, so I grabbed my coat and started off down the road in search of a *supermarché*.

The afternoon had turned into one of those bright spring

days where it almost dazzles the eyes to look up. All I had seen of the town so far was the brisk walk from the station to the bakery, which was a muddled nighttime view of cobbled streets, closed shutters and little else. But walking out onto the street in the daylight lifted my heart in a way I didn't think possible. It felt like being transported onto a movie set; every clichéd idea I had about a French town was here. Now, the natives weren't wearing berets or striped tops with garlic tied around their necks, but they just had an air of self-importance and sophistication. And even though the women were dressed quite casually and not in haute couture, their sense of style truly set them apart from their European cousins. However, the smoking rate, especially among the teenagers, was alarming. 'Think of your teeth!' I wanted to shout at the younger girls, but then I vaguely remembered what it was like to be so young that you felt invincible and I kept my advice to myself.

Not to be outdone in the fashion stakes, I pulled the collar of my expensive cream coat up against the chilly breeze and set off once again. Our cobbled street was home to a host of other distinctively French establishments. A traditional *crêperie*, with a similar timber facade to the bakery, held an enviable position on the corner of three streets, followed by a *tabac* (or a newsagents for all intents and purposes) and a *salon de thé*, or a tea room. Looking at this street, it was easy to imagine that the French had nothing better to do than sit around indulging their appetites. However, it seemed that we were not the only ones taking a long lunch – everywhere was shut. It was remarkable to see how our cultures differed – these kinds of shenanigans would be unthinkable back home.

I wandered along, taking turns here and there, passing a

picture-postcard scene of a group of old men playing *boules* or *pétanque* in a beautiful park named Parc de Songeons. Everything had such a languid feel to it, the trees swaying in the breeze, the men having a good-natured argument about whose ball was the biggest, or the closest probably. Turning right past the river, I found myself in the more modern part of the town where brasseries buzzed with patrons sitting outside, soaking up the atmosphere. It was like coming out of a time warp to see banks, offices and bustling traffic, and for some reason, it felt a little overwhelming. The smart pale-stone facades with white shutters seemed full of their own importance and a little too perfect. I found a Monoprix supermarket and was completely spoiled for choice when it came to fresh produce like cheese and fruit, but other staples were a little more difficult to track down. The closest thing I could get to proper tea was English breakfast tea and the milk situation was so confusing, I ended up leaving without any.

I worked my way back to the Rue de Paris and had a look at the curious exterior door on the eastern side of the building that led to the basement where the ovens were. The street was on a slope at the gable end, so while the shop was at street level at the front and had three storeys, it looked much larger at the side with the basement door in view. The door was painted a deep blue and featured a decorative brass handle that must have been an antique. It looked as though no one had ever used that entrance and I began to wonder how on earth ingredients got in or bread got out. Surely everything didn't go through the shop?

I glanced surreptitiously up and down the lane before reaching out to turn the handle. I didn't know why I was doing it, I was sure it would be locked, but to my surprise it yielded easily. I looked around me again, unable to shake the feeling that I was being watched. I had barely opened the door a crack, when it slammed shut again, as though a gust of wind had pulled it back from the inside. I reached for the handle once again, only this time it was jammed shut and no amount of jiggling would open it.

Chapter Four

Back in my little crooked house, I cobbled together a snack of crackers, grapes – and camembert cheese, which smelled like socks that had been through something terrible, so I resigned myself to the idea that it would be an acquired taste. I washed it down with some weird black tea that lent an odd bitterness to the clash of flavours in my mouth.

'Well, that's quite enough of that,' I said to myself before tipping the remainder down the sink and washing my one, lonely cup. I could hear noises in the apartment below me and began to wonder if that was indeed where Madame Moreau lived. I hadn't presumed to ask the night before and she was not exactly a woman to shower you with information. I flopped down on my sofa-bed and tried once again to make friends with the strange sausage-shaped structure that lay at the top of the bed where my pillows should have been. I pondered over my first few hours in France, which, frankly, had felt like a lifetime.

That's what happens when you are out of your comfort zone – time stretches like an elastic band, prolonging your discomfort and unease, accentuating your isolation. Had I expected a grumpy old woman for a boss and a matchbox for a home when I had answered that ad all those months ago? Did I really think that plonking myself in a foreign country would erase all the painful memories of the last eighteen months? Was I deluding myself that a dream of living in Paris could really make me happy? Every thought in my head was telling me what an idiot I had been and that leaving now would be smarter than prolonging the agony. But my heart wouldn't let me; despite the frosty welcome and the downright idiocy of acting on a childhood whim, my heart was holding out for something amazing to happen. And who was I to stand in the way of that?

I worked with a singular focus all afternoon. *Just get through today*, I silently encouraged myself, hoping my confidence would grow with each new customer. Sure enough, there were quite a few tourists who wandered in, mostly to take photos of a quaint *boulangerie*. It was a relief to speak to people in English after a long day of broken French and improvised sign language. I took an order of coffee and eclairs to a man sitting at one of the tables outside. He had a cute little terrier on a lead and I brought him out a bowl of water.

'Is that an Irish accent I hear?'

'It is indeed,' I said, taking a moment to catch my breath

and let the fresh air fill my lungs. 'And that's definitely an English accent. Are you here on holiday?'

'I've lived here for about twenty years now,' he said. 'And yourself?'

'Oh,' I said, sucking air in between my teeth and checking my watch, 'about twenty-four hours.'

'Ah, well, in that case, welcome to Compiègne. I'm Geoff, by the way,' he said, shaking my hand, 'and this sweet little girl is Ruby.'

I bent down and gave Ruby a quick ear-scratch.

'I retired over here a few years ago from Bristol. Well, I say retired, I'm working part-time as a tour guide, mostly for war buffs coming to see the Armistice Memorial,' he explained, before tucking heartily into his eclair.

'So what is the … armistice, did you say?'

'Well, it's one of the most important sites in France in regard to both World Wars,' he began, switching into tour-guide mode. 'The Allies signed the armistice with the Germans in the First World War in a train carriage in the Forest of Compiègne. In 1940, the French signed an armistice with Nazi Germany in the same clearing; Hitler's way of humiliating his enemies. It's really very interesting, you should visit if you're going to be staying here a while.' He handed me his card, then said, 'If you don't mind me asking, what brought you to Compiègne?'

'Fate,' I replied, hoping it was true.

~

As the evening turned the sky dark and all the residents of Compiègne set off home with their baguettes in hand,

Manu returned to help shut up shop. Like most teenagers, he had few words for anyone, but there was an obvious bond between himself and Madame Moreau. She never had to tell him what to do since he was industriously following a time-honoured routine they had forged long before my arrival. As for me, my feet were burning with pain from standing all day, but I wouldn't give anyone the satisfaction of seeing me take a break. I could tell from their attitudes towards me that neither Manu or Madame Moreau expected the foreigner to last very long, and despite myself, I was inclined to agree.

Manu and I began lifting all of the chairs onto the tables so I could begin mopping the brightly tiled floor, while Madame Moreau counted the money in the till.

'Ça va?' he asked softly, lifting his head and casting a glance around the bakery, as if to say, 'Are you settling in OK?'

'Ça va, I think,' I smiled lopsidedly. His gentle words almost cracked the hardened veneer I was trying and failing to keep. I wiped my eyes as though from tiredness.

With a swift nod, he headed over to the kitchen, poured himself a large glass of water from the tap and gulped it down in one go.

'J'y vais,' he said, taking more boxes with him and once again piling them on the Vespa outside.

I knew that meant he was going somewhere, but where? I figured that was the end of our deep and meaningful conversation.

'Does he make deliveries, I mean, livraisons at this time of night?' I asked Madame Moreau as she locked the door behind him, the clock just striking eight.

Instead of just answering the question like a normal person, my new boss had a way of making you feel like an idiot for having asked it in the first place.

'*Non.*'

'Right, understood, or *bien compris* as you say here. Do not ask ridiculous questions, you foreign simpleton,' I mumbled, cleaning the glass shelves below the counter, when she appeared suddenly beside me, like a ghost.

'He delivers to the church, Mademoiselle *Édith, pour les gens SDF, Sans Domicile Fixe.*' To my blank stare, she added, 'People who 'ave no place to live.' With that irritated response, she shut the lights off and threatened to see me at the same time tomorrow morning.

'Oh, yes, Dad, the people here are just so welcoming and I've really hit it off with the owner, Madame Moreau,' I told my father later that evening on the phone. In a strange way, it felt kind of nice making up the French dream I had expected to have before I got here and I was so good at it, I almost believed it myself.

After a long day at work, I decided to go for a walk around the '*quartier*' to breathe the cool, crisp evening air. It did my heart and soul good to get out and explore my surroundings a little. The streets were lit up by elegant street lamps that curled like a shepherd's crook. Compiègne's picturesque thoroughfares certainly held their charm, but I felt so far from home and pathetically alone. This whole following-your-dreams thing was not at all how I had imagined it. Where were all the fun friends I was supposed to meet, the fun experiences I was supposed to be having? I'd watched enough films to know what should be happening when you chase after your heart's desire, but none of that big-screen magic seemed to be happening here. It was just boring, lonely and a bit scary. Everything that had happened since the plane touched down at Charles de Gaulle had only confirmed my suspicions that coming here was a mistake.

I passed by a hairdresser's on the busy Rue Solferino and saw a photo of a model sporting an Audrey Hepburn-style gamine hairdo. Her hair colour, a kind of dark chestnut, was quite similar to my own. Yet while my long, shapeless do lacked any kind of style, her cropped locks were the essence of chic. I touched my hair absent-mindedly and wondered if I could carry it off.

'*Ca vous irez bien,*' came a man's voice.

I turned around but he was already walking away down the street. He turned back momentarily, revealing a flirtatious grin, but before I had time to say anything, he had turned down another street and was gone. I think he meant that the hairstyle would suit me.

Maybe Compiègne wasn't such a big mistake after all.

Chapter Five

The following morning began much as the one before: Madame Moreau stacking the hot, crusty baguettes into baskets, me piling the golden, flaky pastries on the counter and the sweets in the glass display, while Manu packed his boxes for delivery. It still felt strange to be transplanted into this completely different environment, but less so than the day before. At least now I knew what to expect when the doors opened and the regulars poured in. I filled the baskets with warm *pains au chocolat* and almond croissants and stocked the display case with a delicious-looking tray of *éclairs au chocolat*.

Madame Moreau was still stubbornly clipped in her dealings with me, though she oozed personality with her customers. Of course I couldn't understand everything she said, but it was obvious she was something of a neighbourhood character – always with a sharp quip to throw her opponent off-guard, and a wit and intellect to rival any French philosopher. This made me keenly aware of the fact that she and I were polar opposites. I tried too hard to make people like me, and for the amount of time I succeeded in this endeavour, it hardly made all the effort worthwhile. Yet this cantankerous old dame had everyone eating out of her hand.

On the plus side, I was beginning to pick up some charming phrases while dealing with the customers, such as *'Je vous en prie'*, which literally meant 'I beg of you', but it seemed to be used as more of a 'you're welcome' or 'oh, it was nothing' kind of phrase. It was interesting how, if you heard a phrase used enough times in the same situation, you kind of construed your own meaning, without the need to consult a phrase book. My accent was still frightfully clunky, like a pair of steel-toed boots clodhopping over all the delicate French phrases, but the customers seemed to appreciate the efforts I made.

Before closing at noon, it was announced that I was to have the afternoon off. That was how Madame Moreau operated: she made things known, rather than telling you straight to your face. Apparently two days spent in France without the proper papers was two days too long.

'Il faut aller à la préfecture pour chercher votre carte de séjour,' Manu advised, in a failed attempt to make things clearer.

'I have to go where to get my what now?' I asked, squinting my eyes in an attempt to understand.

Madame Moreau hefted herself onto the stool in the kitchen just behind us, showing for the first time some signs of her age. She looked tired and it was clear by the way she rubbed her wrists that there was a stiffness there.

'It is a residence card. If you are living in France for more than three months, you must 'ave one.'

Three months? I wasn't sure if I was going to last three days, but I wasn't about to argue with an afternoon off. After all, how hard could filling out a few forms be?

Wrong again!

After spending the best part of an hour trying to find the right building (which was eventually marked out by its grey walls and grey people), I waited two hours in an unending queue of foreign students, immigrants and a lot of tired and forlorn-looking people, only to be informed that I could have done the entire thing online. The receptionist, a kind enough woman with an obsession for bangles, loaded my arms with half a rainforest's worth of leaflets. I spent the rest of the afternoon in a café trying to make sense of everything I needed, with four strong coffees and a dictionary. I ended up with a list that looked something like this:

- Passport
- Birth certificate
- *Attestation de residence* (proof of residency)
- *Attestation de bourse* (proof of income)
- *Timbre fiscal* (some special stamp that, quite frankly, sounded makey-uppy)
- E111 Health Insurance
- 4 passport photos
- Photocopies of all of the above

I can't say my enthusiasm for form-filling to remain in a country that obviously did not relish my presence was at an all-time high. But when it became clear that *une carte de séjour* was the key to opening a bank account and actually getting paid, I returned to the bakery and began rooting through my suitcase, which was only partially unpacked. I felt just like that suitcase – still undecided as to whether I wanted to be here or not. I found the E111 and my passport, but I knew I'd have to call home for my birth certificate. I reached for the phone that I'd left on the bed and sat cross-legged on the floor in front of my open case. The wooden floorboards were worn smooth and felt warm to the touch. I hadn't really taken a moment to just be since I'd arrived. I closed my eyes and took a deep breath. It seemed like I was always running. Another deep breath. My shoulders relaxed a fraction and my fingertips gently grazed the floorboards, feeling the warmth from the floor below.

Mindlessly, I began to trace patterns along the wood and wondered if I'd ever be able to stop running away from myself … my life. I'd only been in France a few days and I already felt as though I had failed in some way and so I wanted to run again. One final deep breath. My fingers caught in a groove. One floorboard was slightly uneven and jutted upwards. Without opening my eyes, I used my nails to pull at it and with a soft rasping sound, it lifted. I opened my eyes and looked down. One of the floorboards had been cut and this small section, no more than ten inches, revealed a tiny nook. Inside, I could see a small notebook. I almost held my breath as I reached inside. It had a scarlet-red cover, curling at the edges. In a neat script on the front in black pen was written *Les Recettes*.

What was it doing hidden up here? I opened it to the first page. The paper was yellowed with age, but the black ink was as clear as if it had been written yesterday.

Pierre, 1945

I was completely bemused by its presence and bewitched by what secrets it might hold inside. Had it been concealed under the floorboards all this time? And who was Pierre? Had he lived here once? I turned the page and found the first recipe.

Chocolat chaud pour réchauffer l'âme

I understood that it was a recipe for hot chocolate, but I had to type the remaining words into Google Translate.

'To warm the soul,' I read aloud. 'Hot chocolate to warm the soul.'

I couldn't help thinking that this recipe was written especially for me. Of course that was a ridiculous thought, but as I looked across at my little kitchenette, I spied a small copper pot. I didn't even have milk, never mind any of the other ingredients. I looked down at the recipe again and noticed something that looked unfamiliar.

Une cuillère de liqueur vanillao

Vanillao? The name stirred something at the back of my mind. I'd seen it somewhere before. Then I remembered…

I walked briskly down the stairs and into the kitchen.

No one was there, so I grabbed the large tin of icing sugar and then opened the small cupboard where Madame Moreau stored the boxes of sugar cubes. Right at the back was a small bottle with a cork stopper sealed in wax and a handwritten label that read *Vanillao*.

I turned around, half-expecting someone to be there, but I was completely alone. I hesitated before opening it. For all I knew it could've been poison. But they'd hardly keep that beside the sugar. I really wanted a hot chocolate by this stage. I grabbed a large sleeve of dark chocolate from the tin on the counter, a carton of milk and the rest of the ingredients, before trotting up the stairs to my apartment and locking the door behind me, like some kind of kitchen thief.

I switched on the hot plate to medium and heated the milk and cream slowly. A quick glance at the recipe and I noted that it said not to rush the process but to take a moment to indulge the senses. I didn't know who the author was, but they certainly knew how to make the experience something special. I checked the ingredients' measurements again...

200g chocolat noir (dark chocolate)
Une cuillère à café de sucre glace (teaspoon of icing sugar)
350ml lait (milk)
100ml crème entière
2 gouttes de liqueur vanillao (drops of vanilla liqueur)

Just as bubbles began to form around the edges, I took the pan off the heat and added the broken chocolate, found a whisk in the drawer and returned it to the heat. Gently, I began to stir and watched the alchemy of the dark chocolate melting into the creamy milk. The teaspoon of icing sugar counteracted the bitterness in the chocolate. Just as the liquid began to thicken, I took the glass bottle in my hand. There were vanilla sticks inside, so I was pretty confident that there wasn't anything untoward in there. Breaking the seal, I uncorked the lid and the scent of brandy filled the air. Once the alcohol evaporated, my nostrils picked up on something far more delicate. The sweet, blossomy vanilla bloomed, but there was something else I couldn't quite put my finger on. I carefully added two drops and then took the pan off the heat.

I found a small turquoise cup and saucer at the back of the cupboard, underneath the worktop. After a quick rinse under the tap to remove any dust, I placed them on the table and began to pour the thick, syrupy liquid. It looked sinfully dark and I couldn't help but smile at the decadence of it. I'd never made hot chocolate like this at home. We'd only ever used the cocoa powder from a tin that always ended up tasting like some kind of chocolate broth and never truly satisfied. This recipe seemed to have enough for two small cups, but I figured it was far too rich to drink two. Even if death by chocolate didn't seem such a bad way to go.

I lightly whipped some cream and placed a dollop on top, finishing with a light dusting of cocoa powder. I had to stand back for a moment and admire it. It looked like a tiny work of art. But now came the true test. I used a spoon to gently give it a stir, not too much, then raised the cup to my lips. The surface was almost solid and met my lips like a kiss, before breaking and sliding onto my tongue, filling my mouth with an intense, velvety taste. As I swallowed the dark liquid, I felt a mixture of ecstasy and contentment – it was the kind of completeness I hadn't felt since— And just like that, a memory dislodged itself from some unknown place. I was with my mother at a Christmas concert and we were singing along to carols and there were twinkling lights overhead and I remembered feeling that life was the best thing ever because there would be more days like that. I felt woozy at the recollection. I hadn't thought about that time in years; in fact, I'd all but forgotten it. I took another mouthful and I could almost smell the sulphur from the sparklers we'd held in our hands, like burnt matches. Without my realising it, a tear was rolling down my cheek. But I wasn't sad exactly, just present with myself. I hadn't been present in a very long time. It was as though the hot chocolate unlocked something within me. I suddenly felt ravenous, but there was nothing to eat.

'Good job you live above a bakery,' I joked to myself, wiping the tears away.

Back downstairs, all remained quiet. I uncovered the basket of choux pastry balls with chocolate hazelnut Chantilly crème inside and devoured them with an appetite I hadn't felt for years. I might not have stopped there, but I saw Manu arriving on his bike through the window and realised it was time to open up again. I licked the cream off my fingers and tried to straighten myself up. I had no idea whose recipe book I'd found, but they certainly knew a thing or two about hot chocolate!

Chapter Six

Pierre Moreau

1920

At fifteen years of age, Pierre Moreau began his apprenticeship at Maison Angelina in Paris. Having grown up on a small farm in rural France, Pierre had always felt that fate had something special in store for him. Whilst feeding the pigs or tending to the vegetable garden, he would daydream about a life far away, rich with excitement and opportunity. He had never quite fitted in at home, but when Pierre was old enough to follow his mother's recipes, something changed. In the kitchen, he was more sure of himself, and the warm, tasty pies he produced using apples from the orchard or berries from the roadside earned him the goodwill from his siblings that was in all other circumstances non-existent. Offering food, it seemed, held a kind of magical power to elevate people out of the ordinary and into the realm of contentment, even bliss.

And so it was that Pierre made up his mind to become a baker at the very finest establishment in all of Paris. Maison Angelina was a place of opulence and style, attracting all of high society to sample its exquisite patisseries. It was owned by an Austrian confectioner by the name of Anton Rumplemayer, who was awarded the honour of *Hofzuckerbäcker*, Confectioner to the Court, by the Empress Elisabeth in Vienna. Why did this matter so much to Pierre? Because Pierre was a perfectionist and nothing would do but to learn from the very best. He worked long hours at the bakery, rising so early in the morning that it hardly felt as though he had gone to bed at all. He was passionate about baking and the idea that bread could nourish not only the body, but also the soul.

It was at Maison Angelina that he learned to achieve the perfect lamination in the flaky pastry of the croissant. He also learned of its origin, the Austrian *kipferl*. Created in Vienna following the end of the Ottoman siege and shaped to resemble the crescent moon on the Turkish flag, the French renamed it 'croissant'. They also improved upon the recipe by using layers of puff pastry and butter. Rumplemayer told Pierre that it was Marie Antoinette herself who brought the croissant to France, but that story is for another time.

Despite the clattering of pans, the sharp clang of whisks and the intense heat of the ovens, there was a quiet orderliness to the kitchen that Pierre loved. Each cook was deeply immersed in their own work, only emerging to pass the process on to the next person, in what appeared to

Pierre like a dance. Baking was a meditative process and Pierre felt closer to God in those moments of intense focus than he ever did in a church.

As the years passed, Pierre began to think about his future. He had a little money put aside, but not nearly enough to open his own elegant patisserie in Paris. As much as he loved working with Rumplemayer, there was a desire within him to make his own name. It was on a very ordinary Tuesday, while Pierre was enjoying an afternoon to himself, that he took a stroll to the market in Le Marais. Among the stalls selling fresh fruit, cheese and the finest cuts of meat, he stumbled across a strange man who claimed to have journeyed from Madagascar, an island off the south-eastern coast of Africa, bringing with him a rare form of vanilla bean. He told Pierre that native peoples grew their vanilla orchids from the roots of the cacao tree, and this botanic wonder produced a bean with the rich, earthy essence of chocolate and the sweet floral aroma of vanilla.

The man cut open a vanilla pod and scraped out a small number of seeds onto Pierre's fingertip. Perhaps he was expecting a slightly nuanced flavour, something the customers might not be able to identify, but the taste almost suspended Pierre in mid-air. It had an intoxicating perfume that blossomed within him. Clocks stopped, the market around him fell into silence, and as clearly as he was standing on a street in Paris, all at once he was back in the town of Compiègne, eating a tart filled with fresh fruit and crème pâtissière, with his friend from school, Jean-Yves. In all these years he had never realised, until this moment, until the memory came unbidden, that he had been in love with Jean-Yves.

With tears blurring his vision, Pierre turned back to face the strange man, who had a knowing smile on his face.

'What is this?' Pierre asked.

'Your heart's desire, my friend,' the man replied, placing his flat palm on his chest.

All of a sudden, Pierre knew exactly what he wanted to do. He would return home and open a bakery so the humble people of Compiègne could taste the elegance of Paris. But more than that, with this special ingredient, he would melt their hearts.

'I'll take everything you have.'

'I hesitate to tell you, Monsieur Moreau, but in all good conscience I must, this building has something of a … history,' said the agent, Monsieur Dujardin, who was a nervous type and ensured that no gap in conversation went unfilled for long. Pierre had hardly said one word since they arrived.

'Every building has a history,' Pierre said, matter-of-factly, descending the stairs from the apartment above. It was perfect. He could live above the bakery and there was already an oven in the basement. It might need some attending, as it hadn't been used for many years.

'Quite right, quite right,' said Dujardin, relieved that he had dispatched his moral duty without having revealed anything of the building's more unusual qualities. It was said that a woman had opened a bakery here. Well, that alone was cause for alarm. Everyone knew that women and business should never mix. Far too emotional, and indeed it was this that started all of the trouble. But Monsieur Dujardin did not trade in tittle-tattle nor did he believe in old wives' tales. Especially when it stood between him and his fee.

'I want to make an offer,' Pierre said, in his calm, composed manner.

'Oh, how delightful. What I mean is, naturally, it's a fine building of character, Monsieur Moreau and dare I say, a very competitive price,' Dujardin prattled on, alluding to another buyer who was purely a figment of his imagination.

Pierre handed over all of the money he had saved, which was just enough to secure the purchase of the building. He would need a loan to buy some furniture and most importantly, ingredients, but now that he was a man of standing, he trusted that everything would come good, as it did. Just as they shook hands on the deal and stepped outside into the street, Pierre saw his old friend Jean-Yves. The shock made his mouth dry and his legs feel suddenly hollow. There, by his side, was a beautiful young woman holding a swaddled baby in her arms.

'Pierre!' Jean-Yves called and the two men embraced warmly. 'You have returned to us.'

Pierre could hardly speak, but smiled at his friend, and at his new bride.

'Tell me, my friend, how was Paris?'

'As spectacular as you can imagine,' Pierre finally replied.

'You must be a great pâtissier now!'

Pierre looked at the child in the young woman's arms,

who slept soundly. He felt his heart straining to beat, as though all of the blood had drained out of it.

'I can create many wonderful things,' he said, 'but you, my friend, have the best thing of all, a family.'

Jean-Yves invited Pierre to stay with them until the bakery was habitable.

'You are a part of our family now,' he kindly assured him.

Pierre wanted to turn down the kind offer, but in truth, he had nowhere else to go. It was during those few weeks, whilst witnessing the love that this little family shared, that Pierre made a decision. He told himself that love would not be his destiny, and so he would pour all of his heart into his baking.

When Pierre opened the doors to the Boulangerie et Pâtisserie on Rue de Paris, he began infusing his dough with his special ingredient. The unusual flavour transported those who tasted it to a place beyond imagination. This would be his gift to the people of Compiègne, who now became his family. Even Pierre himself could not explain it, but this mixture of decadence and sweetness could, with the right balance, cause the heart to blossom.

Chapter Seven

On my one-week anniversary, I decided to treat myself, so when the bakery shut for lunch, I grabbed my coat and headed straight for the hairdressers. It was a short walk from the cobbled Rue de Paris to the very modern and trendy Rue de Solferino. I felt a little less intimidated by my unfamiliar surroundings and found myself admiring the smart shopfronts and their stylish patrons. However, as I walked into the salon, I was again transported to another era. The decor was a retro nod to the fifties, with the entire salon painted with bright, ice-cream pastels of pink, peach and cream. To the right was a nail bar with stools that looked for all the world like they had been stolen from an American diner. The rest of the salon was similarly kitted out with white leather styling chairs and pink-framed mirrors. I half expected them to set my hair in rollers with a polka-dot scarf round my head. A glamorous woman with a peroxide blonde bouffant, which would not have looked out of place on Marilyn Monroe, approached me with red talons and made me retreat.

'*Bonjour, Mademoiselle,*' she welcomed me in a sing-song voice, red lips grinning. '*Une coupe, les couleurs ou le brushing?*'

'*Bonjour,* I um … I'm not sure,' I hesitated, pleased that for once someone had spotted I wasn't married and didn't assume that at my age I should be.

'*Ah, vous êtes une Anglaise*? *Pas de problème – ma fille parle un peu anglais,*' she explained, followed by a banshee wail of '*Nicole! Viens ici.*'

I smiled politely and took the seat she pointed to. In her best English she manufactured the words '*Juste* one moment pleese,' with the most adorable accent I had ever heard.

Nicole's entrance caused my jaw to drop – I had never seen anything like her. Her curves had been poured into a black-and-white polka-dot dress and she wore a red scarf tied neatly around her neck. Her hair was jet black and styled in a simple ponytail with a quiff at the front. The words Betty and Boop came to mind.

'Hello, my name is Nicole,' she said, stretching her hand out.

I fumbled to look less starstruck by her and failed miserably. 'I just love your look,' I said sincerely. 'And I'm Irish by the way. My name is Edith, but please call me Edie because everyone pronounces my name in a way that makes it sound like "edit" or "eejit" and I can't bear either.' I realised I was babbling, but Nicole just smiled.

'I don't think you want to do that,' she grinned, 'with the accent on the E, people will start to call you "Eddie"!'

We both laughed and for the first time since boarding the plane, I felt as though I could let my guard down.

'How long 'ave you been in France?' she asked as she deftly lifted my hair and placed a gown around my shoulders. A coffee also appeared in front of me, and I caught her mother winking at me in the mirror as she went back to her other client.

'A whole week,' I sighed, the strain evident in my voice.

'Hmm, and already you are changing your 'airstyle? This can only mean one thing, a man,' she pouted.

'No, no man. I just, I needed a change, you know?' I didn't want to get into all the complicated reasons I had for coming here with little or no plan, but something in her eyes made it clear she understood. 'Your English is so good by the way, you even have a bit of a London accent,' I said.

'Oh, thank you, yes, I made my Erasmus in London. It is where I met my husband, Johnny.' She smiled instinctively. 'I was doing business, he studied history and now we have our little Maximilien,' she said, pointing to a photograph peeking out from behind the mirror of a toddler.

'He's so cute,' I said, and I meant it, for his dark blond hair had also been styled into a quiff and he sported nothing but a nappy.

'Thank you, he's nearly three years old now,' she said, shaking her head in disbelief. 'My God, time really goes so fast, *non*?'

I nodded in agreement. 'That's why I came to France to work in a bakery, carpe diem!'

'Ah, don't tell me, you are the new replacement for Maria at the *boulangerie* on Rue de Paris?'

'Guilty.'

'Well then, we are going to take very special care of you,' she said, placing her hands on my shoulders.

'What happened to Maria?' I asked, suddenly feeling uneasy.

'I'm not really sure. One day she was here, the next day, hop! Gone.'

I gulped hard. 'Hardly surprising, if she'd received the same warm welcome from Madame Moreau that I had.'

Nicole smiled warmly. 'Madame Moreau, she appears tough, but there is softness there. The years have made her that way,' she explained.

I decided to reserve judgement.

'Now, the hair, what would you like today, Mademoiselle?' Nicole slipped into professional mode and ran her fingers through my tresses, which felt divine.

'Well, I was thinking of cutting it all off, actually, and going for the gamine look,' I announced courageously.

'Aye-aye-aye, everyone who comes to France wants this gamine, girly-girl look, *hein*? *Non*, is not for you, *ma belle*,' she replied.

I was taken aback by her candour; most hairdressers at home would just go along with whatever you said but proceed to do the opposite – they would never challenge you.

'Well, something drastic has to happen,' I said, taking a quick sip of my coffee. Taking a leaf out of her book, I decided to say exactly what I thought, rather than be my usual overly polite self. 'I want the kind of hair a man wants to play with!' As soon as I said it, I couldn't help but laugh and thankfully, so did Nicole. But there was no disagreement this time, as she walked me to the sink and set about changing my personality from the head down.

When I arrived back at the bakery for the afternoon shift, Madame Moreau hardly glanced my way and if she did notice my new hairstyle, she said nothing. Nicole and I had settled on a layered bob just above my collarbone with a sweeping fringe that grazed my eyelashes when it fell from behind my ears. I felt like a new person, and as I passed by shop windows on my way back, I hardly recognised myself. I looked younger, more vibrant and inexplicably flirtatious. As far as I could see, I was becoming 'French'! I even ducked into a pharmacy across the street and bought fire-engine-red lipstick. Nicole was a breath of fresh air and, to my great delight, invited me to my first soirée at a jazz club to see her husband Johnny playing bass in a gypsy jazz band. It was marvellous how, in the blink of an eye, everything had begun to change and look a lot rosier. I couldn't remember the last time anyone had invited me out on a Saturday night back home. Perhaps this whole idea wasn't harebrained after all.

Monsieur Legrand approached the counter and with a newfound confidence I greeted him by guessing his order.

'*Une tarte au citron?*'

'*Justement, Mademoiselle Édith,*' he said, putting his hat on the counter. 'You are acclimating well, I see?' he said, nodding at my new hairstyle.

'*Pas mal,*' I agreed, placing the tarte into a small box. 'If it wasn't for all the paperwork.'

He gave me a questioning look.

'*Carte de séjour,*' I said.

'Ah yes, we do enjoy our protocols here. If ever you need my services,' he said, handing me his card.

'*Merci, Monsieur Legrand,*' I said, taking it and slipping it into my apron pocket. 'You'll be my one phone call from prison.'

'Let's hope it won't come to that,' he smiled.

'*Deux chocolats chauds et deux tranches de flan, Édeet, tout de suite,*' Madame Moreau croaked, making it clear that chit-chat had a time limit. So I tucked my sexy hair behind my ears and set about being the best *serveuse* in Compiègne.

Chapter Eight

L ife on Rue de Paris began to settle into a rhythm and the days no longer felt so exhausting. Every mistake I made in the early days made me feel as though I was on a crash course for dummies, but my second week felt a little less bruising to the ego. To my surprise, the weekend rolled around again quite quickly and Madame Moreau informed me that my wages had been paid into my bank account.

'Oh, good, Mr Grumpy at the Prefecture must have received my birth certificate from the embassy,' I cheered. I half expected to be told that baguettes and board were payment enough, but she stunned me further by handing me my share of the tips.

'*Pas mal*,' was all she said. 'Not bad.'

It annoyed me to realise just how much her approval meant to me. Still, she wasn't to know that, so I just agreed. '*Je sais*,' I said, and thought I saw the trace of a smile, but it was probably a trick of the light, for she had already switched off the main lights, leaving us in relative darkness.

'*À lundi*,' she said, bidding me farewell until Monday.

I was looking forward to having Sunday all to myself and not having to get up with the birds. Although this made me recall the noises that had woken me up every night since my arrival. Feeling bold, I decided to ask her about them.

'Madame Moreau, do you know what all the banging is at night? I keep hearing noises in the building.'

That familiar veil of irritation came over her face as she grunted, '*Ce bâtiment est très vieux, Mademoiselle* – all old buildings make noise – zey 'ave to breath, *non*?'

'That's what I thought, all the old timbers and everything. Unless you're getting up each night and dancing Riverdance on the stairs!' I said this extremely quickly in a thick Dublin accent, still she pretended to understand and gave a withering nod before mounting the stairs to her apartment.

'Charming as ever, Madame Moreau, pleasure working with you,' I scoffed in her absence. This kind of encounter would have really upset me back home, where being polite was like an extreme sport. But here, I was getting used to people speaking directly and I was finally saying what I really meant.

Back in my own little room, which I was really growing quite fond of, I indulged in my preparations for the night ahead. I turned on the old-fashioned radio high on the shelf above the stove and found a station playing all American jazz. It was like the old days at home with my mother; Ella Fitzgerald, Louis Armstrong and Ol' Blue Eyes – Frank Sinatra – serenaded me as I showered and pulled on my trusty little black dress. I longed for Nicole's curves, but realised I would soon have my own if I kept wolfing down the bakery's products. Like a true *française*, I enjoyed a fresh baguette with my evening meal and even took to eating a croissant every morning for breakfast.

Trotting through the cobbled streets in a pair of kitten heel shoes, I almost lost my balance once or twice as a sparkling night frost set in. Following the directions Nicole had given me, I made my way to the club through the winding streets of the old *quartier*. From the outside, it looked very unassuming with blue velvet drapes covering the windows and those plastic coloured beads that scream student flat forming a curtain at the front door. The name overhead, written in blue neon lighting, read '*Nostalgie*', which sounded close enough to the name Nicole had given me. Although I tried to act like meeting friends in a bar in France on a Saturday night was just routine, secretly my stomach tingled with nerves. As soon as I walked through the door however, I saw Nicole's face keeping an eye out for me, and her genuine smile on seeing me made me relax.

'Hey, Edie!' she called over the music and embraced me with a kiss on each cheek. 'You look *ravissante*!' she declared, beaming.

She looked ravishing herself, in a red strapless dress with black pearls.

'This place is…' I trailed off.

'*Petit*?' She finished my sentence. 'I know, it's not much to look at, but it's the only jazz bar in town and Johnny's band has their residency here.'

Looking around, I could see why the regulars stayed loyal to the place. It was unpretentious and unique, with its abstract paintings and burgundy-coloured walls. The tables were huddled closely together for a cosy feel and lit by little candles in wine bottles. The waiter was covered in tattoos and sported a gravity-defying quiff. Nostalgie seemed to be the kind of place where standing out meant fitting in. I'd always felt slightly out of step with my peers, probably because I spent so much time at home with my mother watching old films and listening to music from another age. I knew it wasn't healthy to keep retreating into the world my mother and I had created. But in this place, with these people, I finally felt like I belonged somewhere.

Nicole ordered the drinks – Mai Tais all round. The deliciously dark rum warmed my throat after my chilly walk and loosened the tight grip of wariness I wore like armour.

'Edie, I want to introduce you to my sister, Cathy, and her girlfriend, Cécile,' said Nicole, leaning back so we could all go through the kissing hello process again. 'This is my Irish friend Edith.'

A chorus of *'Bonsoir!'* followed and I felt my shoulders relax a little. Unlike the reception I got when I arrived at the bakery, this place and the people were full of warmth.

'Now, tell me, how is life at *la boulangerie*?'

'Oh, you know, Madame Moreau simply can't do enough for me, like even today, she gave me a bonus in my salary for being the employee of the month.'

Nicole tilted her head to one side, looking confused.

'I'm being sarcastic; she still ignores me for the most part and grunts at me when she has to. It's working out fantastically well.'

Nicole laughed a deep throaty laugh. 'You are a funny one!'

'Well, I'm glad my French adventure is amusing someone,' I smirked.

It had been so long since I'd connected with anyone or had a conversation with someone who didn't know all the heartache of the past year and a half. For a wonderful moment, I allowed myself to sense the promise of belonging somewhere, as myself.

'Manu is a sweet kid, even though he never has much to say for himself,' I continued.

'Manu is a smart one, you know, he will take over the bakery after Madame Moreau...' Nicole trailed off delicately.

'Are they related or something?' I asked, unable to imagine why a bright young teenager would want to spend his days working with a cranky old dinosaur.

'I'm not certain, but he has been at the bakery since he was a child. It's so long now that I cannot remember. But I know he wishes to, how do you say, make an apprentice to become a master baker. Perhaps he will be the next Monsieur Moreau.'

Monsieur Moreau? This was news to me. 'Madame Moreau's married?' I gasped.

'No, no, it was her father or her uncle I think. He's dead for some time now.'

'Oh.' I felt a pang of sympathy for her. 'So, I wonder who the master baker is now, then? I've never met him and she's hardly mentioned it – except to say that I am not to enter the basement on pain of death.'

'I will ask my mother, if you like. She grew up in the neighbourhood, so I'm sure she will remember.'

Just then, a group of musicians took to the stage and began warming up their instruments.

'Look, is my husband Johnny on stage.' Nicole waved at a tall, muscular man with dark blond hair swept to one side, revealing a close shave on the other. He wore long black baggy trousers with black braces and spun his bass around as though he were dancing with it. The band leader introduced the musicians – Johnny on bass, Frankie on the snare drum, Laurent on violin and himself, Stéphane, on guitar. They were a raggle-taggle group of musicians if ever I saw one, all sideburns and thin moustaches and with clothes that looked as though they came from a vintage shop. Yet when they started to play, it all made sense. Nicole stood and cheered loudly as they broke into an up-tempo number I didn't recognise, which just oozed cool. I sipped my cocktail happily as I watched my feet take on a life of their own to the rhythm.

'You like?' Nicole yelled over the crowd.

'I love!'

I was living all of my Hollywood movie fantasies. I glanced around the bar at my fellow patrons, chatting animatedly and carrying off the style of the forties and fifties with aplomb. It was then that I noticed a solitary figure emerging from a tussle with the beaded curtains and taking the first available seat at the bar. He was in a dark grey suit with a black tie loosened at his neck and had a look of someone far too serious to enjoy jazz. Then again, I reasoned, that was probably how I looked when I was alone and uncomfortable. From my vantage point, I could clearly see him, while I remained hidden behind a conveniently placed palm tree. He seemed strangely familiar to me, but it was only when he spoke to the barman that I recognised him. He was the guy from outside the hairdresser's that day. My heart began to skip some beats. His blond hair was neither long nor entirely short either and it had a slight wave that gave him a boyish look. His eyebrows were knitted together in a stern look and his high cheekbones only exaggerated his slender physique. However, when the barman brought him his drink and he smiled a thank you, his dazzling blue eyes almost pierced my heart from across the room. As if that wasn't enough, his lips transformed into the most endearing smile, as the corners turned down slightly, creating little dimples in his cheeks.

At this stage Nicole elbowed my arm and asked what I was looking at.

'What me? Oh nothing really, just enjoying the place.'

'*N'importe quoi* – or should I say whatever, *ma belle*, you've spotted someone. Like a lioness and her prey. *Allez*, tell me who it is,' she insisted.

I felt like a schoolgirl again, pointing out the guy I liked.

'Ah, yes I see, *il est mignon, non*? He's cute. Why don't you go over and talk to him?' she suggested, just like that.

'What? I wouldn't know what to say!' She might as well have asked me to take all my clothes off then and there. It was unthinkable.

Nicole rolled her eyes in that impatient manner she had with dilly-dalliers.

'You don't have to say anything. Just walk by on your way to the restroom and give him *the look*,' she replied.

'The look?'

'The look, you know, the look that says, "Come and get me."' She laughed, before pouting seductively.

I thought about it for a second; I mean, here I was, starting a new life, and things were actually beginning to fall into place for me. I felt good about myself, my hair was coiffed, my red lipstick was on, what did I have to lose? Besides, sitting around and waiting for the man to come to me seemed ridiculously old-fashioned, even for me.

'Right, I'll do it!' I announced, knocking back the rest of my cocktail, which unfortunately went down the wrong way, inducing a temporary coughing fit.

'*Allez*, come on, you're fine,' Nicole soothed, giving me a napkin. 'Just walk over there and be hot!'

'Will do!'

I shimmied my way through the maze of tables, trying to seem as though shimmying was my natural state. As I was about to pass by the bar, my target's features had returned to those of a brooding grizzly bear, so I aborted the entire operation and took a swinging right turn towards the gents. Backtracking along the blue velvet drapes at the rear of the club, I managed to edge my way along to the ladies and dived into a cubicle. My heart was racing, as though I had just cheated death.

'So much for being hot,' I whispered to myself, hoping no one had witnessed yet another one of my most embarrassing moments. After a couple of minutes I opened the cubicle door and stood at the sink.

'Oh, well, maybe next time,' I muttered half-heartedly before reapplying my lipstick. I would just have to resign myself to the fact that I would never be a movie siren, just plain old Edith. I walked back into the club, which at this stage was really humming with smooth jazz and hard liquor. I gave a sideways glance at the bar and, to my disappointment, I noticed that ol' blue eyes had left his seat. I knew it shouldn't really matter. I mean, I didn't even know the guy and the chances of him already having already met someone with an ounce of confidence were disappointingly high. But I felt my heart sink a little at not getting to find out.

People had taken to dancing wherever they happened to be and I almost ended up in something of a *ménage à trois* in an effort to get past a couple lost in a slow dance. So I didn't even notice when I returned to my seat that Nicole was now chatting animatedly to a man in a grey suit. When he looked up into my face and gave me an ever-so-cool nod of recognition, my heart actually stopped for a second, as did everything else in the room.

'Ah, Edith, I would like you to meet Hugo Chadwick. Hugo, this is my friend, Edith, from Ireland.' Nicole did the honours without the faintest trace of guile in her wide, innocent eyes.

I instinctively went to shake his hand, forgetting all about the obligatory kisses, whereas he stood to embrace me appropriately or *'faire la bise'*. This miscommunication meant that I had embarrassingly greeted his groin while he lightly kissed me on my temple as I bent forward.

'Enchanté,' he said, kindly overlooking my faux pas. I couldn't remember anyone in my life ever having been genuinely enchanted to meet me. His deep, sultry voice reverberated in my ears and sent ripples along my skin. As we all sat around the table again, an awkward silence descended.

'Hugo has just arrived from London.' Nicole spoke to me as though speaking to a child unwilling to take advantage of an opportunity that had dropped neatly in her lap. Her widening stare provoked me into action and I grabbed the lifeline with both hands.

'Oh, you're not French, then? I thought with a name like Hugo…' I trailed off, aware that my voice sounded remarkably nothing like me.

'Half and half. My mother is French and my father is English,' he replied, still with that serious look that made it difficult to decipher whether he liked you or was simply tolerating you.

'*C'est comme Johnny et moi!*' Nicole interrupted, then realised that neither of us were really listening and so excused herself to move closer to the stage.

I was ridiculously nervous and my heart began to thump in double-quick time. Here was this attractive, intelligent, cosmopolitan guy and I couldn't think of the first thing to say. *Do you come here often* swam around my head a few times before I formed a less clichéd question.

'What brings you to Compiègne?' Well done, Edie, I thought, that almost sounded like something a normal person would say.

'Oh, this and that,' he said with a non-committal shrug, but to my delight, he moved to Nicole's chair to sit closer to me. I took a large gulp of my Mai Tai.

'Do you like jazz?' he countered.

Before I could even answer, he began shaking his head, as though he'd said something wrong.

'Sorry, I'm a bit out of practice.'

I couldn't believe it. He seemed nervous, which oddly put me more at ease.

'Actually, I love jazz,' I said. 'I grew up listening to all of the old standards, so this place is like heaven for me.'

His features brightened a little.

'Oh, good, because my French side was thinking of asking you to dance.'

'What was your English side thinking?'

Oh, my God. I was actually flirting. Where had that come from? He gave me a sidelong glance and it felt as though his mind grazed lightly on my figure.

'Now that would be telling,' he said playfully, before taking a sip of his drink.

I giggled, yes, giggled like a foolish teenager and pretended to look at something very interesting on the dancefloor.

'Well,' he said, leaning closer to my ear. 'Do you want to dance?'

'What, here?'

'Well, preferably on the dancefloor, I think that's what they generally had in mind when they set the tables up around it.'

I burst out laughing. His deadpan delivery was very disarming.

'Are we doing this?' he asked, standing up and offering me his hand.

Was I, Edith Lane, about to dance with this gorgeous guy? It felt as though there was some kind of catch. But watching him standing there, waiting for me to place my hand in his, I suddenly felt like all of my Christmases had come at once and maybe, just maybe, this was how life could be if you just said yes.

Chapter Nine

Once I fell into Hugo's embrace, I think we both knew where the evening would lead. I could have blamed the Mai Tais or the fact that Johnny's band began playing 'Let's Do It (Let's Fall In Love)', but the truth was that something was happening inside of me. I wasn't sure what it was, but something was becoming unstuck. When Hugo asked me to dance and the band sang about birds and bees doing it, my fate was sealed. Had we sat chatting at the table, we might well have gone our separate ways that night.

He didn't strike me as someone who would make a good dancer: his professional veneer and English reserve made him appear quite stuffy. But when we started to move on the dance floor, his French genes must have taken over, for he directed me in a practised manner with ease and confidence. We didn't speak very much, words seemed superfluous, but I felt so connected to him on a physical level that my inhibitions around him vanished. When the band finally wrapped up with a version of Benny Goodman's hectic 'Sing, Sing, Sing', we admitted defeat and returned to the table where Hugo ordered another round of drinks.

'Where did you learn to dance like that?' he asked.

'I was just following you,' I said, slightly out of breath and wishing I'd worn more comfortable shoes. I surreptitiously rubbed the side of my pinkie toe, which was probably already blistering. Taking a sip of my drink, I looked up to find myself the subject of the most intense stare.

'What is it?' I asked.

'Nothing,' he said, looking away and self-consciously rubbing the back of his neck. 'Or everything, actually'.

'What?'

'Do you want to get out of here?'

Just then, Nicole, her sister and her husband Johnny, arrived back at the table. Nicole made all of the introductions and while I was pleased to finally meet Johnny, the timing couldn't have been worse. It was clear they were mad about each other, as he caressed Nicole's neck and placed kisses on her cheek at every break in conversation. A soundtrack of cool jazz began playing over the sound system replacing the live musicians, and the tempo slowed to a soft sway. Chet Baker crooned, 'I Fall in Love Too Easily'. The whole atmosphere was intoxicating and I felt like I was starring in my own Hollywood romance. I gave Nicole a theatrical wink and said I needed the loo.

'What do you think?' I asked, as she followed me. I

suddenly realised that I was looking for guidance from a girl I had only just met, about a guy we hardly knew.

'He's very handsome. Do you like 'im?'

'Well, he's undeniably charming,' I said, smiling so hard that my cheeks hurt. 'And when we danced together, it was like ... every touch was just magical.' I hadn't realised that I'd closed my eyes and when I opened them, Nicole was grinning at me. 'He's asked me to go on somewhere else, but to be honest, I'm shattered,' I said, squinting at my watch. 'It must be all of these early mornings.'

'Why not ask him to walk you home?' she enthused, putting on her bright berry lipstick.

'Eh, I don't know, maybe because I hardly know him and he could be an axe murderer?' I pointed out.'

'Really?'

'Well, no, probably not, but—'

'Listen, *ma belle*, you came to France to change your ideas a bit, *non*? So follow your heart this time. It is OK to have some fun sometimes, you know!'

'You're right, you're right,' I said, smacking the palm of my head against my forehead. I was tired of being so sensible all of the time. Always assuming the worst and waiting for the other shoe to drop. I hadn't realised how hard it would be to break free from the old me, but there and then I felt the desperate urge to take a holiday from myself and all of my rules.

'You have my mobile number if you need me, *d'accord*?' she said, rousing me from my thoughts. 'Now stop over-thinking everything and get back out there!'

~

'So, Edith, you haven't told me what brought you to Compiègne,' Hugo asked, as we walked along the riverbank. The heightened sense of enjoyment I got out of hearing him say my name made me feel like a complete nerd, but his accent was so delicious I couldn't help it.

'Um, something of a clerical error,' I joked, sounding decidedly less posh than Hugo's tutored English accent. The cool night air came as a shock after the hot and sweaty atmosphere of Nostalgie, yet I somehow felt buffeted against the cold when Hugo offered his arm in such a chivalrous move that it made my heart glow a little brighter. 'I had always planned to come to France,' I said, sounding very cosmopolitan, 'but Compiègne was ... how can I put it?'

'A twist of fate?' he offered and I nodded in agreement. It certainly sounded better that way. 'And what do you do here?'

'I'm a singer.' I'd blurted it out before my brain had time to restrain me. I had no idea why I said it; all I knew was that I wanted to sound a little more interesting than a mid-life-crisis victim working in a bakery.

'Really?' he asked, genuinely impressed by my not so run-of-the-mill answer. In fact, he seemed so impressed that I was reluctant to correct him. Besides, what harm would it do to tell a little white lie? As Nicole said, I wasn't marrying the guy.

'Yes, well, I mean, I'm working in a bakery here until I get my big break, but yes, I'm a singer.'

'What genre of music do you sing? Do you write your own songs?' he enthused, unaware of the pressure he was putting on me to make up the answers.

'Mainly jazz,' I said, trying to keep it vague and nonchalant.

'Ah, hence Nostalgie,' he concluded.

'Mmm … and what about you? You never said what it was you do,' I deflected, buying myself some time from my ridiculously tall tale.

'Um, well, I do some photography,' he said.

'Really, oh, that sounds so interesting! What kind of photography?' For a moment I imagined him doing nude portraits. I crossed my fingers.

'Streetscapes, mostly, I'm not very good at it, though.'

Phew! Humble and artistic, he almost seemed too good to be true.

'In fact, I'm off to Paris in the morning to take some shots on location,' he added

I emitted a kind of strangled noise.

'What is it?'

'Oh, nothing. I just … I didn't get to see much of Paris when I arrived.' I decided not to tell him what a moron I'd been, confusing the name of the bakery.

'Well, I have an apartment there. You can use it, if you like…'

Who said things like that? *I have an apartment in Paris if you want to use it.* I felt like I'd accidentally stepped into someone else's life for the night. I hoped it wouldn't all end at midnight.

We came to a bench that offered a beautiful view of the Pont Solferino bridge, with its lights reflected in the flowing waters of the River Oise. Despite the chill, the late hour and the absurdity of it, we both instinctively sat down, wishing to prolong the evening.

71

'So do you live here, or…' I didn't want it to sound like an interview question, but I was curious to fill in the blanks.

'Not anymore. I grew up here, but we moved to Paris when I was about seven. It's funny,' he said, looking out towards the bridge and the lights of the buildings, 'I always remember it being bigger than it is.'

'That's childhood memories for you, half of them are inventions.'

'What makes you say that?' he asked, turning to look at me, with an unreadable smile on his face.

'Oh, I don't know.' I really didn't know. I'd been trying to block out the painful memories for so long now, it was difficult to recall what actually happened, what was true and how my childhood brain had interpreted it. 'Two people can have the same experience, yet still have completely different memories of it.'

He looked out at the water again, as if trying to solve some puzzle.

'Have you read Proust?'

I burst out laughing.

'What?' he asked.

'Sorry, it's just so random!'

We both began to laugh. It seemed like a ridiculous question to ask someone, half drunk, that you'd just met in a bar called Nostalgie. He reached into the inside pocket of his jacket and pulled out a beaten up old paperback and handed it to me.

'*Swann's Way* by Marcel Proust,' I read aloud.

'It's the first volume of *In Search of Lost Time*. I think you might like it. Besides, you're living in France now so you have to read Proust. I don't make the rules.'

'And you just happen to carry a copy around with you, like a prop,' I said, flicking through the pages.

'What can I say, I like to have a paperback on my person at all times.'

'You're not really like anyone I've ever met before,' I said, letting my guard down momentarily.

'I hope that's a good thing.'

So do I, I thought to myself.

I felt his fingertips brushing against mine and looked up at his face. God, I wanted to kiss him. I wasn't sure if I was leaning towards him or if the earth tilted on its axis, but before I knew it, our lips were touching. I could feel his stubble grazing my top lip, his hand reaching up to cradle the back of my neck and it felt like a romantic film. There wasn't a sound, just the breeze blowing in the branches overhead. He kissed me softly and deeply, the warmth of his breath on my skin intoxicating. It was the most beautiful feeling of complete abandonment, and I did not want it to end.

I felt light-headed when we stopped and I didn't know what to say.

'That was…' he murmured.

'Yeah,' I agreed.

He held my hand in his and eventually we found some words and began forming sentences again. But none of it really mattered. It was all secondary to whatever unspoken thing was happening between us.

'Do you make a habit of kissing strange women on park benches, Mr Chadwick?'

'On a scale of one to ten, how strange are we talking?'

I smacked his arm playfully and he leaned in to kiss my ear. Oh, God, I was really falling for him.

'In fact, I have a very strict rule about kissing women on benches after midnight,' he continued.

'Oh, and what is that?'

'Well, you see, the thing is, they have to sing me a song.'

Oh dear. I had well and truly landed myself in it. When he'd asked me what I was doing in France, I'd felt compelled to embellish the truth and for some reason, a long-forgotten dream I had had about being a singer just popped into my head. I used to sing for my mother all the time but I had never done anything about pursuing it. It was as if I had now become possessed by my younger self, who was intent on living out all of the dreams I had never been able to fulfil.

'I really couldn't,' I began nervously.

'I know, the crowd must be putting you off.' He waved his hand to gesture at the family of ducks sailing obliviously past us on the river's gentle current.

'I just can't, I'd be embarrassed. There's no music for starters,' I complained, knowing this was going to be a losing battle, as he had begun to kiss my neck, all the while whispering gentle encouragements. I'm not sure if it was the drink, the magic of the star-speckled night, or if it was just him, but I started to think, what did it matter? I'd probably never see him again, so why not live out this little fantasy until the dawn arrived and broke the spell?

Taking a deep breath and a giant leap of faith, I closed my eyes and sang my old favourite, 'Dream a Little Dream of Me'. I hadn't sung in so long, I knew I was a little rusty, but there was something in the tone of my voice that even surprised me. It was richer, deeper and more emotive than ever before.

Stars shining bright above you
Night breezes seem to whisper 'I love you'
Birds singin' in the sycamore trees
Dream a little dream of me…

'Gosh, you have a beautiful voice,' Hugo said, his voice breaking slightly.

'The last time I sang that song was for my mother,' I told him. 'She's … she's passed away now.'

He said nothing, but took me into his arms. I didn't cry, but I just let myself be held and it felt like such a relief. I hadn't told anyone here the real reason behind my sudden decision to come to France, and even though this was probably the most inopportune moment to open up, not to mention the wrong person, it just happened.

'You OK?' he asked in a soft voice.

I just nodded. I was as OK as I could be.

'It doesn't get any easier, does it?' he asked, somewhat rhetorically.

'I'm just not sure who to be now. Or how,' I said. 'That probably sounds silly—'

'No, I know exactly what you mean. Unfortunately. I lost my brother.'

'Oh, I'm so sorry.' I looked up at his face, but he wore that same mask we all did, those who are left behind, trying to carry on. The club no one wants to be a member of.

'It's about six years ago now. I was twenty-five. I mean, we didn't even get on, but still it changes everything.'

He was right. It did change everything; so much so that I had to change who I was in order to gain some kind of control over my life again.

I wanted to stay there indefinitely, but the cold had finally broken through to my skin and I was desperate for a warm drink.

'Do you want to come back to mine for coffee?'

'Is that a euphemism or actual coffee, because I'd murder a coffee,' he said drily.

This garnered him another smack on the arm.

'You'll be lucky if you do get a coffee at this rate,' I said, failing to hide my smile.

'I'm being assaulted here, you know. Oi, gendarmes, arrest this woman!' he shouted at some students passing over the bridge who responded with all sorts of taunts and gestures that happily I did not understand.

The walk took far longer than necessary, because with every few strides, we were both drawn to each other's lips. My arms reached under his overcoat and embraced the warmth of his body as we kissed by the crêperie then the tabac, before we eventually reached the *boulangerie*.

'So, this is me,' I said, just like they do in the movies. 'But Madame Moreau, my boss that is, lives in the apartment below me so you'll have to be quiet…' I could see his features changing completely. 'What is it?'

'You work here, for Madame Moreau?'

'Yes, why, do you know her? She's not exactly boss of the year material, but I'm really growing to like the place and the accommodation is free so…' I smiled, but Hugo's expression remained unchanged.

'You know, I'd best be getting back,' he said. 'I have an

early meeting in Paris in the morning and I don't want to cause any trouble with your boss.'

'Oh.' I failed to keep the tone of disappointment from my voice, so decided to make up for it by babbling on endlessly about Madame Moreau. 'You're probably right, I've only been here a fortnight and she might start to question my morals along with everything else if I bring a guy home.'

He smiled and held my hand, and looked at me as if in two minds whether to tell me something. In the end, I made the decision for both of us.

'Thank you for the book, Mr Chadwick. And for walking me home.'

'The pleasure has been entirely mine, Miss Lane,' he responded, lifting both of my hands and kissing each of them tenderly. 'I hope to see you again,' he added, lifting those piercing blue eyes.

'Well, if you ever need a baguette, you know where I am,' I smiled.

He pulled me close then, and gave me a ravishingly good kiss on the lips, leaving me with a slightly tipsy feeling.

'Goodnight, Edith,' he said, as he turned to leave.

'Goodnight, Hugo.'

I climbed the creaky old stairs to my apartment, still in a daze. I hung my coat up by the door and slipped out of my shoes, smiling inanely all the while. No sooner had I turned on the lamp by the window looking out onto the street when I heard stones ricocheting off the glass. I skipped to the window and looked down at Hugo about to take another aim.

'Oi, what are you doing, you'll wake the dragon!' I hissed.

'Ah, what light from yonder window breaks,' he called amusingly.

'Quit goofing around or you'll get me the sack, Romeo,' I said, unable to conceal my pleasure at seeing him standing down there, acting like a romantic fool for me.

'I just wanted to ask if you'd like to go out to dinner next time I'm in town.'

'That would be lovely,' I whispered down to him.

'It's a date, then,' he confirmed.

'Yes, it's a date,' I echoed, almost in confirmation to myself. I couldn't really believe this was happening.

'*Bonne nuit*, Edith.'

I waved silently and blew him a kiss, which he caught and held to his heart, then half collapsed as if I had shot him. All too soon, he turned to go and I could have sworn I heard him whistling the tune 'Dream a Little Dream of Me', but I couldn't be sure.

Chapter Ten

My mother had been ill for a long time. She had known from a young age that her time would be limited once she was diagnosed with cystic fibrosis, or sixty-five roses as I used to call it when I was a child. But it was not a life sentence that damned her – quite the opposite, in fact. She was determined to live life to the full and make the most of every experience. She had to spend a lot of time in hospital, dealing with infections and other complications, so we had to try our best to make it fun. She and my father were what you would call high-school sweethearts. She always said she knew he was the one when, after she told him about her illness, he told her they'd just have to hurry up and live a life's worth of memories in half the time.

'Telling someone you have an incurable disease is a surefire way of separating the men from the boys,' she often told me.

That's why they decided to have me when my mother was only twenty. My father was twenty-one at the time and got a job as the desserts chef in a top café in Dublin. He packed it all in when Mum began to get really sick and took on work as a taxi driver, which still meant long hours, but at least he could work the shifts that suited him. The average life expectancy for cystic fibrosis sufferers is forty years, so we cherished every year we shared beyond that. They both made it quite clear that I didn't need to stay at home. 'I can get home help,' my father would always insist. But I was their only child. It had always been the three of us against the world and it just didn't feel right to abandon them when they needed me the most. With Dad's help, I converted the garage at home into a little studio apartment, so I had my own front door while still living at home. We managed quite well between us and, despite their protestations, I knew my parents were glad to have me close by.

With the hindsight that only time can give, I realised too late why they wanted me to make a life for myself. There are some things that are better done when you're young and foolhardy and unafraid of failure. That's the time when you build your career, meet your future husband, carve out your own space in the world. But I couldn't do it and never once regretted the time I spent laughing, crying, watching old films or sharing a box of chocolates with my mother. She stayed at home a lot to prevent any risk of infection, so we turned it into our own little world indoors.

I'd avoided the big bad world for so long, but now I would have to turn the natural order of things on its head. At thirty years old and something of a late bloomer, I was determined to finally live my student years.

I awoke to church bells ringing and, for the first time since I had arrived, I realised I had slept the night through. Picking up my phone, I saw the time was 9.30am, and despite a medium-sized hangover, I felt well rested. My thoughts instantly turned to Hugo and I couldn't help the smile that kept creeping across my face as I replayed our evening together. When I eventually got around to taking a shower, I absent-mindedly began humming to myself and, to my complete embarrassment, remembered singing for him.

'Oh, my God!' I screeched, putting my hands to my mouth, while the water cascaded down my back. I shoved my head underneath the temperamental spout that changed force on a whim. Still, I couldn't help but laugh, because the entire night had been so surreal. Even telling him about my mother only seemed to forge a stronger bond. 'Hugo,' I whispered, just wanting to say his name.

My last boyfriend, Barry, was a postman. My mother always joked that the only way I would ever meet a man was if he came to our house and knocked on the door, and strangely enough that is exactly what happened. He seemed happy-go-lucky and always did his best to make me laugh. When he asked me out, I didn't really feel butterflies, but rather a practical resignation to it all. I felt like the chances of me meeting someone were slim, so I thought I'd better make the best of this one chance. I ignored my lukewarm feelings for Barry as long as possible, because I really did want to love him and marry and maybe even start a family. It would have been ... well, it would have been convenient. But while I was feeling guilty about not loving him, I didn't notice that in some ways, he was taking advantage of me. I was spending nearly every night at his flat and without understanding why or how, I sort of became his housekeeper. I was constantly cooking, cleaning and basically taking care of him, on top of taking care of my mother at home. It all became too much in the end and I finally snapped when he asked why I hadn't bought flowers for *his* mother on Mother's Day.

'Oh, just grow up, Barry!' I shouted, before leaving his apartment for the last time. I thought I might even be a bit sad, but all I felt was relief. My mother just smiled and patted my hand.

'You'll know when it's right,' was all she said.

Wrapped in a towel, I tiptoed across the floorboards to where my phone lay flashing on the bed. A text from Nicole inviting me to Sunday lunch at her mother's house. She couldn't have picked a better time to reach out the hand of friendship, for all these thoughts of home were making me pine for some familial company.

I heard Madame Moreau returning home, most likely from Sunday mass. I wondered if she was lonely and whether she had any invites to Sunday lunch. I pushed the thought from my head. I would be seeing her soon enough in the morning.

Wearing my go-to jeans, ballet flats and oversized cardigan, I set off to find Nicole's family home. It wasn't far from the centre and despite the maze-like nature of the town, I found it easily enough. On Rue Sainte Antoine the detached houses all seemed to have their own unique character and design. Nicole's mother's house had a curved roof that made room for one little window at the top of the house and then gradually stretched out to incorporate more windows on the first floor. An iron gate opened onto a gravel drive with shrubs lining the way up to the steps at the front door, which was painted a spring-like green, with coloured glass panels on each side.

'*Bonjour, bonjour.*' Madame Dubois hugged and kissed me like a long-lost friend and insisted that I call her Jacqueline. Looking every inch the glamour puss in a leopardskin blouse and matching skirt, she invited me in and took my coat and bag and hung them in a cupboard under the stairs, only to discover a little monster waiting inside who almost knocked her over with fright.

'*Maxi, mais qu'est ce que tu fous là-dedans?*' she admonished him lightly, wagging her finger and making lots of gestures he happily ignored. Nicole's little boy ran across the parquet floor straight towards me and then stopped just as fast. He pulled a toy gun out of his pocket, carefully took aim and shot me in the stomach. I couldn't see anything for it but to play along, so I folded in two with pain etched across my face. His laughter rang through the house, and when he even offered a tiny hand to help me back up, I knew I had passed the test.

'*Max, essaie de ne pas tirer sur nos amis, s'il te plaît!*' Nicole, coming out of the kitchen, begged her son not to shoot the dinner guest. She embraced me warmly and brought me down into the kitchen, which took up the entire back of the house, with windows onto the garden at the rear. A giant table with countless chairs sat in the centre of the room, while an old range heated pots and pans in the corner. It was vintage yet chic, old-fashioned but timeless. Johnny appeared rather incongruously from the garden, with a handful of rosemary.

'All right, Edie? Good to see you again,' he said, kissing me. It felt weird doing 'la bise' with an Englishman, but as they say, when in Rome, or Compiègne, in my case. 'How's the head?' he teased, but Nicole elbowed him into silence.

We ate a hearty meal of roast chicken with lemon and rosemary and lots of roast garlic potatoes on the side. I had brought the dessert, which was a raspberry tart with crème anglaise. I passed on the wine, insisting that I would need a clear head to be up at six the next morning. I knew Nicole was desperate to ask me about Hugo, but as she sensed I wasn't keen to discuss it in front of everyone, we talked about the bakery instead. It seemed Madame Moreau and Jacqueline went way back.

'Geneviève Moreau? Je la connais depuis des années,' Jacqueline began, Nicole beside her, translating in case there were any parts I didn't understand.

'Monsieur Moreau, Geneviève's father, died in the late sixties and she's been running the place herself since then,' Nicole explained, bobbing Max on her knee as he recreated a war scene with some soldiers and leftover raspberries on the table. 'She must be at least eighty years old.'

'Bloody hell! Eighty? But she struts around that shop like a spring chicken!' I gasped, waiting for Nicole to translate. Finding out her Christian name was also something of a shock. The name Geneviève was somehow too sweet for the tough woman who greeted me with a scowl every morning.

'She's had a hard life, according to *Maman*. My grandmother also remembers the regime having several run-ins with Monsieur Moreau during the war.'

This was such an eye-opener for me. All I had seen was a grumpy old woman, with little or no time for pleasantries. This was creating an entirely new picture of a young girl who had lived through the war with her father, withstood the tyranny of German occupation and still managed to keep his legacy alive.

'So, who has taken over the baking since Monsieur Moreau's death?' I asked. 'The basement is strictly off-limits for me,' I added, still stung by Madame Moreau's lack of trust in me.

'*Je ne sais pas*,' Jacqueline admitted.

'It's strange because I've been there for two weeks now and I never see anyone going in or coming out. And unless they're milling their own flour underground, I don't know how they're getting it in, because no deliveries show up, either.'

Johnny brought a large pot of coffee to the table along with a glass jar of biscotti. Even though I felt fit to burst, I couldn't resist the golden, amaretto-flavoured biscuits.

'Sounds like you've got a bit of a mystery on your hands,' Johnny said. 'The haunted bakery, where no one is seen going in and no one is seen going out, whooo!' He began to laugh, while Max imitated his not-so-scary ghost impression.

'I'm serious,' I persisted, 'Madame Moreau has all the bread stocked up and Manu has loaded his deliveries before I even get up. There's never any sign of the baker. I just assumed they brought up the bread themselves from the kitchen, but why not let me go down? I mean, I'm supposed to be taking over as assistant manager, for God's sake.'

'Assistante manay-jar?' Jacqueline repeated in a cute French accent, and I smiled.

'Well, that was the job title. I think she's going to have to retire soon. Even if she finds it difficult to let go of the reins, her arthritis won't let her carry on without help for much longer.'

'*Maman* says she must like you – the last girl, Maria, only lasted two days.'

I knew this was meant to comfort me, but somehow it didn't. Again, I wondered what had gone wrong with Maria.

'I know, we'll all start keeping a closer eye on the bakery and see if we can't catch them out. Maybe they're laundering money down there or cooking up some class A drugs!' joked Johnny.

'You'll have to eat your words when I discover a … I don't know … a secret dough society or something,' I said, playing along.

As the dark evening sky settled in around the house, I made the reluctant move to go home.

'*Merci pour tout,*' I said to Jacqueline, kissing her warmly at the door.

'*Je t'en prie, chérie,*' she said, as if it was nothing.

Max was asleep on a little settee near the fire and Nicole didn't want to wake him just yet for their walk home. They lived in an apartment near the university, which was convenient to her mother's house and the salon.

'I will walk Edith to the end of the road while you wash the dishes, Johnny, *d'accord*?' She smiled at him sweetly.

'You see what I have to put up with, Edith?' he said, kissing me goodbye. 'They treat me like their English slave: cooking, cleaning and I won't say what else to save your blushes!'

Nicole threw a tea towel at his head to quieten him, but it didn't work.

'We'll see you at Nostalgie next week, yeah?' he shouted after me.

'Oh, yeah, I'd love to. Your band was amazing, I really enjoyed it,' I said sincerely. 'But who's that Django guy you kept talking about? Was that his music you were playing?'

'Oh, my God, you're joking, right?' he asked in all seriousness. 'Django Reinhardt – you don't know who he is?' he asked.

On seeing my newly acquired Gallic shrug, he begged us to wait for five minutes while he dug out a vinyl from his collection.

'Django Reinhardt is only the king of gypsy jazz,' he informed me, barely excusing my philistine ignorance. 'You've got to take this home,' he said. 'Listen to it, familiarise yourself with it and we'll pretend this conversation never happened, right?'

'Not everyone has a record player, Johnny,' Nicole reminded him.

'Right, well, stream it, then. Obviously it won't have the real, authentic sound…'

'I'll listen, I promise!' I said.

A drizzle had begun, so I told Nicole she needn't bother stepping outside.

'But I wanted to hear all about Hugo!' she said.

'It'll keep, nothing happened. Well, nothing and everything,' I admitted hopelessly.

'OK, tomorrow, meet me after work for a glass and tell me everything, yes?'

'All right, everything, I promise.'

Chapter Eleven

Hugo Chadwick

Hugo heard the wrought-iron and glass doors of his apartment building click behind him. He liked the feeling it gave him, walking out onto the street from his third-floor apartment, just steps away from the Jardin du Luxembourg in the 6th arrondissement. His father had gifted an apartment each to him and his brother when they'd turned twenty-one. At the last evaluation, it was worth 1.5 million euros. Hugo never really felt any sense of ownership over it, though. He hadn't worked for it or earned it. But now he was coming to realise that the apartment was a downpayment of sorts, an unspoken commitment to Chadwick Holdings and his father. His future was already bought and sold. There was a time when he might have rebelled, but after Stéphane's death, the weight of responsibility outweighed any personal feelings. He had to make up for what had happened.

Walking down the Boulevard Saint-Germain towards the Seine, an old shopfront caught his eye on a side street, just before the Quai d'Orsay. Now trading as a *salon de thé*, it had once been a flower shop, with large windows and an unusual shape, as it hugged the corner of two streets. He was already running late, but couldn't help himself. Slipping his rucksack off his shoulder, Hugo took out his trusty Nikon D780. The shop itself was tiny, but there were brightly coloured tables and chairs outside for the patrons to enjoy their flavoured teas. An old wooden sign over the doorway still had the faint outline of the original name and artwork, '*À l'eau de rose*', with cerise pink roses intertwining the letters. In the morning light, it looked almost like a dream. If it weren't for the sound of the traffic and the deliveries, Hugo could almost imagine he had stepped back in time. He looked down at the little screen and scrolled through the images he'd captured. A smile crept across his face as that familiar feeling of satisfaction glowed within him. He couldn't explain it exactly, but there was something about capturing the world the way he saw it – or rather the way he wanted everyone else to see it – that gave him a sense of fulfilment and joy that nothing else could match. It was a passion project he kept mostly to himself. Apart from his mother of course, who understood that creative urge to make something. His father would mock him and his brother, when alive, couldn't see the point in it.

Hugo took a deep breath, put the camera back in his pack and continued on his way to the office.

～

'As you know, my wife inherited the building many years ago and we have now acquired the adjoining premises—' Raymond Chadwick halted as his son walked into the boardroom. The look he gave him was imperceptible to the partners around the table, but Hugo knew what it meant. Resentment. The words had never been spoken, but the meaning was clear: the wrong son had died.

'We've made an offer on the corner building,' his father then continued, 'and I'm confident that we should have acquired the entire street by the end of the month. My son here will be heading up the negotiations with the hotel group,' he finished, concealing any doubts he might have had as to Hugo's ability.

'Yes, in fact I've already been liaising with the design team and they're quite adamant that they wish to retain the original facade,' Hugo said, taking out some brochures and handing them around the table. His father gave him another of his covert looks, but, as always, was careful not to betray his emotions in public. Hugo was counting on this as he added, 'I must say I tend to agree, as we want to keep the local council on our side. There will be a lot of disruption to the area—'

'As well as regeneration, employment, increased business rates…' his father countered.

'Absolutely,' Hugo said, swallowing hard. He had to win this argument. 'However, retaining the historical facade would go a long way towards ingratiating the local businesses—'

'Gentlemen,' Raymond cut in, oozing fake charm, 'I am sure you all appreciate my son's enthusiasm for the genteel aesthetic, but let us move on to more important matters and touch base with the negotiating team once they've secured the contract for the final property.'

With that, Hugo was excused, like a child who'd been pestering the grown-ups. It was utterly humiliating, but he had to risk his father's ire if it meant retaining something of the property in question's original features. If his father had his way, every piece of beautiful architecture would be replaced with angular concrete and glass. All Raymond cared about was profit, and yet the more money he made, the more miserable he became. Hugo couldn't understand what was driving his father anymore. Win at all costs, that was his motto. But win what, exactly?

Walking home that evening, Hugo passed by the old flower shop again. The light had completely changed, and even though the facade was just as ornately beautiful, it lacked the vibrancy he had caught this morning. That's what he loved about photography – the conditions were so happenstance, you could never capture the same image twice. In a habit he could hardly recall forming, Hugo touched the left inside pocket of his jacket where his paperback should've been. Then he remembered: Edith. He shook his head with a smile at the memory. She must have thought him so contrived. But it was true – he carried that book everywhere like a talisman. In some ways it was a symbol of protection – something that was stopping him from turning into his father. And yet he could feel himself slipping.

When Stéphane was alive, he was the centre of attention.

He was naturally full of charm, and as the first-born son his every achievement was lauded, every indiscretion indulged. Hugo had always looked up to him as some sort of demigod. Yet it was only after his death that Hugo realised how much of a buffer his brother had been between him and his father. As long as Stéphane was the high achiever, the heir apparent to the Chadwick fortune, his father was happy and this allowed Hugo to pursue the life he wanted. Being the younger brother, he didn't feel any pressure to carry the mantle of his father's expectations. In fact, he wasn't sure that much was expected of him at all. Stéphane had been the golden child. But in the end, all of that pressure began to weigh down on him. And now it was crushing Hugo, too.

Taking photographs of old buildings began as a hobby, but it had become so much more than that. It felt as though keeping some kind of connection with the values of the past could keep him connected to his soul. In the dying light of the evening, he now saw his camera lens as a doorway, some kind of threshold between the life he was living and the idealised version of it he'd once had. The gulf between these two realities was beginning to swallow him up.

Chapter Twelve

On Monday morning I awoke at my usual time of 6am. I pulled the shutters and stared out the window at every opportunity, with a toothbrush in my mouth or a hairbrush tangled in my hair, looking for signs of any clandestine behaviour that might betray the Moreaus. The street was quiet, nothing stirred. I would have to get up a lot earlier if I was going to catch the baker using the basement door. I skipped breakfast and tumbled downstairs for 6.30am, but Madame Moreau, who had seemingly risen at some unthinkable hour, was already unloading baskets of freshly made bread onto the shelves. Manu was yet to arrive, but the boxes awaiting delivery were already neatly stacked by the door. How did she do it all? And at her age?

'*Bonjour, Madame Moreau,*' I said, startling her.

'*Bonjour, Édith,*' she replied.

I thought she looked a little tired this morning, so I

offered to make her a coffee before we opened. This really took her by surprise and even though she turned me down, I felt something alter between us. I quietly went about my work, and opened the door for Manu when he arrived. The rain was pouring down and I really felt for him, having to get on that scooter and deliver bread. He wrapped a small tarpaulin over the boxes and zoomed off without much ado.

'He's a good lad, isn't he?' I said to Madame Moreau. '*Il est bien*,' I repeated.

'*Il travaille bien, oui*,' she agreed, giving very little away.

'*Il habite près d'ici*?' I pressed on, trying to find out if he lived in the area or who his family were and, perhaps, how he ended up working here.

'*En haut*.' She lifted her head briefly, signalling above our heads.

'He lives with you?' I said, unable to hide my incredulity. Thanks to this little faux pas, I was back to receiving grunts and hand signals that I should get on with my work. And with that the first few customers of the morning came in and there was no further time to think about it.

Working with freshly baked goods all day brought back so many of the wonderful childhood memories that I had stored away for a long time. When my father gave up his position as pastry chef, he turned our kitchen at home into a playground for his artistic expression. My mother and I were often treated to light and airy profiteroles, oozing with cream and smothered in chocolate, or dark chocolate tortes with roasted hazelnut crusts. My favourites were the cakes, and at his side I became quite proficient myself and made a mean spicy carrot cake. He would always say that you could tell a lot about a baker by his choice of ingredients. Needless to say, I was intrigued to meet the master baker who'd reinvigorated my appetite with his delicious breads and sinfully good pastries. Yet he remained shrouded in mystery, hidden in the Moreaus' basement.

In an effort to become better acquainted with his produce, at least, I spent my lunch time doing a little taste test in the café. I told Madame Moreau that I wished to become more familiar with the different kinds of bread and she just shrugged indifference. Having the place to myself, I set my phone up to play some of the Django Reinhardt music that Johnny had recommended. As soon as the guitar began to play, I instantly fell in love with gypsy jazz and found myself swaying along to the rhythm as I began picking out breads to try. Leaving aside the well-known baguettes and traditional *pain de campagne* and *pain complet* (white and brown), I gathered the more unusual-looking breads into my arms and found myself salivating with the scent of fresh, crusty bread. So I sat down at a little table by the window and, using a breadboard and knife, I cut into the first round of bread, labelled *'pain au levain'*, which I determined from its tangy flavour to be sourdough. I remembered my father making a sourdough starter at home, and leaving it to ferment overnight. I used to love watching it transform and come to life.

'See the bubbles, Edie?' he used to say. 'That means wild yeast from the air and the flour itself have started making themselves a home in your starter. They will eat the sugars in the flour and increase the acidity of the mixture, preventing other "bad" microbes from growing.'

It was like a culinary science experiment. Once the

sourdough became frothy and fermented, it was ready to use. My mother insisted he keep his 'experiments' in the utility room because of the pungent smell. He would then bake a loaf of delicious bread (which went a long way towards making up for the stink) but hold back a portion of the sourdough, 'feed' it with flour and water, and keep the process going. He said some bakers would have kept a sourdough 'mother' going for more than a hundred years. I used to think it was a bit strange at the time, growing bacteria to make bread, but tasting this light and airy loaf in the bakery made me truly appreciate this time-honoured tradition. I also wondered how old the Moreaus' sourdough was and who had made the starter in the first place.

Next, I tried a round *pain aux raisins*, which I knew to be raisin bread. I instinctively tapped on the base of the loaf, hearing a wonderfully deep echo that sounded the guarantee of a thick, dark crust. The crunchy bread was tantalisingly good and the sweet, swollen raisins gave it an extra dimension. After a large glass of milk, I gluttonously moved on to a wholesome *pain aux noix*, a walnut bread made with wholewheat flour. In France, the walnut was the king of the nuts, so they simply referred to this loaf as nut bread, as if walnut was the only nut worth eating. With just the right balance of acidity and crunchy walnuts that were almost whole (meaning they must have been added after the kneading process), this bread was my favourite. It was moist and slightly darker in colour than the others, and I could have happily gorged on the entire loaf. Of course I ate them all smothered with butter, like a true Irishwoman. By the time I got to the *pain bis*, a rye bread, I was completely stuffed and full of respect for our reclusive baker. I wasn't an expert or anything, but from the flavours and textures of the breads, my suspicions that they were baked in a wood-burning oven were confirmed. I pushed back my chair and looked towards the rear of the shop. There was a swinging door that led to a small room with a sink and a small worktop for preparing *tartines* or sandwiches and a little electric *chauffe grille* for toasting.

Without consciously making a plan, I got up and strolled over towards the back, fixing things and wiping counters as I passed. I looked back out onto the street, which was quiet at this time of day, and listened for any sound of Madame Moreau upstairs. I could just about hear her little television, probably some kind of afternoon quiz show. Satisfied that I would not be disturbed, I snuck into the kitchenette. I had seen a tiny door there before, just beside the miniature fridge, but had simply assumed it was a cupboard, such was the size. It was painted a pale eggshell blue-grey colour, with two panels of frosted glass obscuring what I now realised must be the basement just beyond. Madame Moreau, being small in stature, would have easily fitted through, but I would have to crouch. I gently turned the little glass knob, but to my disappointment, it was locked. I just stood there looking at it, willing it to open. Then inspiration struck, and I quickly swung the door of the kitchenette open again. The unisex toilet was just on the other side of the kitchenette and although I wasn't sure what access could be gained from the loo, it was worth a try. The loo was quite posh as it goes, with some kind of vintage wallpaper, repeating scenes of the well-to-do taking part in various outdoor pursuits. The taps were gold-plated, as was the mirror, and it felt at once both homely and chic.

To my delight, I spotted a grille plate on the floor behind the sink that looked down into the basement. An old iron thing, I lifted it easily with my pen and for the first time I had a partial view of the baker's domain. It was incredibly authentic and I realised that things must have changed very little since Monsieur Moreau's time. The walls were simply exposed bricks and the floor plain concrete, and everything was dusted with a fine layer of flour. No wonder the bread tasted so good, I mused, they were probably using age-old recipes and baking them in the wood-fired oven. I could just see the side of it from my rather awkward vantage point, but I didn't even need to – I could smell the rich scent of burnt wood. I could just make out the bags of flour stacked against the wall – marked '*Farine*' – and tall wooden shelves holding antique moulds and sheet pans, slightly warped from the intense heat of the ovens. The only thing missing was the baker himself, but I assumed he must have finished for the day, as he would have started baking at 4am. My knees were hurting from the tiled floor and I was about to heave myself up when a voice startled me.

'*Eh, ça va, Édith*?' asked Manu, clearly bewildered by my behaviour.

'Oh, Manu, I didn't see you there,' I replied a little flustered. 'I, eh, just lost my earring,' I bluffed. '*J'ai perdu* my earring,' I repeated, laughing at my own stupidity and sliding the grate back into place with my foot. He nodded, but I knew he wasn't convinced. I just had time to tidy up after my little taster session when Madame Moreau reappeared, unceremoniously turning off the music. She seemed irritated, which was nothing new, but something about the music had affected her. There was no chance to question her, as it was time to open again and I needed to go and freshen myself up. Climbing the stairs, I still couldn't shake the feeling that Manu and Madame Moreau's inimical facade was an attempt to hide something. But what? Were they really doing something illegal down there? It hardly seemed likely. But I could tell from their strange behaviour that something was going on and I was determined to get to the bottom of it.

That evening, I met Nicole for a drink in a café overlooking the river. Walking down the lamplit streets, and taking the familiar turns towards the city centre, I realised that Compiègne had indeed become familiar to me. It seemed like a lifetime ago since I'd arrived on that unexpected train journey from Paris, full of disappointment at my sheer bad luck to have taken on a job in some outlying village. I had come a long way in a few short weeks, in every sense. Nicole was sitting at the bar chatting amiably with one of the bar staff when I arrived. I had never met someone so comfortable in their own skin, and the ease with which she bonded with people left me feeling a little envious.

'So…' she prompted, after ordering me a glass of wine and a snack of pâté and bread. Both were exceedingly delicious and bursting with strong flavours.

'So, he … I mean, Hugo, walked me home,' I began,

though it felt strange saying his name out loud. It was such a magical night and while I had tried my hardest not to daydream about it since, I sometimes wondered if it had ever happened at all.

'Yes, and…' Nicole said impatiently.

'Well, we talked a lot and… Oh, you know he's a photographer?' I said.

'*Très bien, et…*' she prompted, eager to get to the good bits.

'OK, OK, we kissed!' I swooned like a schoolgirl and didn't even have the dignity to hide it. The memory of his soft lips came rushing back to me and I actually blushed. 'God, he was such a good kisser.'

'*Voilà – je l'avais dit*! You're going to have fun in France, *non*?' she purred. 'Are you meeting him again?'

'Well, that's just it: he said he had to go back to Paris for some work thing. Actually, I don't know when he's coming back, he didn't say.'

'Did he take your number? I'm sure he'll call,' she said matter-of-factly, flipping her dark hair over her shoulder and revealing giant white hoop earrings.

'Eh, no, he didn't,' I realised with a sinking feeling. 'I didn't even think to ask.'

'Hmm, but he lives here, yes?'

'I don't think so. He said he has an apartment in Paris.' Now that I was saying this aloud to Nicole, the whole thing began to sound a bit sketchy. 'Oh, God, you don't think he's married, do you?'

'*Pourquoi*, what makes you think that?' Nicole asked, clearly less concerned about the possibility than me. She was French, after all.

'Well, when we got back to the bakery, I invited him up and he just said something about having to get up early. At the time I thought he was being chivalrous, you know? I mean I'm not completely deluded, I'm sure he was interested, but it's like he stopped himself. Now I'm thinking it was guilt that made him hesitate.'

'*Non, je ne pense pas*. He did not have that vibe of a married man.'

'What vibe?' I asked.

'Well, it's hard to describe, but he was too uneasy to be married. You know, married men are just more relaxed, probably because they know they have someone at home. Nah, he was too tense to be married.'

'That's ridiculous, tense people get married. Relaxed people marry and become tense! What kind of reasoning is that? You're just trying to spare my feelings.'

'Maybe,' she admitted. 'But look, there are so many other men here.' Her gaze took in a room full of couples.

I tilted my head with an ironic look.

'OK, well not *here* here, but why are you putting all your apples in this basket?'

'It's eggs,' I corrected her.

'*Ce n'est pas important*,' she sighed, exasperated. 'You really like him, eh?'

I nodded helplessly.

'Perhaps he was being, how did you say, chivalrous? He is part English after all.'

I gulped the rest of my wine with a hard swallow. 'He was such a good kisser,' I repeated, looking out of the window.

Just then Nicole's phone buzzed and she clicked open the message. Her relaxed features suddenly tensed.

'Everything OK?' I asked.

'*Zut alors*. The rent is overdue again.' She slumped a little.

'Oh,' I winced. I couldn't think of any platitudes and didn't want to intrude on Nicole's private affairs.

'Never marry a musician, Edith!'

'Sorry. If there's any way I can help,' I said lamely, knowing that there was nothing I could do.

'Well, if you hear of any jobs going for a qualified historian, let 'im know.' She rolled her eyes.

Here I was thinking that they had the perfect life, but everyone had their problems.

'Anyway, tell me about Hugo again. So … he is a really good kisser?' she encouraged me. And I talked about that, and the romance of the evening with him, until we were both smiling again. Confiding it all to Nicole helped to restore my belief that I would hear from him again.

When I got home that night and let myself into my little apartment, I noticed something on the mat as I opened the door. Picking it up, I realised that it was a postcard with a black-and-white image of the Eiffel Tower. I flipped it over and straightaway saw the name 'Hugo' signed at the end. My heart skipped as I threw off my coat and sat on the bed to read it properly.

Miss Lane,
Still dreaming a little dream of you
Hugo x

Short, sweet and incandescently romantic. He hadn't asked for my number, but he had remembered my address. There was something so wonderfully old-fashioned about sending a postcard, rather than texting me. God, he's smooth, I thought to myself, for he now had me, hook, line and sinker.

Chapter Thirteen

I couldn't sleep that night. At home in Dublin, I often had sleepless nights after Mum passed away. Partly because I didn't want to dream about her, only to wake and find her not there. The last few years had been like living suspended in mid-air, always waiting for the other shoe to drop. Thinking about it now, in this place, with the distance it put between me and the past, I began to realise that I'd lost a part of myself back then. In the process of becoming Mum's carer, I had to abandon some of my own needs. And while I had no regrets about that and would do the same thing in a heartbeat if I could have her back, I was beginning to wonder if those missing parts would ever return. And who would I be if they did?

I looked at my phone. 3.11am. Switching on the light, I reached for Hugo's book on the nightstand. *In Search of Lost Time.*

'Same, Proust, same,' I sighed and opened it to the first page and the first line.

For a long time I used to go to bed early.

I had to smile. Maybe Proust was more accessible than I'd thought. I followed his thought process, gentle and rambling, but still no sign of sleep. When I checked the time on my phone again it was almost four in the morning.

I should try counting sheep, I thought, but then I had a better idea.

I left my squeaking mattress behind and got up to make a hot chocolate with the special vanilla liqueur. With my dressing gown wrapped tightly around me against the chill of the old building, I went downstairs to put on a saucepan of milk. It wasn't far off dawn, and with little or no sleep, I knew I would struggle later today, but somehow it didn't really matter. I found the little bottle in the cupboard and followed the recipe just as it was written in the book. I poured the warm, dark liquid into a bowl and sat at the counter and wrapped my hands around it. It took a little while for me to realise that the far-off noises echoing underneath me were voices. Multiple voices? I strained to hear by lifting my head and turning it to one side, just like a dog, and confirmed that yes, I could hear two people speaking. But it wasn't coming from the street outside, it was coming from the basement.

Of course. I shook my head at my own stupidity. There were two bakers. I put the pan in the sink to soak as my thought processes figured it all out. They must have just begun burning the wood in the ovens, while they started the day's baking. It made perfect sense now. One was in charge of the breads, the other of the pastries. I knew it was too much work for one person. But then I heard her.

Madame Moreau's guttural discourses were unmistakable. But what on earth was she doing down there?

I launched myself towards the bathroom door and deftly lifted the grate by the sink, through which I had spied the basement the day before. It was difficult to see anything at first, the light was so dim. I could feel the warm air rising from the ovens and that sour smell of the yeast proving and turning plain old flour and water into something magical. With a shuffling of feet, Manu came into view, wearing a white apron around his waist and his sleeves rolled up.

'So he is making an apprenticeship,' I remarked, a little surprised. It took a lot of time and dedication to become a top baker, and at fifteen years old it seemed an ambitious undertaking. In an odd way I felt sort of proud of him. Nothing would have got me out of bed at 4am when I was his age, or any age for that matter. I couldn't see Madame Moreau, but I could hear her giving orders.

'*Maintenant, tu fais exactement comme lui,*' she said, directing Manu to do exactly as the baker was doing.

With flour-dusted hands, Manu began kneading a large pillow of dough and I tried to follow his eyeline to see if I could spot the head baker. At first, I couldn't see anything; he seemed to be staring straight at the ovens. Then I began to notice a flicker … once, twice. A person, a man, I thought, but his outline seemed hazy. Instinctively, I rubbed my eyes, thinking this would give me a clearer view. Gradually, a strange feeling came over me; a heaviness that had not been there moments earlier. That was when I fainted.

❧

I awoke in my bed with absolutely no recollection of how I had gotten there. I had a terrible headache and my body felt bruised and sore. The memories of the night before swam just out of reach. Perhaps it was all a dream, the result of an overactive imagination. I reached for my phone and almost pole-vaulted out of bed when I saw that it was gone eight o'clock. I pulled on a T-shirt and jeans and popped my feet into a pair of pumps, before thundering down the stairs and yanking my layered locks into a ponytail. I burst into the bakery with such a force that I almost ran into Monsieur Raynard, a kind elderly gentleman who came in for his coffee and *tartine* every morning.

'Oh, *excusez-moi*!' I said, flushed, and he kindly said the fault was entirely his for standing in front of the door. They just didn't make them like him anymore (although secretly I hoped they did).

I was prepared to beg forgiveness from Madame Moreau for my tardiness, but to my complete shock, she cut me off by saying that Manu had already made my excuses and that she hoped my headache had improved.

'Erm, yes … thanks,' was all I could muster, before putting on my apron and getting stuck into the usual tasks. But as the day wore on, it became clear that Manu and I would have to have words.

~

I called my dad that afternoon when I took my coffee break. Choosing my favourite *croissant aux amandes* with its yummy frangipane centre, I sat outside at a little square around the corner as the afternoon sunshine warmed my face.

'Happy birthday!' I cheered, trying to make up for the fact that I wouldn't be there for his birthday.

'Ah, Edie, how are ya, love? I got me card – didn't understand a word of it,' he laughed.

'I'm sorry I'm not there,' I said, trying to ignore the niggling thought that I'd abandoned him somehow.

'You missed a cracking barbecue,' he said. 'A few of the lads came over to watch the rugby.'

'Oh, the weather must be nice, then?'

'You must be joking, it rained all weekend, so I had to light the barbecue in the shed!'

'I'm not sure that's very safe,' I said, grimacing at the thought.

'Anyway, how are them frogs treating ya?' he asked.

'I don't think it's politically correct to say that,' I reproved.

'Well, have you made any friends over there yet?'

I filled him in on Nicole and her family and he sounded genuinely reassured that there were people looking out for his not-so-little girl. I didn't mention Hugo, or things that go bump in the night, even though I wanted to, badly.

I kept to myself at the bakery that afternoon, focusing all of my attention on our patrons while keeping my distance from Madame Moreau. I waited for Manu to return that evening, but Madame Moreau insisted I knock off early, saying she thought I looked a little pale. I couldn't understand her change in attitude, but I was rather tired and I had a mountain of laundry to get through before bed. I had put off the *lavage* since my arrival, as it appeared there was no washing machine in the building and this meant spending hours in a launderette.

After lugging what felt like a dead body around on my back, I found one open near the university campus and dumped my sports bag on the counter. The noise of the machines droned mercilessly, as comatose students sat watching their clothes circumnavigate the drum. It was self-service, so I separated the lights and darks and put money in the two machines. After five minutes of watching them spin, I turned to my phone and saw that Nicole had sent me a photo from our night at Nostalgie. It was Hugo and I, dancing. I'd never seen a picture of myself like that. I looked so happy and carefree. He was smiling, too, and looking at me in a way that made my entire body tingle even then, just at the memory. Why the hell didn't I get his number? I put my phone back in my pocket. After a failed attempt to read the local newspaper that someone had left on the seat beside me, I resorted to staring out of the window until the machine thudded and clicked to a halt.

That night, I got into bed early with my Proust and a hot-water bottle I had bought at the pharmacy. It brought some comfort against the cold and confirmed my status as an antiquated saddo. But an antiquated saddo who now read Proust. Once again, I found myself hypnotised by his verbose style that challenged you to slow down and not speedread to find out what was going to happen. It was the very antithesis to scrolling social media, which sometimes left me feeling jittery. In fact, I was almost transported back to his time, when everything moved at a slower pace. Then something interesting caught my eye.

I feel that there is much to be said for the Celtic belief that the souls of those whom we have lost are held captive in some inferior being, in an animal, in a plant, in some inanimate object, and so effectively lost to us until the day (which to many never comes) when we happen to pass by the tree or to obtain possession of the object which forms their prison. Then they start and tremble, they call us by our name, and as soon as we have recognised their voice the spell is broken. We have delivered them: they have overcome death and return to share our life.

I began to wonder about what I'd seen in the basement. Could it be true? Could a lost soul be held captive in a place? Somehow, in the midst of these imaginings, I'd drifted off to sleep with the book on the pillow beside me. But just before 4am, I woke and sat up rigid in the bed. I'd had strange dreams about a campfire and old wooden caravans – like the kind they used in old European circuses. There were horses and people speaking a language I didn't understand. I was trying to find my way back somewhere, but I couldn't. I woke with tears on my face. I turned on the light and got up to get a glass of water. I felt such a sense of sadness that I couldn't quite explain and I wasn't sure if it was coming from me or this place.

All was quiet and just as I got back into bed and switched off the lamp, my phone came to life, playing Django Reinhardt's 'Minor Swing'. Had I been a cat, I would have been hanging from the ceiling by my claws. I didn't dare breathe, but as suddenly as it came on, the phone went silent. I became alert to every unfamiliar sound. After some tense moments of negotiation with myself, I dared to reach my hand out from under the sheet and switch on the lamp. Everything sat motionless and ordinary, as it should be. I slowly began to allow myself to breathe again and took the courageous step of getting out of bed and checking underneath it, in some childhood belief that if all was clear under there, I'd be OK. Of course, there was nothing there, but the goosebumps on my skin told me there was something not quite right in this bakery.

My first instinct was to pack. I could toss my clothes into a bag in less than five minutes and get out of there. Get the early-morning train to Paris and take a standby flight home from the airport. Yet I didn't move. My second thought was to go to Madame Moreau's apartment, bang on the door and demand answers. Yet I didn't do that, either. I couldn't explain it rationally, but somehow I got the feeling that whatever was going on in this bakery was a key to unlocking something deep within me.

A thought grazed the surface of my awareness. It wasn't a memory, exactly, but more like a clue. I grabbed my shoes, pulled on a coat and tiptoed down the winding stairs as lightly as I could. Once inside the bakery, I found the keys to the front door in the drawer beneath the cash register. I turned the key in the lock and felt the mechanisms clink. Then I pulled the bolts back at the top and bottom of the door with a bit too much gusto and worried I'd made too much noise. I stood still for a moment and listened. All was quiet. Phone in hand, I stepped out onto the dark, cobbled street. Without the sound of any cars and with only streetlamps to light the way, it almost felt like stepping back in time. The buildings around here hadn't changed in over a century. I walked around the side of the building and down the little lane to where the blue basement door lay half in shadow on the gable end. I tapped the torch on my phone and shone it onto the door where I saw a brass plate. I had hardly registered it the first time, but there it was, just as I'd seen in my mind's eye. Stencilled in gold letters was the name 'P. Moreau'. *Pierre.* The same name I'd found on the recipe book.

Chapter Fourteen

Pierre Moreau

1942

Pierre began his morning as usual by firing up the ovens and tying his white apron around his waist. From a burlap sack of flour, he took several large scoops and sieved the powder into a bowl. He no longer needed to measure the amounts, he could tell by eye alone. Then it was time for the sugar. There was hardly any left. The shopkeeper had promised last week that the sugar delivery would arrive that very day, although given that was what he had promised a fortnight before, Pierre decided to hold back a little. Having folded the flour into some beaten eggs, he finally mixed the batter into melted butter, giving the madeleines their distinctive golden taste. Within minutes, they were in the oven and filling the basement with the warm scent of sugar caramelising.

Pierre was a rather shy man. He kept himself to himself, but to his customers, he was the most reliable man alive. He could always be depended upon and ran his bakery like clockwork. Of course, there was some idle gossip as to why such an eligible bachelor remained single, but such was the magnificence of his pastries, they were willing to ignore this seeming oversight of not having found a wife.

'Perhaps he is not attracted to women, eh?' Arnaud, owner of the nearby tabac, used to say. Every community has an Arnaud. The one who must immerse himself in everyone else's business. As if knowing everyone else's private business will give them some kind of advantage and shield their own inconsequential lives from scrutiny. Not only did Arnaud sell the newspapers, he invented his own news about everyone in the town. Idle gossip was one thing, but in wartime, someone like Arnaud became very dangerous indeed. He stood in his doorway, watching the comings and goings of everyone on Rue de Paris.

He bellowed a loud 'Bonjour!' and waved at Pierre, without smiling, on the morning he had set off to deliver some baguettes to the station master. No one would have guessed by Pierre's stoical demeanour that he was struggling to keep the bakery going, what with the rationing of every essential ingredient he needed to bake. Butter, milk and eggs were all in short supply. But it was the ingredient that made his pastries extra special – that was the ingredient he missed the most. His precious vanilla beans, whose flowers grew at the base of cacao trees in the jungles of South America. At the start of the war, the seller he had met at the market had simply disappeared and along with him Pierre's secret ingredient. One last jar remained and so he preserved the contents in a brandy liqueur, saving their precious effect for only very special occasions.

For now, it was his duty to feed the inhabitants of Compiègne and so he cycled down the street, five golden baguettes jostling in the wicker basket. Trucks passed him by on the road and threw up dust into the air. At the back of one truck, the cloth cover opened slightly to reveal rows of German soldiers sitting on each side, holding their rifles, laughing and joking in the midday sunshine. It gave Pierre a nauseous, churning feeling in the pit of his stomach. How could they smile like that? Knowing the suffering that they were inflicting. It seemed so unnatural and inhumane. And yet they were human beings, made of the same flesh and bone as Pierre.

'*L'espoire fait vivre,*' he whispered to himself, believing that to give up hope was to let the enemy win.

Just as he arrived at the station, a train was pulling in. The harsh sound of metal and machine coming to a halt, something that used to excite him as a child, held no such wonder for him now. He took the bread from the basket and walked along the platform towards the station master's office. He caught sight of his reflection in one of the carriage windows. He had lost weight and his tall, lean physique had narrowed with every passing month of the occupation. He took off his cap and ran his fingers through his dark hair. He needed a haircut. Caught in this absent-minded thought, he didn't notice them at first: the woman and the little girl. She was staring back at him from the other side of the glass. There was something desperate in her eyes. She hurried out of the carriage, hardly taking her eyes off of him, as though he were the finishing line to a race.

The platform, at this point, was full of people, and soldiers, too. The woman walked right up to him and gave him an imploring look, but no words. The war had robbed everyone of their beauty, it seemed to Pierre, but this woman was lit from within. Even he could see that. The child clutched her hand tightly, her grimy face streaked with tears. He looked back to the woman and that was when he noticed her split lip and the bruise just above her eyebrow. It must have only been seconds, but to Pierre, everything seemed to be moving in slow motion.

'*Cheri!*' the woman said loudly. One of the soldiers turned to look at them and all at once, Pierre understood.

'Welcome home, my darlings,' he said, embracing these two strangers as though they were his own.

Little did he know that day, this woman was about to change his life.

Chapter Fifteen

Another postcard arrived first thing the next morning. I just about managed to refrain from kissing the postman, for my heart leapt at the thought of Hugo and his intense eyes that sought to know me on that magical night. I had been intermittently going over that evening in my head, wishing things had turned out differently. Our premature goodbye had left me feeling as though I'd missed my chance, so these postcards kept my foolish hopes alive.

The picture this time was of a beautiful building, La Musée Carnavalet. An exquisite stone mansion, featuring an inner courtyard with café-style seating and giant parasols. *Ah, Paris,* I sighed. On the back it simply said –

Thinking of you, Miss Lane,
Hoping it wasn't all just a dream.
Hugo x

I knew I shouldn't have been so affected by his words, but I couldn't help it. I had a major crush on him and in a way, I had sort of resigned myself to whatever would result from it. A fling, a heartache, a lifelong relationship; either way I was bound to see it through. I cringed at how his handwriting piqued my curiosity even further. I was desperate to know more about him, to find out if he felt the same way I did. At the same time, there was also a sense of being overwhelmed by my feelings, and that made me want to run and hide. I put the card in the pocket of my apron and went to wipe down the tables outside, humming a little tune to myself.

'I don't need to ask what has put a song in your heart,' came Nicole's voice, as she stopped by the bakery that morning to pick up some pastries for the salon and have a quick chat.

'He is very, you know, old-fashioned, with his postcards and calling you "Miss Lane",' she said, sipping a quick espresso at the counter after I'd shown her the postcard.

'I know, I think that's what's making this so unbearably romantic!' I agreed, rather enjoying the drama of it all.

'He still does not say when he's coming back,' she added, flipping the postcard over in her hand.

I left the statement unanswered and popped some *pains au chocolat* into a brown paper bag for her to take back to the salon.

'*De toute façon*, it's better than dating apps, *hein*? *Mon Dieu*, you should see what's on there,' she said, draining the last of her cup.

'You're replacing Johnny already?' I said, jokingly.

She gave a raucous laugh. 'Don't believe the stereotypes,

not all French people take lovers. Honestly, with work and little Max, where would I find the time? No, it's my mother. She and my father divorced some years ago and I suggested she go on a date.'

'The man who gets to go on a date with your mother will be one lucky guy. She's a total stunner, inside and out!'

'As I keep telling her, but the men on these sites? Aye-aye-aye. I don't even think their profile pics are real.'

'Well, if I meet any millionaire bachelors, I'll send them your way,' I assured her, as she headed for the door.

'Don't forget, Johnny is playing in Nostalgie on Thursday night, so you have to come, yes?'

'Sorry, it's way past my bedtime. I'm hardly getting any sleep as it is.'

'Too busy dreaming of you-know-who,' she winked, as she sashayed out of the bakery.

Madame Moreau was at the specialist that afternoon for her arthritis, so for the first time I was left in charge of the bakery. It felt wonderful. This was what I had imagined when I left for Paris all those weeks ago. I decided to give Django Reinhardt another go, even though he'd almost given me a heart attack the other night. I had fallen in love with his swinging guitar style and served the customers with a rhythm that made me feel as though I were dancing around the tables. I felt completely in control and I so enjoyed being my own boss and not having Madame Moreau's constant presence like a long shadow over me. Since it seemed impossible to impress this woman or get any kind of validation from her, I had lost the urge to try and I knew she sensed the change in me. Our interactions were purely perfunctory and it worked better for both of us that way. Manu on the other hand was entirely different with me, and I with him. I sensed that he was hiding some kind of secret and that it was only a matter of time before he would come to search me out.

When I closed up that evening, I decided to go out for a bite to eat. Madame Moreau had not yet returned from her outing and I didn't feel entirely comfortable being in the building on my own. I went to the brasserie where I had met Nicole the previous week and sat at the back of the restaurant on a banquette. The staff were kept on their toes with a decent number of patrons eating out on a Monday night. I ordered a 'Salade Roquefort', a blue cheese and walnut salad that packed a punch, with a glass of equally bolshie red wine. That was one thing I was coming to appreciate about France – their ballsy flavours and simple presentation. Bread, wine and cheese could happily sustain the population for breakfast, lunch and dinner. I was so tired and preoccupied after a long day at work that I didn't really mind eating out on my own – something I never would have done at home in Dublin. I'd always thought people either looked lonely or ridiculously self-confident when eating out alone. I felt neither just now in my absent-mindedness. A thought was forming in my subconscious, and it was only as I mopped up the dressing with my bread that it came to the fore.

'I'll Google him!' I actually said it aloud without realising, but thankfully no one seemed to notice. I quickly typed 'Hugo Chadwick photographer' into the search engine. The first result was for a genealogy website, where a woman was searching for a Hugo Chadwick who had died in the late 1800s. The second was for a country pub in

England called The Chadwick Arms and after that there were a few photography studios in Australia and America with the name Chadwick, but nothing for my Hugo. I deleted the word 'photographer' and hit search once more. This time, the first result was a Facebook page for Hugo Chadwick. My heart jolted, then my conscience had a serious argument about looking too eager if I sent him a message and quite possibly ruining the old-fashioned correspondence we had going on. Still, I need not have wasted my energy worrying, for when I clicked on the link I found a black-and-white picture of a Colombian bodybuilder. Not too hard on the eye, but still not my Hugo. I felt a bit deflated and hardly noticed the next link for Chadwick Holdings Incorporated. My eyes glanced over the first line or two, with terms such as 'principal investor', 'commercial properties' and 'asset management', none of which held much meaning for me. Just out of curiosity, I noted that their registered office was in London with a subsidiary in Paris. In the end, I decided to abandon my background search. I didn't want to feel like a stalker and satisfied myself with the belief that if he wanted to tell me more about himself, he would. Besides, it was nice to have this air of mystique. If he looked me up online he wouldn't find much. The very *raison d'être* of social media was having something to show the world, and up to now, I didn't think my life had anything worth bragging about. In fact, I was actively trying to hide myself and the blank spaces where all of my milestones should have been. And that was when the doubts crept in. Why would someone like Hugo be interested in me?

I didn't want to indulge these negative thoughts, so I

paid my bill and left before I had a chance to over-analyse the situation any further. Walking home, I bumped into Geoff, who was taking his dog for an evening walk in the square.

'Settling in OK?' he asked.

I bent down to pat Ruby.

'I am actually, thanks.'

'Better than Paris?' he asked, recalling our conversation.

'Do you know what? I'm starting to think Compiègne was meant to be.'

'Tell you what, why don't you come on one of my tours? If you're planning on sticking around, it might be good to find out about the history of the place.'

I wasn't really the type for tours and large groups of people, but I recognised the hand of friendship when I saw it and decided to say yes. I agreed to go on my next day off. If nothing else, it would distract my thoughts from Hugo Chadwick.

Chapter Sixteen

The minibus was parked at the south side of the river and I was the first to arrive.

'The perks of waking up at 6am every day,' I explained to Geoff, who was standing on the footpath with a large colourful umbrella, presumably to make him visible to his tour guests.

As it was a Sunday, the bakery was closed, but I had brought some day-old pastries along with me.

'Perfect way to ingratiate yourself,' he said, picking a madeleine out for himself.

'My dad always brought some nice pastries when we'd go for a day out,' I said, suddenly stricken with a pang of homesickness that caused my eyes to water. 'Sorry, gosh, I've only been gone a fortnight!'

Geoff gave me a handkerchief and I did my best not to ask whether it had been used or not.

'We all get lonely, sometimes,' he said.

'Do you ever miss home? The UK, I mean?'

'Oh, you know, I get back now and again. There's just my mum left now. She's in a home in Bristol.'

I nodded. There was a sad sort of finality to it. It was the natural way of things, but it didn't chase the empty feeling away. Thankfully, people began to arrive in threes and fours and before I knew it, the minibus was almost full and Geoff started the engine.

We drove east out of Compiègne on the N31. It felt strange leaving the city and seeing the outskirts for the first time. Rue de Paris had become my entire world since I arrived; so much so that I had almost forgotten that there was an entire country to be explored. Within minutes, we were driving into the Compiègne Forest. It was beautiful, so peaceful and verdant. Passing by the massive Alsace Lorraine Monument – a huge sculpture depicting a sword cutting down the Imperial Eagle of Germany – it became clear to me why so many war historians held this place in such high regard. We parked in a small car park and walked along a wooded path to an extraordinary clearing. In front of us lay railway tracks leading to the centre of the memorial. To one side there was a statue of Marshal Foch and ahead, between a tank and a gun, stood the museum; a nondescript low white building with flags fluttering in the breeze.

Although the area itself was green and lush and smelled of sap, there was a sense of something solemn that had taken place. Even though I was, as yet, incognisant of what had happened in this place, I could sense the gravity of it. We entered the small building and Geoff explained that this was the Armistice Museum. He purchased our tickets and went into full tour-guide mode. Despite myself, I was hooked on his every word. He looked the part, too, in his mustard corduroy trousers and V-neck jumper.

'Now listen up, everyone! This is a replica of the railway carriage used by Marshal Foch and his officers, who included the English First Lord of the Admiralty, Sir Rosslyn Wemyss, and the French Chief of Staff, General Weygand. It was here that they met with the Germans to sign the armistice to end the horror that was the First World War – The Great War. It was signed on November 11th at 5.10am.'

'And who was Marshal Foch?' I asked.

'Basically, he was the Commander-in-chief of the Allied Armies. The head honcho. He was revered as a great military theorist and fought the Germans back into their own territory. He did predict, however, that the armistice was not a permanent peace and that after twenty years, war could break out once again. He was right; twenty years and sixty-five days later, the Second World War began.'

It was chilling, not like history lessons at school, where books containing old photos of dead generals did little to convey the realities of war. There was a lot of First World War memorabilia in that room, with yellowing newspaper articles, photocopies, old cameras showing pictures from the various fronts, flags, objects made from shells, old hypnotic film footage that flickered and eerily reminded me of the ghostly baker.

For such a small museum, the atmosphere was extraordinary. The simplicity of the display and the objects was so affecting, drawing visitors into those past events.

'What about the Second World War?' a woman with a

Spanish accent asked. I remembered then what Nicole's mother had said about Madame Moreau's father living under 'the regime' during that war, so my ears pricked up.

'I'm coming to that just now, Madame,' Geoff replied.

He really came into his own when talking about the past – you could tell it was his passion and I felt really lucky to have this knowledgeable guide all to myself.

'Right, so this space covers the events of 1940, which were a very different story for the French. The Battle of France was lost; the enemy was in Paris, and France was about to be cut in half. A request for an armistice was made, and here in the forest, at what was called the Glade of the Armistice, the French and German delegations met on June 21st 1940. Talks were conducted in the very railway carriage that had been the scene of Germany's defeat. Then the armistice was agreed – a deliberate and highly effective means of humiliating the French.' He paused to let the significance of the site sink in.

'During the German occupation of France, from 1940 to 1944, the site was cleared and the carriage taken to Berlin. Later, as the war went badly for Germany, it was moved to the forest of Thuringe and destroyed by fire in April 1945.

'Now, this wasn't the end of the story for the forest clearing known as the Glade of the Armistice,' he said, and I absently wondered if he could get his own documentary series on TV. He was so good at presenting complex information. 'On September 1st 1944, Compiègne was liberated. In November, General Marie-Pierre Koenig, the best known Free French leader after General de Gaulle, led a military parade in the Glade watched by crowds that included British, American and Polish officials.'

'Wow, so this place really played a pivotal role in France's history,' I said.

'As I keep telling you, Edith, you haphazardly picked one of the most important locations in all of Europe! And that's why I'm kept very busy with tourists who want to come here and see it for themselves. In fact, on November 11th 1950, a replica railway carriage was officially opened containing the objects that you see today.'

We spent some time walking around and quietly absorbing the exhibit. I could hear American accents as well as British and Italian. I was a bit embarrassed at how clueless I was about the whole thing; what the war really meant for the French, who shared their border with the enemy. I thanked Geoff for being such an engaging tour guide and promised that there would be plenty of eclairs in it for him.

We all got back onto the bus for our next stop on the historical tour. I sat directly behind the driver's seat so I could have the best view.

'Maybe I should get a car,' I said, leaning forwards so Geoff could hear me. 'It's nice to get out into the countryside.'

'Well, you don't really need a car to get around. I used to cycle when I first arrived. It's much more cycle-friendly weather than back home in Britain, and you can bring them on the trains, too.'

'Gosh, I haven't cycled in years,' I said. 'I'm not sure I'd remember how!'

'It's easy – just like riding a bike,' Geoff winked.

'You've really got to work on your material, Geoff.' I laughed, comfortable in his company.

As we travelled along the main road, Geoff pulled the minibus over to what appeared to be a forest path. We walked along until we reached a gravestone. Everyone gathered around and once the chatter had died down, I looked at him questioningly.

'This marks the spot of the last train from Compiègne to Buchenwald on August 17th 1944, carrying 1,250 men to the death camp.'

The silence was visceral. It was one thing to read about these things, but to actually stand on the ground where such unthinkable crimes against humanity had occurred was truly humbling.

'What? You mean, trains left from here for the concentration camps in Germany?' I couldn't believe the words I was saying. German occupation, Nazis, the Holocaust, these were things that were a million miles away from my life.

'In fact there was an internment camp here that held many Jews and French Resistance soldiers. They detained them here and eventually shipped them off to the labour camps where most of them perished.'

I felt numb with shock. This place seemed so peaceful; it was impossible to imagine such traumatic events had taken place here. The stark realisation affected me deeply and I asked him how he could bear coming here, time after time.

'People need to remember, Edith, otherwise their deaths and the thousands of people who sacrificed their lives trying to protect them will have been for nothing.'

His words were so powerful. Remembrance was the best way to honour people. As the other members of our tour began making their way back to the minibus, I hung back for a bit.

'My mother always loved France,' I said. 'Sometimes I wonder if I'm living her dream or my own.'

He paused for a while, then took out a pack of cigarettes. I had never smoked in my life, but for some reason it seemed like the right thing to do in this instance. I coughed and wheezed as he lit it for me and I tried, unsuccessfully, to inhale. He lit his own and slowly gathered his thoughts.

'She's no longer with us, is she?'

No,' I replied, glad that I didn't have to explain.

'Tell you what, why don't I show you some place that both you and your mother would have really loved?' he said, patting my arm. He reminded me a bit of my own father and that wasn't just the seventies sideburns. He had a no-nonsense attitude that made him easy to be around. 'It's not far,' he assured me.

We headed back towards the city centre as the sun began its descent into soft lavender clouds. Just as he had promised, it did not take long before we entered another car park, but this time we were at the entrance to a grand castle, set in stately gardens and surrounded by woodland. My fellow passengers made lots of appreciative 'oohs' and 'ahhs' before slipping on their backpacks and getting out of their seats.

'What is this place?' I said, shaking off the shadows of the forest.

'This,' he said, taking off his seatbelt, 'is where I bring all the wives when they get fed up following their husbands around all the war museums. It seems to do the trick,' he added casually.

I was completely taken aback by the scale of the castle. As we walked up the steps to the terrace, lined with magnificent classical statues, I mentioned to Geoff that it kind of resembled Buckingham Palace.

'There are similarities, yes. Indeed, Château Compiègne is an example of the First French Empire style from the eighteenth century, but the Compiègne estate dates back to the Merovingian dynasty.' Geoff was back in tour-guide mode and again I found myself grateful to have his fountain of knowledge on tap, if I could just keep up with what he was talking about.

'The who dynasty?' It sounded made up, like something out of *The Princess Diaries*.

'In the fifth century, the Merovingian dynasty ruled the Franks for three-hundred years in a region known as Francia. It's believed that all French kings descended from them.'

'I had no idea,' I said, realising that history was like a vanishing point that just kept moving further and further away. 'So who lived in the castle?'

'The castle itself was built as a royal residence for Louis XV and was later restored by Napoleon. Even before the château was constructed, Compiègne was the preferred summer residence for French monarchs, primarily for hunting – given its proximity to Compiègne Forest.'

'You're kidding me? Who knew Compiègne was so … important! To think, I was so upset because I wouldn't be living in Paris,' I told him.

'We like it,' he said, looking around as though it were his playground. 'We don't have time today, I have another tour to do in the afternoon, but maybe when you get your own wheels you can come back and visit the Second Empire museum – it's full of Empress Eugénie's clothing and marriage paraphernalia.'

'I'd love to come here again,' I said, genuinely. 'You must be pretty busy?'

'You might be surprised, but I've actually had to turn people away. I can't keep up with the demand, especially once the season gets going. If I'm being honest, I could do with taking someone on, but I haven't been able to find the right person. There aren't very many people who have the historical knowledge as well as the communication skills to make it interesting. It's like a performance in a way.'

My eyes lit up. 'You need an assistant?' I said.

'Yes, would you be interested?'

'I have my hands full with the Moreaus for now, but I might know the perfect candidate,' I mused, thinking of Johnny. If anyone knew how to perform, it was him, and hadn't Nicole said he'd studied history?

'Right, back to the castle,' he said as we walked around the grounds and joined up with the rest of the group.

The building itself was spread out over a large area of about five hectares and was indeed very grand, but not as fussy as the pictures I had seen of Versailles or other French châteaus. I could see the long avenues leading off into the forest in the distance and could just imagine the royals hunting on horseback and having a jolly old time of it.

'Now, it was built in a neoclassical style – and what is neoclassical style, you might ask? It's when simplicity and clarity govern the design. In 1750, the prominent architect

Ange-Jacques Gabriel proposed a thorough renovation of the château. During the French Revolution, the château passed into the jurisdiction of the Minister for the Interior. In 1795 all furniture was sold and its works of art were sent to the Musée Central. However, in 1804 Napoleon made the château an imperial domain and ordered it be made habitable again. Its layout was altered, a ballroom added, and the garden was replanted and linked directly to the forest. They say that 'Compiègne speaks of Napoleon as Versailles does of Louis XIV'.

'Bravo!' I clapped, impressed by his ability to memorise so much detail. 'This really is your passion, isn't it?' He gave me a shy grin and I envied that sense of fulfilment he exuded. This was how it felt to be doing something you loved.

As we strolled around the gardens, the enormous château and its extensive grounds put my own life into perspective. There was so much history here, centuries of kings and queens, life and death, and yet it was the building and the forests that remained. It called to mind the shadowy figure I had seen in the basement of the bakery. I wasn't sure how to put it, other than blurting it out.

'Geoff, do you believe that places like this, with all their history, do you think they could be haunted?' I tried to say it casually, conversationally.

'What, do you mean ghosts?'

'Maybe, you know, or just, I don't know, like "a presence" of some sort?'

'I don't really believe in all that palaver, but I suppose somewhere as old as this must have the odd ghost rattling about. I've heard stories,' he added, 'on the old battlefields, but that could be just a load of old twaddle!'

I nodded and didn't mention it further. It felt good to get away from the bakery for the day, but there was something drawing me back there – a mystery that needed to be solved.

Chapter Seventeen

I was humming an old Julie London tune, 'I'm in the Mood for Love', as I walked along Rue Solferino to see Nicole at the salon. I looked up at the beautiful sandstone buildings, as the sunlight glinted off wrought-iron balconies festooned with flower boxes. Oh, to live in an apartment with those floor-to-ceiling windows! I was lost in a daydream of polished wooden floors and billowing white curtains and almost walked past the salon entirely. I'd brought some treats as well as some good news, and to my surprise I saw Johnny through the window and it felt like fate.

'Perfect timing!' I said, as I greeted both him and Nicole. I handed her the bag of pastries.

'Guess who's looking to hire an historian?'

They both stared at me blankly.

'Geoff Harding, he's a local tour guide.'

'O-kay,' said Johnny, stubbornly refusing to connect the dots.

'He's completely overrun with tours at the moment and he's looking for someone who not only knows about history,' I paused for dramatic effect, 'but is also able to entertain a crowd!'

My smile was beaming strongly enough to power every streetlight in Compiègne. Johnny's was not.

'*Mais, c'est geniale*, what a perfect opportunity!' Nicole agreed.

'Who said I needed a job?' Johnny said in a tone that left me in no doubt. I had totally put my foot in it.

'I … um, well, nobody really. It's just, I went on one of his tours…'

Nicole began speaking to Johnny so quickly in French that I had no idea what was going on. They kept the volume low, but the guttural emphasis on each syllable made it clear that this was an argument.

'He's really lovely,' I added, though they were no longer listening to me. 'I'll just, yeah, I'll just get back to work,' I said sheepishly and left without them even noticing.

I wasn't singing on the way back, that was for sure. I realised too late that I should have told Nicole first, let her tell Johnny herself. Or better yet, I should've just stayed out of it. Trying to help people wasn't such a straightforward business after all.

After a long, stressful afternoon of worrying about whether I'd just messed up my friendship with Johnny and Nicole, I began closing up for the evening and spotted someone getting out of a Range Rover across the street. I did a second take when I realised it was him. Hugo.

'*Bonsoir*,' he said.

'*Bonsoir*.' My smile was proof enough that I was happy to see him. He looked ridiculously handsome in a crisp white shirt and chinos. And that tan. I had to bite my lip to remind myself that I wasn't imagining him and this was, in fact, happening.

'I was just in the neighbourhood – actually, scratch that. I wasn't in the neighbourhood at all. I had a meeting in Paris today and thought I'd swing by on the off-chance you might be free for dinner.'

It was the kind of line that could sweep a girl off her feet and I was well and truly swept. Still, I knew how to play the game. I checked my watch and considered for a moment.

'I guess I'm free,' I said and watched as he smiled a knowing smile.

'Right, OK, good. Shall we?'

'Oh, I should change first, right?' I asked, looking down at my breton top and jeans.

'Personally, I wouldn't change a thing…'

I rolled my eyes playfully.

'I'll be down in five,' I said.

All of the women's magazines had me believing that going from 'day to night' would be a significant part of my adult life, and reading all of those articles had finally paid off! I had to think fast. I slipped off my ballet pumps and found the only pair of heels I'd brought with me – a pair of black, open-toed boots. There was no time to change my top and I couldn't find any jewellery to jazz it up, so I threw on a red neck scarf that Nicole had given me to tie up my hair. I sprayed myself liberally with perfume and loosened my hair from the clip I wore at work. I combed my fingers through it as I stumbled into the bathroom and found some red lipstick. A quick lick of mascara on my eyes later and I was done – day to night accomplished! I threw my black jacket over my shoulder and locked the door to the bakery.

Hugo was standing with the passenger door open and gave me a nod of appreciation.

'So, where are you taking me?' I asked, once he'd got in and turned the key in the ignition.

'It's a surprise.'

Twenty-five minutes later, we arrived at our destination. A long driveway lined with cypress trees led up to what, at first, looked like a weathered old barn. But as we got closer, I could see lights strung over a trellis outside, with tables set for dinner.

'What is this place?' I asked, surprised and relieved that we weren't going to a posh restaurant.

'It's an old vineyard. A friend of mine took it over last year,' he explained, turning the wheel and deftly slotting the car into a space. He was out of the car and around to my door before I had time to open it. 'Allow me,' he said, holding it open for me.

'You're setting a dangerous precedent here,' I said.

'I'll take the risk.'

I felt like I was already a bit tipsy. Was this actually happening? To me, Edith Lane, terrible map-reader and average waitress?

'Jean, *comment ça va*?' Hugo said, shaking his friend's hand as they walked into the barn, which I now saw was a winery.

'*Eh, mon ami, content de te voir,*' Jean replied. 'And you have brought a guest?'

'Oh, *bonsoir*,' I greeted him with a kiss on each cheek. 'This place is beautiful.' I could see inside to the rows and rows of oak barrels and a small bar at the front for tastings.

'*Merci, Mademoiselle,*' he said.

We sat at a table that overlooked the vineyard below, sloping away southwards and now shimmering under the moonlight. Although it was still early spring, it was lovely to be outside in the night air, listening to the crackle of wood logs burning in a small chiminea. There were sheepskin rugs on the seats and blankets to stave off any chill. The other tables were filled with couples and groups of friends, their light conversation providing the perfect soundtrack.

'I don't think I've ever been anywhere like this,' I said.

'It is quite special.'

Oh, boy, he brought me to a special place. This *meant* something. Butterflies crashed into each other in my stomach. A waiter came and poured some wine, which Hugo, of course, refused.

'Please, go ahead,' he said, when I shook my head in solidarity.

'Well, maybe just one glass, I do have to get up at six.'

'Ah yes, the bakery, how's it going?'

His cool blue eyes fixed on me and I suddenly felt the need to make my life sound far more interesting than it was.

'Oh, you know, it's just a day job. I'm more interested in pursuing my music.'

Oh, why had I said that?

'That's amazing. Any performances coming up? I have to say I really enjoyed the last one.'

Quelle merde, as the French would say.

'Um, yeah, I might do a session with Johnny's band at Nostalgie,' I said, digging deeper and deeper into a hole of lies. What was I saying? If nothing else, I was the last person Johnny would want to speak to right now, let alone sing with. Mercifully, the food arrived.

'*Bon appétit*,' Jean said, placing two giant white plates on the table followed by a small pot. When he lifted the lid, the aroma that wafted towards us was rich and hearty.

'Do you like Coq au Vin?' Hugo asked, as he spooned the delicious-looking chicken onto my plate.

'I'm not sure I've tried it.'

I placed my napkin on my lap and waited for him to serve himself before tasting.

'*Bon appétit*,' he echoed Jean.

The taste was divine. Chicken braised in wine with pearl onions, mushrooms and some salty bacon. The French did simple ingredients so well. There was a basket of bread on the table and Hugo began tearing some up and dipping it in the sauce, a brave move with a white shirt.

'Thanks for bringing me here,' I said, after savouring the first few mouthfuls of our meal. 'It's magical.'

'I had a feeling you'd like it,' he said.

I began to wonder what kind of photographer he was, to be driving a car like that and eating in hilltop vineyards.

'What is it?' he asked, when he caught me looking at him.

'I'm just trying to figure you out, I suppose. On the one

hand, you seem to live this glamorous life, but on the other, you look happy with simple things.'

'Can't I enjoy both?'

I nodded in agreement. Perhaps I'd put my foot in it. He was entitled to live whatever way he wanted. I finished my glass of wine and accepted another from the waiter. I was really out of practice at this dating thing.

'Sorry, that came across a bit rude,' he said, pushing his plate aside and placing his napkin on the table. 'My life is full of contradictions. Like you, I have a passion for the more creative side of things, in my case, photography; but also like you, I have a day job. A boring, soul-sucking, day job.' He drained his glass of water. 'It just pays a bit more than your bakery,' he said, with a wink.

'I didn't mean to sound nosy, it's none of my business really.'

'No,' he said, reaching across the table and taking my hand. 'I'm glad you're interested. Because I'm interested in you.'

Woah! An actual man actually stating his intentions. It was all too much. I was far more used to guys hiding their emotions, disguising their feelings and only revealing a crumb of their true selves after a few pints. So I decided to do what I did best in these kinds of situations. I babbled.

'Did you know that Compiègne has a really rich history? I went on a tour with Geoff, one of the customers from the bakery, he's English. Like you! Anyway, he was saying I should get a bike and I don't know why I didn't think of it myself. I used to love cycling and it would be really handy here, if I'm staying, to have a bike. But not like a regular bike; one of those vintage ones, you know? Maybe with a basket!'

Again, I was saved by the arrival of dessert.

'Cherry clafoutis with a light Chantilly cream,' Jean announced and the other diners broke into spontaneous applause. I had almost forgotten there were other people dining alongside us. I tucked into the soft, spongy cake and almost forgot what I'd been talking about.

'So, you are staying then?'

Was I? I suppose I was. Who was I kidding, of course I was! If living in Compiègne meant more nights like this…

'For the time being,' I replied. *Now* who was playing hard to get? 'I like its old-world charm.'

'Ah, well, if it's old-world charm you're after, you might like these.'

Hugo took out his phone and brought his chair a little closer to mine.

'This is a project I've been working on,' he explained, as he pulled up some photos of vintage-style shopfronts.

'Oh wow, these are gorgeous!' A cobalt-blue shopfront popped out from the screen. 'Oh cool, it's a record shop, Johnny would love that.'

His timid smile betrayed how much this project really meant to him.

'And this,' he said, scrolling down to reveal a faded pink-and-gold window with puppets inside.

'A puppet shop?' I asked, bemused that such a thing existed.

'Yes! The owner has been making puppets, mechanical toys and music boxes since the seventies. It's a seventeenth-century building, the last of its kind in Paris.'

'So, are you going to exhibit your photographs?' I asked, attempting to get my head back out of the clouds.

'What I'd really like is to put them all in a book, but I haven't approached any publishers yet.'

'Why not?'

'I don't know. Fear, I suppose. Anyway, I'm not finished yet.'

'What made you begin?'

'I think I wanted to capture the history before it disappears.'

I thought about the old films I watched with Mum and how I too was trying to hang on to something from the past. A sense of old-fashioned values, belonging and community.

'This one's my favourite, I think,' he said, showing me a photograph of a beautiful wooden shopfront painted in a soft grey with a faded sign on top that said 'Fabrique de Chapeau'. 'It's a bookshop,' he explained, 'and when the owner was renovating he uncovered the old sign.'

'Oh, it's beautiful,' I said, in a longing tone.

'What is it?'

'I just, I'd love to see it.'

'I can take you sometime, if you like.'

Our eyes met, followed very swiftly by our lips. Kissing him was like walking into a wildflower meadow on a warm summer's day. I felt like my heart was shining from the inside out, twinkling like the fairy lights around us.

'Ahem,' Jean said, as he began to clear our plates.

'You still have terrible timing, Jean,' Hugo joked, before ordering coffees.

Chapter Eighteen

'What's this for?' I asked, as Johnny handed me a box of chocolates. It was mid-morning and I was taking my coffee break at a table under the awning outside the bakery.

'An apology and a thank you,' he said, sitting on the empty chair beside me and lighting up a cigarette.

'The tour-guide job?'

He nodded.

'I spoke to Geoff and he's a really good bloke. I'm doing a trial run tomorrow.'

I opened the box of chocolates and ate one immediately.

'I'm sorry, too, I shouldn't have stuck my nose in your business like that. I really did mean well, but sometimes I get carried away with myself. I suppose I'm just—'

'A fixer?'

I grimaced.

'No, seriously, you did me a favour. Things have been a bit tight and I was letting my pride get in the way.'

'How do you mean?' I asked, offering him a chocolate.

'I suppose I had this idea that if I took on a day job, it meant that I was selling out or that I didn't really believe I could make it as a musician. Us creative types are quite sensitive,' he said half-jokingly, before stubbing out his cigarette in the ashtray.

'I totally get it,' I said. 'The truth is, I think you're really brave. You're following your dreams, no matter what.'

'Brave or stupid,' he replied, resting his elbows on his knees and staring down at the cobbles under our feet.

'I used to think that I wanted to be a singer,' I said in a low tone, as though I was in the confessional box. 'But I didn't think I'd be good enough to make a living, so I just abandoned it altogether as a stupid dream. I mean, that's what happens, isn't it? You grow up and face reality, but what you don't realise is that abandoning your dreams is like abandoning a part of yourself. And for what? Because it won't make you rich? I mean, so what? Maybe it'll make you happy, and you can't put a price on that.'

'Eh … wow!' said Johnny, taken aback.

'Sorry, I'm rambling—'

'No, not at all, it's like listening to someone's life manifesto! You *should* sing, Edith, if it makes you happy.'

'Oh, no, I mean, I wasn't talking about me per se,' I said, suddenly feeling exposed and awkward.

'Listen, anytime you want to jam with us—'

'Oh, I couldn't, Johnny, I'm not a performer like you.'

'You think I started out like this? I learned my craft busking on the streets… And do you wanna know what the secret is?'

My eyebrows shot up. I did want to know, very much.

'People think performing is about putting on an act, but it's not. It's about letting people see the real you.'

His words seemed to reverberate, right into my soul.

'*Édith*?' Madame Moreau called from the open doorway.

'And on that note,' I said, rising from my seat and straightening my apron, 'I'd better be getting back to work.'

'OK, but think about what I said,' said Johnny, before walking off down the street with a new pep in his step.

'Thanks for the chocolates,' I called after him, 'and good luck tomorrow!'

What was it about this place that kept causing me to blab my inner thoughts out loud, I wondered?

The evening crowd were forming a queue for their baguettes, and while I was busy serving, I noticed Manu come into the kitchenette behind the counter through the door that led to the basement. It was the first time I'd seen it being used, but before I had a chance to see what was behind it, he closed it hastily and turned a key in the lock. We exchanged an awkward glance when he realised he was being watched. *What's the big mystery?* I wanted to say, but I had a feeling that I'd have to solve it myself. Along with the fact that they hardly had any English-speaking customers. Why had they specified 'English as a first language' in their ad? Something was definitely amiss, but it was hard to keep my focus when my phone buzzed with a text from Hugo. I read it surreptitiously while keeping it in my apron pocket, otherwise I'd never hear the end of it from Madame Moreau. Mobile phones were a no-no at work.

It was so good to see you last night, it read.

When he'd dropped me off, he finally asked for my number.

'You're costing me a fortune on stamps!' he'd said, and as he began punching in my digits, I leaned across and kissed him softly just below his ear. 'Erm, I've completely forgotten the numbers now,' he added, his voice sounding husky.

'Two-zero-three,' I said, all the while placing kisses from his jawline to his collarbone.

'Oh, sod it,' he said, dropping the phone and reaching over until his hand was at the back of my neck, his fingers running through my hair.

The memory of it now was making my legs feel wobbly.

Chapter Nineteen

Hugo Chadwick

Hugo wore his black Ray-Bans to shield his eyes from the morning sun. He clicked the button on his key and heard the Range Rover locking behind him. Walking along the Rue de Paris, he felt that same sense of familiarity he always felt; an inexplicable déjà vu. He didn't need much of an excuse to visit the bakery, but he told himself it was a convenient spot to pick up some coffees, even though it was nowhere near to where he was going.

As the bell rang overhead, he paused in the doorway. Edith was bending down to a little girl who was formally introducing her to her stuffed animal.

'*Il s'appelle Mou-Mou,*' the little girl said, before inviting Edith to kiss the greying mess that might once have been a toy elephant. Edith handled the situation gracefully by opting to shake hands with his trunk instead. Just then, she looked up directly into Hugo's eyes and the smile that lit up her face on seeing him made his heartbeat quicken.

'Oh, hello,' she said, standing up. 'Have you met Mou-Mou?'

'*Enchanté*,' Hugo said politely, before the little girl's mother took her hand and led her back out onto the street. 'You're a hit with the patrons,' he told Edith, lightly kissing her on the cheek. Every cell in his body wanted to take her into his arms and feel her warmth against him.

'Irish charm,' she said with a wink.

Madame Moreau walked between them deliberately and Edith gave him a strained look.

'Doesn't work on everyone,' she mouthed. 'So what can I get you?' she asked in a loud, theatrical voice.

'Actually, I just came by to pick up some pastries. I'm on my way to visit my mother.'

'Oh, does she live nearby?'

'In a sense,' he said. 'I'll take a small fraisier cake, *s'il te plait*.'

Once she placed the strawberry cake into a white cardboard box, fastened with string, she refused to take any money.

'My treat,' Edith said, which made Hugo realise something about her he hadn't noticed before. She was kind. He tried to object, but she insisted.

'It's my pleasure,' she added. 'Actually, hang on a sec.' She retreated into the kitchen and emerged a few minutes later with two takeaway cups. 'You have to try this hot chocolate, it's … special.' Her eyes were twinkling with mischief.

'OK,' he said, 'although I'm not much of a hot-chocolate man.'

'Trust me, you'll like this one. It's very Proustian.'

He couldn't stop smiling for the rest of the journey. He'd taken a sip of the hot chocolate and to his surprise, it was really very good. In fact, it was probably the best hot chocolate he'd ever tasted. It reminded him of his childhood, sitting in front of the TV and watching cartoons with his brother. He had a clear image of them both, bowls of hot chocolate in hand, him feeling like the luckiest boy in the world to have an older brother like Stéphane. And yet the tightness he always had in his chest whenever he thought of his brother now was strangely absent. In its stead was an uncomplicated feeling of warmth and, dare he say it, happiness. He rarely felt this way, especially when visiting his mother. Yet when he drove through the iron gates of the facility, the guilt and shame returned.

It had been three years since she had become a resident of 'Le Retrait'. Early onset dementia, according to the doctors in Paris. At first, it was just the occasional visit as a day patient, but as things had deteriorated, Seraphine Chadwick insisted on returning home for good to her native Compiègne.

Hugo spotted her from the main house, sitting at an easel on the lawn. He smiled to himself; he could almost pretend that she was simply staying at an artist's retreat and nothing at all was amiss. That his father had not moved his mistress into their home in Paris. He shook off these thoughts and walked purposefully down the garden path.

'*Bonjour, Maman*,' he said, kissing her cheek. He was still startled by her shock of grey hair. She'd stopped dying it the platinum blonde he had always associated her with. Growing up, he'd believed she was the most glamorous woman in the world, with her flowing kaftans, brightly coloured bangles and the large wooden beads that she always wore around her neck.

'My beautiful boy,' she replied, smiling up at him and touching his face.

'I've brought your favourite,' he said, opening the cardboard box and revealing the creamy strawberry cake inside.

'Wonderful! But first, you must look at this painting and tell me what it's missing,' she said, turning back to her painting of the lake in the distance.

It was a game they used to play when he was a boy. Seraphine had wanted to sharpen his observational skills, to view the world as an artist might. It was the main reason he'd taken up photography. For Hugo had never had the patience for sitting in front of an easel, dabbing paint onto the canvas. No, he preferred a more immediate form of storytelling – capturing the world in the way he saw it, or how he wished it could be, through his lens.

'A cherry tree in the foreground, no?'

There was something so comforting in the familiarity of his mother's artwork. At least that had not altered. Unlike everything else in their lives.

'I'll just get some plates,' he said, 'but why don't you try this hot chocolate while you're waiting?' He took the cover off the cup for her before disappearing back up the pathway to the house.

As the afternoon sunshine pierced through the clouds, Seraphine raised the cup to her lips and took a sip. In that moment her features transformed, and as the rich dark liquid entered her bloodstream something strange began to happen. Memories appeared to flash through her mind's eye – like old movies but crisp and clear, as though they were happening in this moment before her. An old family story that had been hidden and not spoken of for many years replayed in her mind.

Her uncle, who owned the newsagent's on the Rue de Paris, had been a bitter old man. He was always envious of what other people had and wanted to spoil it for them. Perhaps in a way he couldn't help it. He felt his life had been lacking in what other people took for granted, like love and happiness, but what he didn't realise was that no one is entitled to these things. They must be earned, nurtured and cherished

'I remember something', she announced as soon as Hugo returned with utensils and some plates.

'What is it?' Hugo asked, the air growing taut with expectation.

'This drink, I have tasted it before, in my childhood.'

For an unguarded moment, Hugo had allowed himself to believe that she might have remembered something about him. There were days when she didn't even know who he was, or that she'd ever had two sons. The worst of all was when she forgot that one of them had died.

'Have I ever told you about my childhood?' She looked at him then in a way that strangely made him feel as though he had never really met her before. People always said that as children, we never see our parents as real people, but here now he could see Seraphine not just as his mother but as a woman in her own right; someone with a past, with stories and secrets. 'Did I ever tell you about the Rue de Paris?'

Hugo swallowed hard. Was she confusing his father's business dealings with her own story? He couldn't be sure but there was a lightness in her eyes that he hadn't seen for a very long time. As he watched her take another sip of her hot chocolate, he began to wonder… No, it was an absurd idea.

'During the war,' she said, with a clarity that gave strength to his suspicion. Was the hot chocolate from Madame Moreau's stoking up old memories?

'My uncle, Arnaud, had a shop there. And he did a very bad thing.'

Chapter Twenty

'There's no such thing as ghosts,' I told myself, calmly, having woken to strange noises in the building again. I blamed it on the wind, making a mournful sound as it whirled down through the chimney, but I knew in my gut that there was more to it than that. The wind was just the messenger. I turned on the light and sat up in bed. I wavered between feelings of fear and curiosity, before finally deciding that I had to confront whatever this was. Like Madame Moreau said, it was an old building and even if it did hum with the echoes of past residents, there was no reason to feel afraid. They were people once. With lives. Just like Mum. The thought was sharp as a nail. I still found it hard to think about her death. I took out a notebook and began jotting down some random thoughts. I used to keep a journal when I was younger. It had provided me with a safe space to pour out my thoughts when I didn't want to burden my parents or worry them. I began to wonder why this 'haunting' was happening to me and as I did, the words on the page began to flow. Maybe my fear was misplaced grief. Perhaps I'd been haunted by my inability to grieve properly for my mum. I was caught in a web of so many different emotions, guilt, resentment, sorrow, self-pity … it was hard to deal with one without pulling on the strings of the others. I was exhausted, mentally and emotionally. It was understandable that the stress had caused me to see things that weren't there. It was time to face the unseen and prove to myself that I had nothing to fear. So I got up, put on my dressing gown and went down the stairs.

How wrong could I have been; I was terrified. The fleeting courage I had found immediately deserted me. I mean, who goes out of their way to vanquish a ghost? Stupid people in horror movies, that's who, and we all know how they end up. It was too late to turn back, so I just had to get on with it and trust that my newfound theory was true. Crouching in my usual space below the sink (light years from my Parisian dream), I lifted the grate and searched below for any sign of life – or death, as the case might be. I saw Madame Moreau and Manu working diligently as before, although I could hardly hear their voices over the loud thumping of my heart. I began to have my doubts about the 'presence' I had seen the other night, for they seemed to be alone. Then, just as before, a flickering image appeared by Manu's side and an overwhelming sense of fear bloomed in my chest. I thought I would pass out again. I had to concentrate on my breathing, trying to slow it down, and as I did, I prayed to my mother for courage and understanding. I tried to remember what I had felt upstairs in my room – whoever they were, this person was alive once. Just a normal person with their own hopes and fears. I held my hand on my chest and felt my heart rate begin to decelerate. As I began to calm down a little, I lay flat on the ground (which, in a toilet, is a huge sacrifice of personal hygiene) to get a better look. The man, for he was dressed like a man, appeared to be real. Yet, the more I forced myself to watch, the more he seemed slightly opaque. There was a dim glow to his skin. Otherwise, he was moving around like an ordinary person. That's when I realised, to my amazement, that he appeared to be in the process of kneading bread. There was no dough in his hands and he didn't appear to be touching anything, but his actions were that of a baker kneading dough. Looking across at Manu, I could see him mimicking every move the man was making, the only difference being that Manu's hands were actually connecting with something. Then I heard Madame Moreau speak from the shadows.

'That's it, now you will be able to bake bread like a true Moreau!' she said, her voice breaking with pride, or sadness, or both.

I stayed there for another fifteen minutes, having brought my trusty notebook to take notes so I wouldn't be second-guessing myself later. I had to plan my next move very carefully. It was clear that Manu knew what I had been doing in the toilet that night, and yet as far as I knew he had said nothing to Madame Moreau. In a way, I intuited that he wanted me to find out, but as to why, I did not know. I would not confront them until I did some digging of my own. While living above a haunted bakery might take a little getting used to, I wasn't prepared to run away just yet.

~

I waited for Manu till the end of the day, when the streetlamps popped on, one by one, and he returned to the bakery on his scooter. As was his routine, he began emptying all the leftover bread into a box for delivery to the homeless shelter.

'Why don't I go with you?' I suggested. By this stage I was accustomed to his and Madame Moreau's complete lack of enthusiasm regarding anything I said. If there was one thing I had learned in this country, it was to just barge your way through instead of waiting for an invite.

Manu sort of sniffed and looked out at the scooter. He had a point; I couldn't see myself riding on the handlebars.

'Why don't we walk, eh … *marcher*? I'm sure it's *pas loin*,' I said. 'It's not too far, is it, Madame Moreau? And I can help to carry some of the boxes.'

Instead of her usual shrug, I almost detected what might have been considered a smile. Perhaps I was breaking down her walls after all. With that, off we trudged through the cobbled streets.

'So, you're interested in becoming a baker, then?' I asked Manu, starting the proceedings with a little small talk.

'*Oui.*'

'And you are learning from the baker I saw in the basement last night?' I let the sentence hang there until he worked it out.

'You saw … 'im?' he asked a little hesitantly.

'I saw something, and I definitely wasn't dreaming,' I said, matching his frankness. '*Ce n'était pas un rêve.*'

'*S'il vous plait* … do not speak of last night to Madame Moreau,' Manu blurted, in surprisingly good English.

Up until that moment, I had doubted my own sanity.

Each time that image of the ghost standing there (or hovering there) crept up, I felt slightly weak and spent the entire day afterwards explaining it away. Lack of sleep, a play of shadows, even having a nervous breakdown seemed a preferable alternative to what I knew in my gut to be true.

'I'm not sure what I saw,' I replied honestly, 'but I think I deserve an explanation.'

Neither of us spoke for a while. Manu led the way and took a right turn by the side of a large church I hadn't seen before. At the back, there was something of a hall with a line of windows lit up warmly from the inside and a queue of people extending out the door. Manu greeted some of the people in the queue and quite chivalrously let me go in ahead of him. I hadn't really thought about where we were going, my mind had been so fixed on getting answers out of him. But now that we had arrived, I was both surprised and humbled by what I saw. It was like a canteen with lots of tables set up for dinner, and at the top of the room there was a counter manned by volunteers handing out bowls of steaming soup and a main dish of some kind of casserole. A priest spotted Manu and came out from behind the counter to greet us.

'*Bonjour, Emmanuel,*' he greeted him by his full name. '*T'as amené une petite amie?*'

'*Père Bernard, je vous présente Mademoiselle Lane,*' Manu spoke respectfully. '*Elle est irlandaise,*' he added almost as an excuse for any upcoming blunders I would make.

In that vein, I wasn't entirely sure of the etiquette and whether I was supposed to kiss him, but thankfully, as I put the boxes down on a table, he took my hand and shook it. It didn't help that I suddenly forgot all my French, which I was wont to do on social occasions, but again he took the initiative.

'*Ça vous plaît, la vie ici en France?*'

Did I like living in France? Well, it was a work in progress.

'Oh, *oui, je suis très contente ici.*' It wasn't a lie exactly, my life in France was growing on me in some ways.

'Father says, it is our *responsibilité* to protect the forgotten,' Manu said, filling in the blanks for me.

And these people were forgotten. Many of them were immigrants, who looked as though they had little more than the clothes on their backs.

As we walked back to the bakery later, I had a whole new set of questions for Manu.

'Those people back there,' I began, 'they're not French, are they?'

He eyed me up for a moment before answering. 'They come from many different places. They are refugees.'

'And you and Madame Moreau help them?'

He nodded in response.

'Are you two related?' I pressed on, aware that this was really none of my business, but at the same time, I felt as though I was being drawn into something and had a right to know.

'*C'est ma grandmère,*' he said.

'Grandmother?' I repeated unnecessarily. I let it sink in for a while. I couldn't understand why they hadn't just told me that in the beginning. Perhaps something had happened to Manu's parents, Madame Moreau's son or daughter, and that was why she was looking after Manu.

'*Grandmère* says that, as Roma, it is our duty to 'elp those who are on the outside.'

I knew nothing about Roma gypsies or their culture. All I knew from Ireland was the traveller community and the discrimination they faced every day, negative stereotypes diminishing their rich culture.

'So, can you tell me what really happened last night? Does it happen every night?'

He was obviously uncomfortable talking about it, but he seemed more concerned about me blabbing my suspicions to Madame Moreau than what I would do with the information. Still, he was guarded.

'It's OK, Manu,' I said, feeling a rush of maternal feeling towards him. '*Vous n'êtes pas obligé de tout me dire maintenant. We can talk about it later,*' I assured him. It was clear he wasn't ready to talk to me about it and I wasn't sure how ready I was to hear it. It was enough to know that I wasn't going crazy and Madame Moreau's secret was safe between us for the time being. On that mutual ground, we parted for the night, but my curiosity still tugged at me. I couldn't help but wonder where, or rather when, the apparition was coming from. Had something happened in the town's history, or perhaps the building itself?

Chapter Twenty-One

'*É*dith!' Madame Moreau called. '*Il y a un coursier qui te cherche.*'

'What?' I asked, looking up and seeing a courier at the door, his white van parked outside. I came out from behind the counter and vaguely heard Madame Moreau ask if I was planning on doing any work today. I pretended not to understand, a tactic I employed quite often.

'*Signez ici,*' the courier said, holding out a small electronic machine.

I scribbled my signature on the screen, not knowing what I was signing for, as he didn't seem to be holding a package.

'*Dehors,*' he nodded and I followed him outside.

There, perched jauntily on its stand at the side of the bakery was a beautiful cream-coloured bicycle, complete with a wicker basket.

'What?!' I exclaimed, looking around for some sort of

explanation. I put my hands on the handlebars and saw an envelope inside the basket. I opened it quickly.

I hope you'll excuse the lack of ribbons and bows - the courier company said they didn't do that kind of thing.

Happy travels,

H x

I read the words over and over. Characteristically, Hugo was downplaying it, as though this wasn't one of the most considered gifts I'd ever received. A surprise present was one thing, but it was quite another to realise that he'd listened, really listened on our date and remembered my comment about getting a bicycle. I tried to stay level-headed. It was too much and I obviously couldn't accept it. But I couldn't help it, my heart was bounding ahead of me like a puppy escaping its leash. My entire being felt lit up from within. It was so rare these days to find someone who really paid attention and acted on their good intentions. Hugo had gone from being my French crush to something much, much more. He was a man who was genuinely thoughtful, as well as being incredibly good-looking!

'*Où est Édith?*' I heard Manu call to Madame Moreau. I didn't have the exact translation for her answer, but I thought she said something like, 'That girl is outside smiling like a loon at a bike.' And she was right, I was.

I cycled down to the river on my new bike during my lunch break. I had fully intended to leave the bike exactly where it was and have it returned. I couldn't keep it. But the more I looked at it, the more I realised that I really wanted it. I would pay him back, every cent. I sent him a message saying exactly that. Hugo said he would FaceTime me so we could discuss it over lunch, but he had yet to find out how stubborn I could be when it came to paying my own way.

I brought half a baguette, some Emmental cheese, a red apple and an apricot pastry for dessert which looked like a glowing orange sunrise in golden pastry. Everything tasted so good here! And I even brought a half bottle of white wine with a plastic cup. The weather was bright, breezy and promising summer warmth. I wondered what my first summer in France would be like. I still couldn't believe that I'd done it. Nothing really matches up to the ideas in your head – some things are better, some things are definitely worse – but what you can never anticipate is how you will feel inside. And I felt proud of myself.

Minutes ticked by, and I eventually received a text from Hugo saying that he was stuck in a meeting. I sent him a photo of my picnic on the bench with my beautiful new bike leaning against it. It looked like a postcard scene. I began to wonder what exactly his job was. But then again, perhaps he hadn't spoken very much about it because it wasn't his passion. In my mind, he was a photographer, and with that, I clicked onto his website where he had uploaded some of his photos, and began munching my food. The old buildings he'd captured were so beautiful. There was a gorgeous teal-blue chocolate shop with arched windows and golden letters on the front. My mind ran away with itself as I began to imagine visiting Paris with Hugo – him showing me the sights and then staying in some terribly chic hotel together. Or his apartment. I wondered what that was like? He seemed quite well off, so it was probably beautiful, with a doorman and everything. Not like my atelier, with its dodgy plumbing and spooky noises.

I poured out a glass of wine and watched as a small motor boat sailed past on the water. It was easy to dismiss my fears in the middle of a sunny afternoon, but there was a very real possibility that the bakery was... No. I couldn't even say the word. The very idea was too absurd for words. And yet, something weird was going on. I picked up my phone again and opened the search engine. My fingers typed the words 'ghosts and hauntings'. Scanning down the page, I searched for something that looked reliable. After some browsing on the subject, I discovered that a lot of websites referred to two main types of hauntings; intelligent and residual. Something in my gut made me click on the word 'residual' and when I spotted something on Wikipedia called The Stone Tape theory, I opened it. The explanation I found was eerily accurate.

The Stone Tape theory is a paranormal hypothesis which speculates that during intense moments in someone's life, places can absorb some form of energy from them as living beings. After their death, this stored energy can then be released, resulting in a display of the recorded activity. According to this hypothesis, ghosts are not spirits but simply non-interactive recordings similar to a movie.

I hadn't even registered that I'd eaten the entire pastry while reading. There was a part of me that wanted to know what was going on, but mostly I was hoping it would all go away or that there'd be some rational explanation. I felt ridiculous for even looking it up. I was about to shut down the page when I saw the words '... *like an echo of past events*'.

I thought of the person I'd seen, the man with the phantom glow lighting up his skin and his old-fashioned clothes marking him out as being from another time. Could it have been possible? There was only one thing for it now – I had to confront Madame Moreau. Just then my phone rang and I almost flung it into the river with fright. Then I saw Hugo's name on the screen and tried to compose myself.

'Hello,' I said, fixing my hair. It took me a moment to realise it wasn't a video call.

'*Salut, chérie,*' he said, melting my heart immediately. 'I can't stay long, but I wanted to apologise for not making our lunch date. I will make it up to you.'

'Oh, that sounds promising,' I said, taking a bite of my apple.

'Perhaps I could bring you back a little something from the city,' he said in that seductive accent that fell somewhere between Paris and London.

'Um, you literally just bought me a bike,' I said, leaning across to the handlebars and ringing the bell for effect.

'Does Mademoiselle approve?'

'Of course I do, it's beautiful, but I can't possibly accept a gift like that.'

'Why not?'

'Because it's too generous!'

'And that's bad because?'

'I just – I like to pay my own way.'

'Oh, of course, I didn't mean…' he trailed off.

I was glad I couldn't see his face at that point. Maybe I'd insulted his generosity, but it was just how I felt.

'When I've dated in the past, it was expected,' he said.

'Oh.' I wasn't sure how to respond.

'That sounded weird, like I've time-travelled from the court of King Louis or something.'

'It's OK,' I said, laughing. 'I appreciated the gesture. Very much.'

'What I mean is, if you were serious about someone, you let them know.'

Serious. He'd just used the word serious. About me. I tried and failed yet again to keep my heart from forming promises with his words.

'I wish I'd known that before, I would've said I wanted a sports car!' I said, trying to keep it light-hearted.

'It's all being noted down, don't worry. Any particular colour?'

'Surprise me.'

My cheeks hurt from smiling. In fact, I was pretty sure my smile was visible from space.

Chapter Twenty-Two

The following evening, Manu surprised me by leaving a key on the mat outside my door. It was an old, heavy key and I knew exactly which door it would fit. I set my alarm for 3.15am., so I would have time to get into the basement before Madame Moreau. There was some trepidation on my part, partly at the thought of being in the same room with a ghost, partly at how Madame Moreau would react. I realised that my predecessor, Maria, must have found out about the unsettling secret in the basement and high-tailed it out of there. Geoff had told me that she was also English and left without saying anything to anyone. Not that I blamed her – it's not exactly what you'd expect to find in a quaint little French *boulangerie*. Besides, who would have believed such a story? Unless, like me, they saw it with their own two eyes. I now firmly believed that fate or destiny had brought me here at this mid-point in my life, following my mother's passing. I didn't want to run away without facing the mystery of this place and its past.

I crept downstairs as quietly as I could. I felt more awake than I had done in a very long time, considering that all about me was darkness. Once I reached the kitchenette, I turned on the light and wiggled the key into the lock of the little door leading to the basement. The sound of my heart beating in my ears would have woken the dead, I thought, and immediately hoped that wasn't true. 'What are you doing, Edie?' I asked myself, coldly resigned to the fact that there was no turning back now. I turned the key and heard the click. As the little door creaked open, a blast of cold air hit me in the face. I felt my knees trembling and threatening to give way. I would have reconsidered the whole thing then and there, but I heard noises coming from upstairs, which only meant one thing. Madame Moreau was up and would shortly come down to the basement herself. I steadied myself and took the torch from my dressing gown pocket. Closing and turning the key in the door behind me, I stepped carefully down the small staircase to the basement.

Manu had left a note with the key, advising me where to position myself. Seeing the bakery from the vantage point of the bathroom offered me some kind of safety, but being in the actual room was far too close for comfort. I found the bags of flour that Manu had said to hide behind and took up my position. From there I had a clear view of the great ovens that produced the Moreaus' famously crusty bread and I could see the large troughs they used for mixing the dough, too, which had been obscured from my little spyhole in the toilet. Old wooden shelves lined the walls and were stacked with rose-gold pots and loaf tins. A large weighing scale sat at the other end of the room, where the dough was cut and rolled before baking.

I sat in complete silence, with every hair on my body alert. Something lightly brushed against my ankle and I instinctively shrieked with terror. I clasped my hand over my mouth and hoped to God I wasn't being attacked by a zombie. On closer inspection, I saw that the culprit was the belt of my robe coming loose and didn't know whether to feel relieved or embarrassed.

All of a sudden, I heard the key turn in the lock and realised that Madame Moreau and her grandson were on their way, which meant that 'he' was surely on his way, too. I took whatever breadcrumbs of courage I had left in my hands and tried to steady my breathing. I remembered the information I had read about residual hauntings and tried to remind myself that it was essentially a film on rerun, nothing more. Wordlessly, the two of them entered the bakery, although I could see Manu's eyes darting about for me. If he couldn't see me, then I knew I had hidden myself well. Perhaps he thought I had chickened out. There wasn't much time for him to consider this, though, as straightaway he began loading the oven with wood from a pile in the opposite corner of the room. I noticed the door that presumably led onto the side lane, the one that had pulled shut on me when I first arrived. Could I make my escape through it if things got too much?

As the wood began to crackle and spark, the room filled with the low light from the fire and Manu set about emptying large quantities of flour into one of the troughs. Madame Moreau moved about stiffly, preparing the additional ingredients Manu would need. After a thorough mixing of the yeast and the water, which he didn't bother to measure, he scraped the dough together and transferred it to the worktop. The smell of the flour and the sweet-sour yeast made me feel at home and I almost forgot the reason I was there. Watching him expertly throw the flour over the surface, I found myself becoming lost in the process, until the flickering began and the atmosphere in the room changed completely. It felt as though there was an electric charge running through the air. Gradually, like thousands of shimmering dust motes swirling together, a hazy outline of a person began to appear. I jolted from the shock of seeing him at close quarters and almost knocked over one of the bags of flour that concealed my presence. However, no one seemed to hear me or notice, as they in turn jumped at his sudden apparition, despite the fact they were expecting him. What Madame Moreau said next shocked me even further.

'*Bonjour, Papa.*'

I was frozen to the spot. This was no random haunting; I was watching the ghost of Monsieur Moreau. I had to stuff the belt of my robe into my mouth to ensure I wouldn't scream. Monsieur Moreau, or rather his ghost, seemed completely oblivious to the presence of his daughter and great-grandson, instead focusing intensely on his work. He moved about, not like a regular person, but just as the website had said. It was like watching an old, scratchy film – at one point the light around him would glow, and the next almost fade completely. He reached for objects but never quite connected with them. He seemed unwilling or unable to interact with Manu, who watched his great-grandfather carefully and did his best to emulate his technique. It was startling and amazing to watch. They both flicked out their wrists to spread the flour on the board, then began the process of kneading and adding various ingredients along the way. While the breads were set aside to prove, Manu continued to shadow Monsieur Moreau as he put a pot of steaming water in the oven and, using a long wooden paddle, placed the round breads at the very back and closed the door. The only conversation was between Madame Moreau and Manu, surprisingly ordinary things like 'Make sure the temperature of the water is right for the dough' and 'The baguettes are ready for the oven now.' Somehow, this bizarre and unique set-up had become normal for them. Madame Moreau watched her father lovingly, but was careful not to get too close.

This carried on for over an hour, by which stage my entire body was aching from crouching behind the large bags of flour on a cold floor. It was then I heard Madame Moreau suggest that she start to take the cooked breads upstairs and get ready to open the shop. With that, Monsieur Moreau, or his spirit, vanished, leaving only a strange charge in the atmosphere, like ripples in water. I knew the moment of truth had arrived and I had to make my presence known. I didn't want to frighten them by popping up out of nowhere, but considered that if they had spent the morning sharing their kitchen with a ghost, my presence shouldn't come as that much of a shock.

'Good morning, Madame Moreau,' was all I could say, as I stumbled out from behind my hiding place. She staggered at the sight of me, and thankfully Manu grabbed her arm to offer her support.

'*Mais, qu'est ce que…* You!' she shouted at me with a mix of fury and guilt at being found out.

Manu ushered his grandmother to a stool.

'*Elle veut nous aider,*' he assured her gently.

'He's right,' I added, 'I do want to help, if I can.' I wasn't quite sure what I was signing up to, or why Manu thought I could possibly help them, but I would have said anything at that point, for Madame Moreau looked so pale and shaky, I feared for her health. I went and fetched her a glass of water, which she gulped in one go. She ordered Manu to get the bread ready for the shop and to prepare his deliveries, and she assuaged his worries with a persuasive nod of the head that she would be all right. I didn't know if the same could be said for me. I was still shivering myself and I wasn't sure if it was the cold or the shock. She must have sensed this, so she heaved herself off the stool and bade me to follow her. We climbed the stairs and, with another nod of encouragement to Manu as we passed through the shop, we climbed the next set of stairs to her apartment. I had never seen past her front door up till now and the significance of bringing me into her home was not lost on me. It was, like my own apartment, small and functional, but hers was extremely cosy and homely. It was carpeted and had frilly drapes that hung from the long windows overlooking the street. Her fireplace was home to lots of old photographs of the bakery and what I assumed to be her mother. Then I saw Monsieur Moreau in another frame and recognised him instantly. The thick moustache and neatly gelled-back hair were unmistakable.

'*Assieds-toi,*' she said, pointing to one of two wingbacked chairs arranged in front of the fire. I was glad of the heat and rubbed my hands in front of the low embers. Madame Moreau boiled some water on the cooker and prepared a pot of strong coffee for us both. She placed the cups on a little side table and sat down in the chair opposite me.

'I underestimated you, *Édith,*' she said, with a look of approval on her face.

And there it was – approval. My drug of choice. All I ever wanted was the approval of those around me. Yet now that I had finally won this taciturn woman over, I no longer cared what she thought of me, for I was so angry with her.

'Was this some sort of test? I thought you hired me to become the assistant manager, not a ghostbuster!' I knew I was being facetious, but it seemed the only way to counteract the shock of what I'd just witnessed.

'*Mais non* … of course not,' she argued.

'Oh, really? What about Maria, then? Yes, I've heard about your last employee,' I said, seeing her surprise. 'Is that why you hire people from abroad, so none of the locals will find out your secret?'

'Partly, yes.'

I had expected some sort of argument, for her to tell me I'd got the wrong end of the stick.

'Oh, so you're admitting it?' I could feel the blood rising to my cheeks with rage.

'*Édith, écoute-moi,* I was not trying to fool you or test you as you say. *Mais,* I cannot risk anyone here finding out. They will think we are…' At this stage she tapped her index finger against her temple and whistled like a cuckoo.

'Well, it's not fair, expecting someone to live here

without knowing the truth,' I said, taking a sip of coffee that was thankfully good and hot.

'Would you have taken the job if I had told you the truth?'

I left the question hanging in mid-air. Of course the answer was no, but how could you tell anyone that you had a ghost in your basement without sounding like a lunatic?

'We cannot talk for long now,' she said, checking her watch, 'but I promise, I will explain you everything tonight.'

I regarded her carefully and wondered how we were supposed to carry on as normal for the rest of the day in the shop. Then it became clear to me that she and Manu had done exactly that, for years. It was their reality.

'You have known for some time, yet you are still here,' she said sincerely. 'Why did you not leave us?'

'I'm not sure,' I answered honestly, 'The truth is, I came here to get away from my own problems and despite, well, *this* –' I gestured at the floor below us '– I kind of like it here. It's going to sound strange, but there's something about the place that has given me back my appetite for life, you know?' I wrinkled my nose with a half-hearted smile. I hadn't really understood how true it was until that moment.

'Well, I am glad you stay. *Mais maintenant*, we must work!' she announced and something in her practicality made me put aside my misgivings. As I rose from my chair and prepared to follow her downstairs, she turned and gave me one of her withering looks.

'What now?' I asked impatiently.

'Oh, nothing, perhaps this is your new uniform, *hein*?' she replied, eyeing me up and down.

That's when I realised that I was still in my dressing gown.

'Hang on, did you just make a joke?' I said, smiling triumphantly. She walked away, but we both knew I had cracked her hard shell.

Edie one, France nil.

Chapter Twenty-Three

Commerce always comes first for a sole trader and Madame Moreau was no different. She interacted with her customers as usual from her perch behind the counter, while I carried out my work in a daze. Just before lunch, Geoff popped by for a 'cheeky eclair' as he put it and I was never so happy to see anyone in my life.

'How is my favourite customer today?' I asked while wiping down his table. Madame Moreau must have wondered whether I was going to share her eerie secret with an outsider, but if she was concerned, she did not show it. Her face was an inscrutable mask.

'How's Ruby?' I asked, craving a normal conversation after the extraordinary events of the morning.

'She's having her nails clipped at the salon.'

'Sorry, what?'

'It's a joke!'

'Oh, of course,' I said, rubbing my eyes. 'The early mornings are catching up with me.'

'That yours?' he asked, nodding towards my bicycle that was leaning against the gable.

'Yes,' I smiled, thinking of how happy I'd been when it arrived.

'You should take yourself off for a nice spin, clears the head.'

'You know what, that might not be such a bad idea,' I said, untying my apron. 'I might just take an early lunch and see if I can't cycle my way into a better mood.'

Instead of asking, I simply told Madame Moreau that I was leaving and walked out into the watery sunshine. I unlocked my bike and cycled over the Pont Solferino and past the train station, searching for some unknown object that might make everything seem normal again. I took the tow path along the River Oise, with only the sound of my tyres on the gravel to keep me company.

Seeing Monsieur Moreau that morning had brought up some unwelcome thoughts about death and the afterlife. To think I had come to France to get away from all of that, only to end up coming face to face with a real live, or dead, ghost. Where was his soul, after all? Trapped in some kind of limbo? I wasn't sure if I believed in heaven, but I wanted to believe that my mother was happy, wherever she was. Despite my frustration at being lied to, I couldn't help but wonder what it must feel like for Madame Moreau to see her father like that, night after night. I couldn't imagine seeing my mother in that way: as an echo of herself. On the one hand, it would be so wonderful to see her again, but to not be able to touch her or speak to her? I realised that it would be a kind of breathtaking torture. I wasn't really sure if I could deal with it. I mean, I was still in the process of grieving myself. I pulled hard on the brakes, got off the bike and stood by a nearby bench. Without thinking about it, I took my phone out of my pocket and I called my dad.

'How are ya getting on, Edie?' he greeted me, full of the joys. I could feel the tears stinging my eyes and tried desperately to hold onto them. I was gripping the bench, watching the river rushing by in front of me.

'I miss her so much, Dad,' was all I could say, as the tears came in torrents. He said nothing for a while, but from the sounds he made, I felt he was crying, too.

'Do you want to come home, love?' he asked eventually, his voice hoarse.

'Yes,' I said, snivelling like a little girl who just wanted her father to make everything go away. 'But it wouldn't change anything. Besides, I think they need me here.' It was a revelation as I said it. I remembered how Manu had told his grandmother I would help them and I realised that despite their air of nonchalance in the bakery that morning, they were struggling somehow.

'They're lucky to have you, Edie, you know that,' Dad said with paternal pride.

'You know what? You're right!' I said, as though suddenly understanding my position in the world. Maybe it wasn't my destiny to become a chart-topping singer or a domestic goddess with 2.4 children and a dog. But I had the ability to make an impact on people's lives, if only in a small way, just by being myself – and that was enough.

I began cycling back towards the city centre, and stopped at a set of traffic lights where I spotted a jeweller's on the corner. Something, perhaps intuition, told me I should go in. I stepped off the bike and pulled the handlebars up, lifting it onto the pavement before locking it to a railing. The pretty silver jewellery sparkled in the shop window. A charm bracelet caught my eye; it had a small Eiffel Tower charm and a little bicycle, too. Maybe every tourist succumbed to these clichéd trinkets, but I didn't care. It immediately put a smile on my face and I knew that could only be a good thing. I went straight in and bought it for myself.

That evening, Madame Moreau had me round for dinner. It had begun to rain outside and the temperature had dropped rapidly, so her cosy apartment was a welcome refuge. She had prepared a delicious rabbit stew with lots of comforting root vegetables.

'*Manu ne mange pas avec nous?*' I asked, when I noticed he was not at table.

'*Il sort avec ses amis,*' she said. 'Your French is improving.'

'*Merci,* I've always wanted to speak fluent French – that's why I came here, really,' I said, enjoying the opportunity to open up to this woman who had kept me at arm's length since I arrived. She dished out our meal from a porcelain terrine onto pretty plates with blue flowers, while I poured the wine. We ate in companionable silence for a time, with only the sound of the ticking clock and the sparking logs in the background. As I mopped up the sauce with my bread, we spoke about ordinary things like the weather and some of the interesting characters that came into the shop. She had prepared a delicious *tarte Tatin* with caramelised apples in cinnamon and, despite my full stomach, I cleaned the bowl. After we had cleared away the dishes, we moved to the chairs beside the fire once again and I knew it was time to discuss the elephant in the room.

'You didn't really need an assistant manager for the shop who spoke English, did you?' I said, suddenly understanding the motivation behind the job being advertised abroad. 'You didn't want anyone from around here finding out about your father and risking them telling anyone.'

'I never want to upset or frighten anyone, but yes, it was easier to keep the secret that way. It 'as been difficult – concealing this. That is why we use the tunnel for the deliveries – that way, I can avoid anyone coming into the basement,' she explained, solving the other mystery that had me baffled. 'When my daughter was alive, I did not need any help from the outside. But now, my arthritis is bad and Manu must go to school.' She shrugged.

'I'm sorry, I had no idea your daughter had passed away,' I said genuinely.

Her eyes glistened as she said, 'No parent should see their child go before them.' She searched for a tissue in the pocket of her housecoat and wiped her eyes.

'I'm so sorry,' I said again, the words sounding so small and insignificant. Now I understood what it was like for my family and friends when they felt so helpless.

'It was a car accident. Twelve years ago. She and *son mari*, her husband, were travelling south to Spain, to visit his family. Little Manu, he was sleeping in the back seat.'

It was visibly distressing for her to talk about it, so I

stopped her with my hand on her arm and told her it was OK, she didn't have to explain.

'I lost my mother – I know it's hard to talk about it sometimes,' I said in solidarity. Her face was the picture of empathy; such was the softness of her large brown eyes as she placed her hand on mine.

'*C'est dure la vie, hein?*'

She was right about that, life was hard. In the silence that followed, I understood how my first impressions of Madame Moreau were completely wrong. I'd interpreted her frosty demeanour as hostile and unfriendly, when in actual fact she was merely doing her best to protect her family and her own peace of mind. She stood up and went to a tall mahogany dresser and took a photo album out of one of the cupboards. Sitting back down beside me, she showed me pictures of her daughter from childhood right up until before she died.

'She would have been just a year or two older than you,' she told me in a soft voice.

'Does Manu remember them, at all?' I asked, but she just shook her head, saying he had only been a baby then.

'He's such a bright young man, and a credit to you.'

'*Comment?*' she said, unfamiliar with the term.

'You have brought him up extremely well,' I clarified. Then a thought struck me. 'Your daughter?'

'*Gabrielle, oui?*'

'Did she see your father, too?' I asked.

'But of course, it was she who was learning the old methods from him – she was to take over the *boulangerie*. Not that it matters now,' she added.

'Why do you say that? Manu is doing a good job, isn't

he? My father used to work as a pastry chef at home in Ireland, so I know a thing or two about baking, and Manu really has the flair for it.'

'Ah, yes, I remember this in your application. Manu said it could be useful.' She smiled proudly at her grandson's foresight.

'Oh, I see, so it's Manu I should thank for giving me the job?' I said, smiling too.

'Indeed, but as I am sure you know, small bakeries are not so profitable anymore. People are buying those *moche* … how you say, horrible sliced breads in the supermarket because they are cheaper and with all those preserves that keep it from going stale for days and days, ugh!'

'I suppose the cost of living is affecting everything and people are just trying to save money.'

'*Exactement*, so they do not buy their fresh bread and croissants every day. Things are becoming very difficult for us here. I don't know what future there is.' She stared into the fire and for the first time since I had known her, she looked tired. I didn't want to press her about the small issue of a ghost in the basement, but I couldn't hide my curiosity either.

'So, what about your father?' I asked in as sensitive a tone as possible.

'Ah, yes, well, you deserve to know the truth now, *Édith*, and I will tell it to you. *Mais*, I have to start at the very beginning…'

Chapter Twenty-Four

L'histoire de Madame Moreau

My earliest memories are sitting around a campfire, watching my mother dance. She wore *une robe*, a beautiful dress with flowers in yellow and red that twirled with her body. My grandmother and all the other women clapped, while one of 'ze men played his guitar and my mother tapped her feet on the dusty earth. Her name was Mirela; in Romani language it means 'to admire', which was right because everyone who saw her admired her. I remember the warmth of our brightly painted caravan, and 'ze sounds when the camp stirred at first light, with pots and pans rattling and children laughing.

I know that these are the romantic notions of a child. I mean, what child would not enjoy 'ze freedom of a nomadic life? You are not expected to go to school and you live close with all your family, so there is always something to do and someone to play with. It is life from a child's perspective, but even then I could see the 'ardship for my parents. Roma were very disliked by many of the locals and we were chased from one campsite to the next, *très souvent*. My family were 'Manouche' – a small group of Roma who came to France from Eastern Europe. We were so very poor, but we were a proud people and did what we could to make a living. My father traded in horses and he worked sometimes training 'zem in the stables of the rich. He spoke many languages and in fact it was he who taught me to speak English. We learned how to survive and use our skills to make a living on the edges of society. But there was always uncertainty and our caravans were always on the move.

My memories of that time have become golden; they are so precious to me. When I think of my mother back then, all I remember are the sparks from the fire lighting up the sky and how her body resembled the dancing flames, swaying and diving and lulling us all into a trance. She was *très belle*, with long black hair braided down her back, like one of my father's stallions. They said she had the '*duende*', that she danced with passion and fire in her soul, and people would come from all around to see her.

Things began to change in France, and I could often 'ear the adults talking about the war. I did not fully understand what a war was, but I knew that people were frightened. When France signed the armistice with the Nazis in 1940, I was eight years old. I thought I knew what hardship was, but life was to become much more difficult. The Germans made 'ze French pay for the occupation and the prices for everyday goods inflated. People were already poor, but now there were no jobs, so people were trying to survive on very little. With the curfews and the Vichy Regime punishing anyone who resisted 'ze rules, life in France became *intolérable*. But the worst was yet to come.

For some time, we 'ad 'eard the rumours of German labour camps. Hitler's regime had begun the rounding up of minority groups considered 'racially inferior'. Jews, Poles, Roma, homosexuals and people with disabilities were being sent to labour camps, or they were shot, to protect the Aryan race. Of course, my family did not tell me this at the time, but I remember hearing about a crazy man in Germany who wanted to take over the world. It did not seem real to me. Not until my father disappeared.

We were staying in a camp just east of Paris when a small troop of German soldiers pulled up in their army jeeps. They said the men were needed for work and that we would all be moved to a town in the north I 'ad never 'eard of, called Compiègne. The men had to leave with them *immédiatement*, and the women and children were to take a train. I remember feeling nervous and scared, but my mother reassured me all would be well. She said that *Papa* was a good worker and that was why he was being asked to go in such a hurry. He held me fiercely in his arms and told me to be good for my mother. I never saw him again.

There was some excitement getting on 'ze train because it was my first time, and despite the confusion, I was eager to get moving. I remember how quickly the landscape moved past, not like our caravan and the old horse that clip-clopped along the lanes. It was no time at all before we pulled into the station and I noticed German guards all around. I did not know why at the time, but my mother yanked me up out of my seat and pulled me behind her towards the exit *en vitesse*. She must have spotted 'im as we pulled in, and seized her chance when the guards were distracted, checking papers with the station master. An ordinary man, dressed in an overcoat with a white apron underneath, stood on the platform holding a large basket of baguettes. I 'ad no idea what she was doing, or how she seemed to know 'zis man, but as soon as we alighted from the train she ran to him and embraced him, desperately, and spoke to 'im in what I thought was a very posh accent.

'*Chéri*, you've come to greet us off the train!' she said, kissing his face. *Il y avait un regard*, a look that passed between them then that I couldn't explain. A pause that seemed to last just a second too long. One of 'ze officers approached and was about to say something, when Monsieur Moreau put down the basket and put his arms around us both.

'Welcome home, my darlings, how I've missed you!'

Chapter Twenty-Five

Pierre Moreau

1942

'What is your name?' Pierre asked the woman as they walked back to the Rue de Paris.

'Mirela. And this is my daughter, Geneviève.'

Pierre unlocked the basement door at the gable of the bakery and once they were inside, shut it firmly after him. His shoulders slumped and air refilled his lungs. What was he to do now? He couldn't think. The consequences of sheltering prisoners were known well enough. He went to the sink, took down some glasses and filled them with water before handing them to Mirela and her daughter.

'Thank you, Monsieur, for what you have done for us,' she said, before gulping down the entire glass and handing it back to him. She turned back towards the door, as though ready to flee.

'What will you do? Where will you go?' he asked.

'North,' she said. 'Perhaps we can get a boat from there…'

Geneviève rubbed her eyes and whimpered. She looked weary to her bones.

'The child is tired,' he said. 'Here…' He pulled a bench out from the wall and placed an empty flour sack upon it. 'Let her rest. I will get you something to eat.'

He took some of the remaining apples from a crate at the back of the basement. They were bruised and over-ripe, but they were all he could get. With a knife, he cut off the browning soft spots and sliced the apples into pieces, then put them on a plate with some madeleines. The child, who had up to this point clung to her mother like a barnacle on a rock, gave Pierre and the plate a wary look.

'Please,' he said, reaching towards her. She looked to her mother who gave her a reassuring smile and with the speed of a pickpocket, she took a madeleine and munched it happily.

Pierre smiled. He didn't have much experience with children, but this little girl, her large brown eyes that suggested a quick, lively intelligence… Well. He was quite taken with her.

'You'll never make it to the coast,' he said, getting up to prepare some coffee, which was really just roasted acorns and chicory root. 'I think you know that.' He set some water to boil on the stove.

'I have no choice,' Mirela said.

Pierre looked at them both, nibbling on the small plate

of food. They had barely survived up to now. And he felt sure their survival rested in his hands. Sending them out onto the street now was a certain death sentence. This war had already stolen so much from him, he wasn't going to let it steal his humanity as well. Even if it meant dying for it, it was the only thing worth living for.

'You can stay here.' The words seemed to echo around the walls. It was a life-and-death decision. He was afraid of what would come, but equally, he felt as though he were living up to the nature of his soul, his highest good.

Mirela looked up at him with confusion in her eyes that turned a moment later to some kind of recognition.

'I cannot offer you anything,' she replied, after a time. 'I won't do that.'

The kettle began to whistle and, with a cloth wrapped around the handle, he took it off the boil, then turned to look at her, forgetting about the coffee.

'I don't understand,' he said.

'I love my husband, whether he is alive or dead.'

Suddenly, it dawned on him. She assumed this would be an arrangement of some sort. That he, being a bachelor, would take advantage of her vulnerable situation.

'No, you misunderstand. I am no threat to you, Mirela. I…' The words died on his lips. How could he say out loud the very thing he had kept secret for years. 'I do not see you in that way.'

She stared into his earnest eyes and tried to listen to him with her heart and not her ears.

'Do you understand what I am saying? I cannot love a woman.'

It was as though an electric charge or a current had been

switched off. The tension that had been tying her body in a tight knot released and with that, the tears began to flow.

'*Maman*?' The little girl looked cautiously at her mother.

'I think *Maman* would like some more madeleines,' Pierre said gently. 'Shall we make some together?'

And that was how Pierre Moreau found himself with a family he had never asked for or dared hope for. They decided on a story that, while unusual, could convince the locals. Pierre told everyone that Mirela was his wife. Yes, it was sudden, but in wartime, people did strange things, no? Yes, he would make a great father to the child. Of course, they came from a small village in the country, you wouldn't know it. And that was how they carried on, as an unexpected but happy family. Mirela took on her role as dutiful housewife and Geneviève spent every day by Pierre's side, learning how to bake. Before long, their lives began to resemble something approaching normality, but more than that – joy.

Chapter Twenty-Six

M adame Moreau put some more logs on the fire and fetched two glasses and a bottle of brandy. I was enraptured by her story and stunned by its stark realities.

'So, he saved you from a concentration camp?' I said, hardly believing the dramatic childhood traumas she must have witnessed.

'For a time, yes. *Maman* explained to me that while my father was away, Monsieur Moreau, Pierre, would be like *mon oncle*. But in public, I was to call him *"Papa"*. She said it would not be like betraying *Papa*, because he wanted me to be safe and looked after until he returned. I'm not sure if she believed he would come back, or if that was just for my benefit. My young eyes never saw any artifice. We lived quietly in 'zis apartment for many months. Pierre was a kind, good-natured man. I always remember his funny moustache, curling at the ends and his great mess of dark hair. As long as he was working in his bakery, he was happy. Kneading dough, rolling pastry and turning the hot, crusty bread out of the oven was his passion.

'Bread is a living thing,' he used to tell me. 'If you put your heart into the dough, you'll spread happiness to all who eat your bread!' His *enthousiasme* was contagious and I spent many happy hours working with him in 'ze kitchen. He encouraged my love of English, also, and borrowed many books for me from *la bibliothèque*. Monsieur Moreau was a very well respected man in the community and when he took us in, most of the locals admired his *générosité*. Most of them, anyway. As always, our presence in a town divided opinion … and one day, when I was in the basement playing with some dough and making little animal shapes, I heard shouting upstairs in the shop. I climbed the stairs and peered through the doorway. I recognised the uniforms instantly and to my horror, I saw two soldiers holding my mother. She looked at me, terrified, then composed herself and winked. I knew what 'zat meant – I had to disappear. In the basement, there is a doorway that leads onto an old underground tunnel – it runs all the way to an opening by the river – that was 'ow they delivered the flour in the old days, when the boats sailed down from the mill. But it hadn't been used for years. Monsieur Moreau had told us that if anything ever happened, we could escape from the building through the tunnel. Like frightened prey, I ran through the darkness and never looked back. As soon as I reached the opening, I hid in the thicket along the riverbank until it grew dark. I was sure no one had followed me, as I kept an eye on the opening, hoping against hope that my mother would emerge and take me back with her. But no one came.

After hours of shivering with the cold, I crept back into the pitch blackness of 'ze tunnel and arrived back to find Monsieur Moreau in the basement, sobbing *comme un enfant*. When he 'eard my footsteps behind him, 'e turned and took me to his breast in pure elation. He kissed my head and my face and cried for joy at my return. But I stood limp in his arms.

'Where is *Maman*?' I asked, though I knew the answer.

'I tried to stop them,' he explained. 'And I will do all I can to get her back,' he promised. 'But from now on, you must stay out of sight, Geneviève.'

And so, that was my life until the war ended. I stayed in hiding at the top of the house during the day – in your little apartment – and at night, I worked with Monsieur Moreau in the bakery.'

'My God, I don't know what to say,' I said after some time had passed.

'There is nothing to be said. War, genocide, it exposes the ugliness that some people 'ave in their hearts. But I found that it also brought about the most beautiful kind of humanity. Monsieur Moreau protected me with his life. I was just a young girl, someone he didn't even know and yet he became my father.'

'Geoff, the English guy who comes here? He took me to the Armistice Memorial in the forest,' I said, recalling his commitment to remembering the lives lost during that terrible time in history.

'There was a camp there. That is where 'zey were taking us – Royallieu-Compiègne. My mother used her wits that day at the train station and we were lucky to escape. But I found out later that is where they took her. It was an internment and deportation camp. Between 1942 and 1944 they deported forty thousand people from there to Auschwitz.'

'How did you survive? I mean, how did you carry on after that?' I asked, cognisant of my own struggles after my mother's death, which in contrast to Mirela's was peaceful and dignified.

'Monsieur Moreau,' she said simply. 'He saved me in every way. He gave me an appetite for life again. When the war ended, I began working in the *boulangerie* and learned to bake at his side. We spent every day together, kneading, folding and baking the stuff of life.'

'Do you think that's why he's remained?' I said, recalling my research online and the inability of some spirits to let go.

'I don't care to know why. He said he would always be here for me. Even in death, he stays true to his promise. But it will not last much longer,' she said.

'What do you mean?'

'It used to be that he was here all the time, day and night I could see him. Now, he stays for just one or two hours, that's it. It will all end soon.' She sipped her brandy and let her gaze fall onto the dancing flames of the fire.

I guessed that these residual hauntings couldn't go on indefinitely, but it seemed almost cruel to think of Madame Moreau and Manu carrying on without his reassuring presence. 'But what about Manu? He is going to take over some day, isn't he? I mean, he is learning from the master, I could see that.'

Madame Moreau's eyes shone with pride, then clouded

with uneasiness once again. 'We are being forced to sell the business, *Édith*,' she sighed, 'I have to sell the *boulangerie*.'

'I don't believe it. After everything you've told me? It's impossible!' I had not expected to hear that and couldn't hide my shock.

'You think I want this?' she shouted, her voice full of emotion. She reached to the mantelpiece and took a letter down. It was an official one, and when she showed me the letterhead, I saw it was from her bank. I could guess what the contents were. The Moreaus were in debt and the bank wanted them to sell.

A howling wind had picked up outside and the snow whirled in circles outside the window. Madame Moreau got up with difficulty to close the shutters, her arthritis clearly paining her.

'I've worked hard every day of my life to keep our home,' she said, sitting back down and looking at her hands in her lap. 'But now with these useless things…'

I could see her fingers were curled and stiff. This was why she couldn't go on and why she couldn't pass on the Moreau legacy to Manu. It was physically impossible.

'I married a man with big dreams and a false heart. When he died, he left me with much debt. He gambled, you see. So when my Gabrielle died, 'zere was only me left to take care of Manu. The bills kept coming in, books for his school, his clothes, food and the costs of running the *boulangerie*. I had to borrow a, how you say, *hypothèque*, on our home and I can no longer make the payments.'

'A mortgage?' I said, looking down into my lap. 'Oh, I see.'

'They came last month, the men in their suits with pale

faces, and avarice in their eyes. It would seem there is a buyer, eager to develop the building into a boutique hotel.'

'What? But that's ridiculous; the bakery has been here for years, hasn't it?'

'Since 1920, the Moreaus have been baking their bread here,' she said, distraught at the thought of losing the legacy that had been entrusted to her.

'Surely the town council wouldn't allow it,' I argued, 'I mean, this has got to be a listed building.'

'*Mais, c'est ça le problème.* It's expensive to keep up the building and the developers have promised the council that they wish the exterior to remain the same, but that they will restore the interiors to preserve the building for years to come. These historic societies are very strict about such things – *sensibilité* to the building's origins – but they don't care who is paying for it. The bank believes a hotel will be more profitable, so they are supporting the deal. The developers have promised the council increased tourist numbers with an 'istorical hotel. I don't see what I can do.'

I stared into the flames, trying to take it all in. I had no idea when I arrived that their situation was this dire. In fact, I began to wonder, why had they hired me at all?

'Why did you place that ad online? If you knew things were this bad?' I felt the heat of resentment rising in my throat.

'Manu,' she said, shrugging her shoulders. 'He thinks he knows what is best.' There was a mixture of pride and irritation in her voice.

I suddenly felt ashamed of myself for bringing it up. Given what they were facing, it wasn't the time for blame.

'Anyone can see that baking is his passion,' I said.

'Ah yes, he learns well from *Papa*. But he is just a child. I wanted to give him the home Monsieur Moreau gave to me after my parents died. But now we will lose everything – even him.'

That was when she finally broke down. The pressure of keeping everything together must have been enormous. I knelt down beside her and put my arm around her shoulders while she cried into her tissue. Manu's words in the basement that morning came back to me: '*Maybe she can help.*' What on earth did he think I could do? Well, I couldn't make things any worse, that was for sure. I would have to think of something.

Chapter Twenty-Seven

I woke to the sound of my phone buzzing with a simple
message.

I'll be back in Compiègne next week, Hugo x

My stomach performed a backflip that left me unsure
whether I was excited or terrified, or both. If I was being
honest, I had pushed any thoughts of him to the back of my
mind since my evening with Madame Moreau. Her tragic
story had affected me deeply and raised a lot of issues
surrounding my own mother's passing. I now found myself
feeling unutterably grateful for the time Mum and I had
had together; all those close hours sharing each other's likes
and dislikes, singing songs and eating cake. I realised how
privileged we all were as a family to have shared such a
wonderful life together, and even when I thought of her
lying on her deathbed, I could no longer experience the
grief of loss without it being tempered by gratitude for
having shared so many precious years with my mother. I

knew Madame Moreau's story held far more pain and terror than she had revealed. Not only had she lost her parents, but she had lost her culture as well. She grew up as a French girl, daughter to the local baker, and was never again to speak about her Roma heritage.

I didn't want to keep bombarding her with questions of the past, so I began doing some research of my own. The '*Porajmos*' as some called it, or the Romani Holocaust, was responsible for the near annihilation of the Roma population in Europe, killing hundreds of thousands of people. Just as Madame Moreau had said, I discovered that there had been an internment camp in Compiègne, used for members of the resistance as well as Roma and Jews, before sending them on to camps such as Auschwitz. It made for horrifying reading, but to know someone who had lived through that time, who was now about to lose everything she had fought for to some greedy developers? Well, I simply couldn't let that happen.

'I've got to find a USP, you know?' I said to Dad later that night on the phone.

'A what now?' he said, confused.

'A Unique Selling Point! Come on, Dad, get with the programme. I just thought, with all your expertise, you might be able to think of something that would get the business going again and attract new customers,' I explained. We had already discussed the shift from baguettes to supermarket sliced bread and the ailing European economy.

'Loyalty cards are always a nice incentive for the regulars,' he began, clearly happy to be asked for his opinion.

'Yes, I was thinking that, too,' I agreed, jotting down the first bullet point in my notebook, 'but I'm not sure if that's going to move the needle. We need something more imaginative.'

'You did say it's a bit of a touristy place, yeah?'

'Yes, lots of Brits come here, and people come here from Paris, too, at the weekends,' I said.

'Let's see.' He took a sharp inhale. 'Right, well it is France,' he began.

'Yes, we've established that,' I sighed with impatience, staring up at the discoloured ceiling of my room. The whole place needed a revamp, but there was no budget for anything like that.

'So, there's no point in competing with the finer patisseries,' he continued.

'No, I suppose not.'

'Well, then, I think the best you can do in the short term is to bring a bit of fun to the shop front window – entice the customers in, you know. So I'd say cupcakes. Your only man.'

'Huh?' I felt a bit deflated that this was his big plan for saving the bakery. 'Aren't cupcakes a bit, well, passé?'

'That's like saying the Victoria Sponge has gone out of style! Some things will always sell and it sounds like that's what you need right now – cash in the till.'

'I don't really think Moreau's is a cupcake kind of place,' I said uncertainly.

'It's a gimmick, right enough, but there's good business

sense behind it. You'll earn a bigger return for minimal expenditure. Go on, Google it now while I'm talking to you.'

'OK,' I sighed, failing to keep the unenthusiastic tone out of my voice. 'Oh, hang on,' I said, my spirits lifting. As I scrolled down the screen, I found rows and rows of images featuring the most decadent cupcakes I'd ever seen. Tiny macarons in every colour of the rainbow sat like little confectionery hats on top of cupcakes sprayed with gold and sprinkled in coconut snowdrifts, even entire cakes covered in macarons. 'Wow, these actually look amazing.'

'You're welcome,' he said and I could almost hear his smug grin.

'It could work, but I dunno, Dad. I'd have to make these myself and I only ever baked at home,' I said, doubtfully.

'Don't worry, love, I'll give you the perfect recipe. Just give it a few practice runs and you'll get the hang of it.'

'Seriously though, you think I could do it?' I asked.

'Sure, weren't you taught by the best in the business?'

I laughed despite myself, then thought of Monsieur Moreau. Suddenly, family legacy seemed far more important than I ever realised.

'Look,' he said, with a more serious tone. 'Do I think you can save a business in debt and keep a roof over your boss's head? I don't know, Edie. But do I think you can get more punters in the door with colourful cupcakes? Absolutely!' he boomed with the deep baritone voice that had always kept his sous-chefs on their toes. 'She's lucky to have you on her side.'

That was all the moral support I needed.

He was right, it was a start. And in the meantime, I would try to come up with some sort of long-term business plan that Madame Moreau could take to the bank. I decided to start right away and make use of the kitchen while the bakery was closed for the afternoon.

The next day, I asked Madame Moreau and Manu to have lunch with me in the shop after we closed. It felt quite nice, the three of us sitting together. Madame Moreau had prepared a tasty chicken-liver pâté and served it with a green salad and of course, sourdough bread. Manu was visibly more relaxed than I had ever seen him and he talked animatedly about the future – the day he would finish completely with school and work full-time in the bakery.

'Not until you complete your *baccalauréat*!' Madame Moreau rhymed off, as if this was an habitual argument they had. Having heard about her own lack of formal education, I could understand her vehemence, but Manu was obviously keen to become the next Monsieur Moreau.

'Right, order – I call order!' I shouted to get their attention. 'I've been trying to think of ways we can drum up more business. I've been talking to my father, and we were thinking of maybe targeting the tourists with some high-end macaron cupcakes?'

I half expected tumbleweed to blow through the shop, such was their lack of enthusiasm.

'I don't bake cupcakes,' Manu answered eventually.

'Well that's just it, I'll be making them!'

Another drawn-out silence followed.

'Maybe it's better if I show you.'

I went to the kitchen and opened the cupboard where I'd stored the cupcakes I'd made earlier. I had found my inspiration in Pierre's recipe book. Macarons. A delicate sweet snack, made of simple ingredients but needing a bit of patience to make. Having scoured Instagram for ideas, I had decided to merge my father's cupcake notion with something a bit more chic. I lifted the glass cake cover from the plate like a waiter lifting a cloche.

'I present to you vanilla cupcakes with a white-chocolate buttercream filling, topped with gold-leaf macarons and a Baileys ganache.'

Their eyes, wider than dinner plates, said it all.

'Where did you get these?' Madame Moreau asked.

'I made them, of course!'

I gave them a detailed overview of the process as they ate. Following Pierre's instructions, I had gathered my ingredients and began by whisking egg whites to stiff peaks. Then, the recipe suggested an Italian meringue for a glossy appearance, by heating a mixture of water and caster sugar. At this point, I poured the mixture into the egg whites and gently folded in almond flour and sugar. Then came the tricky part! I cut out a rectangle of parchment paper and traced circles using a small glass. Once I had a piping bag filled with the mixture, I tried to make twenty identical macarons. The recipe said to let them sit in order to finish spreading and get on with making the filling.

I decided to add a bit of Irish flair and make a Baileys ganache by heating some cream and Baileys in a small saucepan, then adding chopped white chocolate and letting it melt. I checked the temperature of the oven and wiped my brow with the back of my hand. I hadn't noticed it happening, but at some point along the way, I had started to really enjoy myself. It felt so good to be creating something and adding my own flair to it. The final ingredient – three drops of *vanillao* bean liqueur – and I spread the mixture on the cooled macarons.

I could see by their expressions that I had gone up in their estimations.

'Not bad, eh?' I said, peeling the paper off one and biting into it. 'I think if we stick these in the window, we might bring in some new customers,' I explained, munching all the way.

'I had no idea you could bake like this, *Édith*,' Madame Moreau marvelled.

'It's all thanks to this recipe book,' I said, taking the red notebook out of my back pocket.

Madame Moreau's features froze.

'Where did you get that?' she asked.

'I-I found it,' I said, feeling as though I had just put my foot in it again. 'It was hidden under a floorboard in my room.' I looked at Manu who shrugged his shoulders. Clearly, he was just as clueless as I was.

I looked down at my hands, holding fast to the notebook. Why hadn't I told Madame Moreau about it before? Had I been too immersed in her story and my efforts to turn the bakery's fortunes around? I should have realised how important this family heirloom would be to her.

She reached out her open hands for me to give it to her. She touched it like it was a priceless artefact, turning it this way and that. Once she opened the cover and saw the handwriting within, her hand went to her mouth.

'I remember when he wrote this,' she said, tenderly caressing the recipe book. 'He filled it with all of my favourite recipes. It was after my mother—'

'I'm sorry, I should have told you about it sooner,' I said, but she batted away my apology.

'I hid the notebook myself,' she said. 'I must have left it there and forgotten about it.'

'I didn't even know who Pierre was when I found it,' I said, although it didn't seem as though Madame Moreau was even listening.

'It's the strangest thing,' she said. 'As I was eating your cupcake, I remembered something that I haven't thought about for a very long time.'

I bit my lip. *So it's not just me*, I thought to myself.

'I once asked Pierre what I should do with all of this love in my heart for *Maman*; love that now had nowhere to go.'

My own heart juddered at her childhood question and for a moment I felt like I couldn't breathe.

'He told me that the love you have in your heart for someone you cannot be with is never a burden to be carried. It is a gift, he said. A gift you can share in other ways.'

'How?' Manu asked, speaking for the first time since we'd sat down to eat.

'Well, for him, it meant he put all of his love into his recipes and baked them for the people of Compiègne. He said it was so that everyone may know love.'

'That's beautiful,' I said, wiping away a stray tear with my apron.

'I like them,' Manu said. 'They remind me of my *maman*.'

Another memory? I wondered. That was it. I had to say something. I got up and fetched the special ingredient out of the cupboard.

'Is there something I should know about this?'

Chapter Twenty-Eight

I set to work the very next day, and began my baking in the afternoons when we were quiet. Manu had assured me that there would be no one or nothing keeping me company in the basement at that hour, which gave me some crumb of comfort. Despite my efforts to understand Monsieur Moreau's residual haunting of the bakery, it didn't make it any less unnerving to be down there.

'Do you think your grandmother has forgiven me for the vanillao yet?' I asked him before he set off for school. In my most Edith of moments, apparently, I had opened the last remaining bottle of Pierre's intoxicating elixir. No one knew where he had sourced this very special ingredient and so they couldn't make any more.

'Forgiven? Maybe. Forgotten? *Jamais.*'

I knew what that meant. Never. I sighed loudly.

'I'm joking,' he said, with a playful smile. 'She said, it is no good having our memories locked up in a bottle. I think she is glad you opened it.'

'Are you sure?'

'*Je te jure*,' he said, crossing his heart. 'I swear.'

I bought a portable speaker and began playing some of my old jazz music down there. I even started learning some French songs and discovered the amazing Josephine Baker. Over time I noticed myself picking up vocabulary by osmosis and the realisation made me smile. Sometimes if you just let things happen, rather than trying to force them, they came easier.

I enjoyed baking again and spent the next few afternoons perfecting my flavours. Down in the basement, I was free to make as much mess as I liked and so I sent clouds of flour puffing towards the ceiling as I tried to get the hang of the old weighing scales. There was a sort of alchemy to it; combine flour, eggs, butter and sugar, and you've got the basis for the most sublime cakes, whose only flavour-limit is your own imagination. I made peanut butter ones, red-velvet dark-chocolate ones and vanilla white-chocolate ones. I felt like the Willy Wonka of cupcakes and relished my new role as part of the Moreau baking team. And it turned out that Dad was right – macarons were not that tricky once you had a good recipe and a bit of confidence in yourself. Baking, it seemed, was a lot like life.

When Manu finished school the next day, he came down and made a good stab at eating all of my frosting.

'I tell the other kids at school about your cakes, so maybe they will stop by,' he said, licking his fingers.

'That's great, Manu, let's hope we have something to offer them when they arrive,' I said, yanking the bowl away from him. 'How are you getting on with our website?'

'We are live tomorrow and already on Instagram we 'ave one hundred and fifty followers!'

Madame Moreau looked blankly at us both.

'On that, I'm going to need your help, Manu,' I explained, as I took out my phone and showed him some of the TikTok accounts I'd been following. Videos featuring preppy home bakers that looked as though they'd been directed by Scorsese and produced by a Hollywood studio were garnering hundreds of thousands of views.

'I want to create something like this, but on a tiny budget,' I said.

'*Ah ouais, mais c'est super!*' he enthused and he arrived back later that day with a ring light on a tripod stand and a wireless microphone for me to wear. I didn't have much by the way of props, but I figured the original ovens as a backdrop were even more authentic than anything I'd seen online.

'OK,' I said, as I stood behind a trestle table we'd set up with a gingham tablecloth. Manu gave me a thumbs-up and began recording on his phone. I looked down at my ingredients; pale blue ceramic bowls were filled with flour and sugar; a jug of milk and some eggs wobbled on the surface of the table. 'I, eh … hang on, can we start again?' I asked, before retying the belt on my apron.

'Take two,' Manu said, before pressing the record button again.

'Welcome to ... eh, what are we calling ourselves?'

Manu pressed stop on his phone again and gave me an impatient look. At this rate, we'd be pulling an all-nighter.

'Compiègne Cupcakes?' he suggested.

'OK, it'll have to do,' I said, nodding at him to press record again.

'Hello, everyone, and welcome to Compiègne Cupcakes!'

Manu gave me a big, encouraging smile and so I carried on.

'So, today, we are going to be making, well, I'm going to be making – baking, I mean. Oh damn!'

'It's OK, *Édith*, keep going. We can fix it after,' he assured me.

But it was a disaster. I kept forgetting to say what ingredients I was adding and my voice was so monotone, I almost put myself to sleep. After I put the batch of cupcakes in the oven, Manu stopped recording and I buried my face into a tea towel.

'This is rubbish,' I groaned. 'I'm crap at this. They make it look so easy!'

Manu sat down beside me.

'OK, so maybe it's not *parfait*—'

'Oh, thanks, don't feel you have to lie to save my feelings or anything,' I said.

'You just need to relax a bit. You are too ... like a robot,' he said, performing a robot dance, in case I hadn't fully understood.

I glared at him.

'We can stop for tonight, if you like. Finish tomorrow.'

'No, I want to do the frosting. That's the best part.'

Baking at home with my dad was usually so much fun. I had the best memories of being in the kitchen with Mum, laughing and singing. That was when it dawned on me.

'We need music!' I grabbed my phone and pulled up the Django Reinhart playlist Johnny had sent me. All of a sudden, it was like I was in my own little world and I hardly even noticed when Manu pressed record. I was smiling, making jokes and whipping up some of the best-looking cupcakes I'd ever made. It felt like something magical was happening, as I mixed the butter and the icing sugar and swayed to the rhythm. I was finding my flow. It just felt right. Everything was coming together in a way I hadn't anticipated. I stopped being so nervous about it and by the end, I felt like my real personality had come out of hiding.

'You're a natural,' Manu says. '

'I kind of am, aren't I? I laughed. I was really enjoying myself. For the first time in my life, I felt like I was starting to shine.

'I knew you would help us,' Manu said as we began to clear up. It was a rare moment of openness and out of Madame Moreau's earshot.

'How did you know that?' I said, rinsing out a cloth before wiping down the surfaces.

'Because you are alone, too,' he replied simply.

'Eh, that's not really a compliment, Manu,' I stuttered. 'I thought you were going to say something like, "You have kind eyes."'

'Well, no – I mean, of course you do,' he explained, backtracking, 'but you see, we're lucky that no one else found you before we did.' He was happy with this cockeyed explanation, although it made me sound like a stray dog.

It was at that point I decided to give him a butter cream facemask.

'*Mon Dieu*, my English is not so good,' he said, wiping the frosting off his face. 'Family is important for you, I see that. So, I am glad you are part of ours.'

Manu's little PR trick paid off, and that afternoon the *boulangerie* was crammed with students from the local *lycée*, all curious to try out *les gateaux irlandaises*. It was a roaring success and Madame Moreau was visibly pleased to see such a young clientele livening up the place. Still, I knew we would have to keep up the momentum if this was going to make any impact on the business plan for the bank. The following morning I went to the printers to pick up our new loyalty cards, offering a free croissant when you bought five, or a free baguette. They were a bit gimmicky, but at least it showed the *boulangerie*'s customers that we were moving with the times and planning to stick around.

'I take it this is your input,' Geoff remarked, when he and Ruby stopped by for their weekly treat.

'Well, you know you can't stand still in business,' I said, not entirely sure of what I meant.

'Looks like it's cupcakes for us today, Ruby,' he said, and the terrier lifted her paw on cue.

Chapter Twenty-Nine

Hugo Chadwick

'I think we should pull out of Rue de Paris. Financially, it's not viable.'

Hugo had his father on speaker phone in the car.

'Listen, Hugo, if you cannot or will not ensure this venture goes ahead, I can easily have someone take your place. There are countless junior associates who would kill to have your position. Not everyone was handed their job on a silver platter.'

Hugo inhaled sharply and took the next exit off the motorway.

'Listen, *Papa*, I am on my way to Compiègne now. I will visit *Maman* first and call you from there.'

'Why call me from La Retrait?'

'I don't know, maybe you'd like to speak with your wife?'

A strained silence followed.

'Just do your job,' he said and hung up.

Hugo unbuttoned the collar of his shirt and let the window down, feeling the wind on his face. He felt trapped. Everyone wanted him to be someone other than who he was. How could it be that no matter how hard he tried, he would always end up disappointing someone? When Stéphane had died, everything changed. It was almost as if Hugo was compelled to make up for his loss, to take his place. And this he did, thinking it would keep his parents happy or somehow soften their grief. But nothing made any difference. His mother's health declined anyway. His father became even more withdrawn, focusing entirely on the business. And now there was Edith. He had let her believe that he was a good guy. When he was with her, that possibility seemed more attainable. But in the real world, he was just another soulless man in a suit.

'How has she been?' he asked, as the nurse on duty at La Retrait walked him towards his mother's room.

'Honestly, she has been quite agitated since your last visit. She keeps talking about an old uncle of hers, something about putting things right?'

Hugo rubbed his forehead. She had begun telling him a story last time, but then became muddled. He didn't think it was very important at the time.

'I'll talk to her,' he said and smiled at the nurse.

The room was filled with a gentle evening sunlight and the window left slightly ajar, letting the curtains sway in the breeze.

'Ah, peonies,' his mother said, seeing him come in with a bright pink bouquet. 'You don't have to bring me gifts every time you visit,' she said, rising from the armchair to greet him properly.

'A son can bring his mother flowers,' he said, unable to shake the feeling that no matter what he did, he was falling short. She should have had two sons spoiling her. She shouldn't have even been in this place to begin with.

'Listen, Hugo, I'm glad you have come. I have something important to tell you,' she said.

He pulled out a chair for her at the small table by the window and poured them both a glass of water from a pitcher by the sink.

'What is it, *Maman*?'

'I-I must tell you, it's important that I remember,' she repeated, frowning slightly.

'It's all right,' he said, putting his hand gently on her arm. 'You mustn't exert yourself—'

'It's important!' she shouted.

His mother hardly ever raised her voice, but he could see the frustration in her eyes. The constant search for fragments of memories, the stories that make a person who they are. She must've felt as though she were losing herself. He was losing her too, as much as he didn't want to admit it to himself. He hated that this was happening to her.

'Well, then, we'll stay here until we figure it out, OK?'

She gave him a grateful smile.

'You didn't bring the hot chocolate?'

'No, I didn't have time to stop by the bakery,' he lied. It would be soon enough going there tomorrow. He was dreading the look on Edith's face already.

'The bakery on Rue de Paris.'

'Yes, you remember!'

'Of course I do. That is where he had the tabac.'

'Your uncle?'

'Arnaud. He was my father's uncle. That is what I wanted to tell you about. He did a bad thing – a terrible betrayal. We must put it right, don't you see, Stéphane?'

'Yes, *Maman*,' Hugo nodded. She would have always relied on Stéphane, the same way his father did. He was always the more practical of the two sons. Once again, he would have to fill in for the son she had lost.

'I know what your father has planned. You must stop him. We must put it right, for the Moreaus.'

'Wait, what are you talking about?'

'He told the Germans that she was hiding there. The woman and her child. He betrayed them and broke his heart. Please, my son, you have to put it right.'

Her words kept ringing in his ears, but none of it made any sense. Who was she talking about? And what did the Germans have to do with Madame Moreau? Suddenly, things had become a whole lot more complicated.

Chapter Thirty

Everything was going according to plan, until *he* showed up. It was Friday afternoon and I was in the kitchen, melting white chocolate for my ganache. I heard the little bell over the door ring, but took no notice of it until I heard Madame Moreau's tone of voice change from welcoming to downright hostile.

'You have no right to come in here,' she said in English, which made me pop my head around the door.

I could hardly believe my eyes when I saw Hugo standing at the counter with another man, both of them sharply dressed and carrying briefcases. A love-struck smile crept across my face as soon as our eyes met, but that soon faded when I heard him speak.

'We have been given permission by the bank and their estate agent to view the property, Madame Moreau,' he said in a clipped tone.

Then the man beside him stepped in. 'You did receive my letter regarding our visit, Madame?'

That was when Madame Moreau broke into a tirade of abuse in French that I could hardly understand. It seemed I had been frozen to the spot while they argued, as I physically had to pull my feet from their entrenched position to go to her aid. I put my hand on her shoulder and guided her back to her stool, giving her a glass of water, despite her considerable efforts to ignore me. I turned back to the men.

'Edith,' Hugo said, in a tone of voice that sounded almost regretful for my presence there.

'Hugo, what is this, what's going on? Why are you here – I thought you weren't coming until next week?'

He looked visibly uncomfortable as he fidgeted with his briefcase.

'Look, I'm sorry about this – I was hoping … well, never mind.' He produced a letter and asked if I would mind giving it to Madame Moreau once she had calmed down.

'I'm sorry, I really don't understand all of this,' I said, glancing down at the envelope. I spotted a logo on the top right-hand corner that looked familiar. Chadwick Holdings Inc. It took some time for the thoughts to form cohesively in my mind, but when I looked up at him, it suddenly became clear.

'Hugo Chadwick. Are you…?'

He turned his head to the side and sighed. 'Will you step outside for a moment? I don't really want an audience,' he said, looking around at the regulars who were all staring at us.

I agreed and closed the glass-panelled door behind me, aware that our audience were all but pressing their noses against the glass.

'My brother was Chief Operating Officer of Chadwick Holdings and now the board wants me to take over,' he explained, as if that would somehow make things clearer to me.

'But they're some kind of property investors, right?' I asked and he nodded in confirmation. 'I don't get it – I mean, you told me you were a photographer?'

This time he just looked at the ground.

'Oh, I get it, that was just some stupid story to impress a girl in a bar.' I turned away from him, feeling utterly foolish.

He reached for my hand and turned me around to face him again.

'I am a photographer; it's just not what I do for a living, that's all. I didn't lie, Edith.'

'No, you just weren't exactly forthcoming with the truth, were you?' I thought back to that night and his reaction when he walked me home. 'That's why you acted so strange when I told you I was working here. You knew all about it, didn't you?'

'Of course I knew,' he said angrily, trying to keep his voice down. 'They're in debt up to their eyeballs,' he said looking at the bakery, 'and my father's company, well, we offer solutions.'

'You mean you find businesses that are struggling and prey on them to satisfy your investors.' I spat out my words.

'Exactly, Edith. Business. This is just business.'

'Listen to me, Hugo, there is so much more to this than you know! I can't explain it all now, but Madame Moreau and her grandson work twenty-four-seven to keep this *boulangerie* alive. They are good people and they don't deserve to have their livelihood taken from under them.'

He sighed and let his head drop. I thought I was winning him over, but he started to shake his head, as though listening to a counter-argument in his head.

'Look, they've had plenty of notice,' he said.

'Oh, well, that makes it all right then. As long as you've given them plenty of notice that their livelihood, no, their legacy is going to be erased by a heartless corporation like yours!' I walked away completely enraged and slammed the door of the bakery in his face. Then I grabbed what I assumed to be the estate agent by the arm, struggled to open the door that had practically come off the hinges and slung him out into the street.

'And don't come back!' I shouted, slamming the door again for good measure. I felt so hurt and the look in Hugo's eyes made it worse. I couldn't tell if he was angry, guilty or relieved that our relationship had gone no further. But then the *boulangerie* broke into a spontaneous round of applause for me, led by Madame Moreau, who had come out from behind the counter. I was shaking so much that I had to hold on to her for support, but on seeing a room full of outspoken, fearless French people applauding my courage, I had to smile. Perhaps they were starting to rub off on me!

~

That night, I lay awake and turned the art of over-analysing into an Olympic sport. My ego was badly bruised, as was my heart. Still, I wasn't sure if I had the right to feel so betrayed. We had only just begun getting to know each other, but it was such a magical connection and I knew he had felt it, too. The postcards, the book, buying me the bicycle; I mean, why would he have done all that if it didn't mean something to him? I reached for the lamp on my nightstand and accidentally knocked Hugo's copy of Proust onto the floor. I leaned over to pick it up, causing the bookmark to fall out. I sighed. I should've dog-eared the pages, that would've served him right. Although I wasn't quite sure anybody deserved that. I took it into my hands and opened a page at random. It was the kind of book where you could do that – just pick up on the author's memories and insights, almost like a journal. I found it comforting to read the thoughts of someone who'd lived years ago, in very different circumstances, and still feel like it was written just for me. I liked how Proust fleshed things out, connecting the dots in hindsight and finding some kind of meaning. Maybe it could work for me too; if I could map out the past, perhaps I could understand myself a little better.

The thirst for something other than what we have …
to bring something new, even if it is worse, some emotion,
some sorrow; when our sensibility, which happiness has
silenced like an idle harp, wants to resonate under some
hand, even a rough one, and even if it might be
broken by it.

Was my relationship with Hugo just that, something new to distract myself? I wasn't sure. Why was it so difficult to understand what was going on in my own head? I couldn't bear the thought of him being a part of the *boulangerie*'s demise. Perhaps if he knew the truth, he would see things differently; convince the board of Chadwick Holdings that this wasn't a good investment. But I knew I couldn't tell him – for starters he would probably think I was insane. Spirits aren't exactly mitigating circumstances for renegotiating your mortgage. Although it didn't seem that the truth ranked high on his list of priorities, and that was what hurt the most. I didn't like being lied to, whatever the reason. Yet there was a small part of me that wanted to believe he had his reasons. Still, that didn't change the fact that his company was going to take over the *boulangerie* and turn it into a boutique hotel. And if that happened, how could there be a future for us?

These thought spirals were getting me nowhere.

'This is useless,' I said to no one and plonked the book back onto the nightstand. I spied the red cover of the recipe book just underneath and decided I might find something a little more comforting and less confronting on its pages. The time-worn paper felt soft on my fingertips. I had begun to cherish it like an heirloom. I flicked from one recipe to the next, looking for something that might speak to me. Chocolate soufflé, millefeuille, eclairs … and then I came upon it.

Crêpes pour un coeur brisé.

Crêpes for a broken heart. 'Perfect,' I whispered to myself, before hopping out of bed and creeping downstairs to get the ingredients together.

The secret to a perfect crêpe is the batter, the recipe said. *You must leave the batter overnight—*

Oh, well, I didn't have time for that and besides, I told myself I could use any leftover batter in the morning for breakfast. I took out a small packet of flour and weighed 125g, mixing it with caster sugar and a pinch of salt. I set a small saucepan on the hob and began melting the butter, before cracking two eggs and lightly beating. Before I knew it, I was humming that old Eileen Barton song, 'If I Knew You Were Comin' I'd Have Baked a Cake'. It was amazing how quickly my mood improved when mixing these ordinary ingredients. The anticipation of the warm, satisfying tasty mouthfuls they would become seemed to release all of my happy hormones. I found a heavy pan in the cupboard and set it on the hob, then mixed all of my wet and dry ingredients well with a whisk. I turned down the heat before it began smoking and added a few knobs of butter. Then the best part; I ladled the batter, just a small amount, onto the pan before taking the handle and tilting it round and round until it spread evenly.

It is a truth universally acknowledged that the first pancake is never quite up to scratch and so should only be gobbled down by the chef. After flipping it over, I plopped a spoonful of Nutella in the middle, before transferring it to a plate, where the chocolate began to melt. With the light touch of a knife, it spread easily and I quickly folded the crêpe into quarters before stuffing it in my mouth. I actually groaned with ecstasy! The edges, crispy from the butter, and then the soft, sweet pancake coated in warm, runny chocolate – it was, in a word, divine.

I looked back at the notebook and began to wonder if

Pierre Moreau wasn't some kind of genius. It was the perfect recipe, simple though it was, for a broken heart. I felt a sliver of hope return and even some optimism for the future. Maybe things could still work out somehow. But that might have been to do with the fact that I'd already begun ladling out the batter for another crêpe!

Chapter Thirty-One

I awoke the next day with renewed vigour. I went down to the basement after the morning rush and began baking my cupcakes.

'*Merci pour hier,*' Madame Moreau said, poking her head around the door.

'Oh, it was nothing,' I said, trying to hide my dilemma. 'We'll find a solution to all of this, I promise.' I knew I shouldn't have been making those kinds of promises, but in a strange way, I think she knew I was limited in what I could achieve. I was sure she must have tried all kinds of initiatives to try and fix things before I arrived, and it obviously hadn't worked. Then again, she wasn't the type of woman to ask for help, and their particular circumstances meant that they had to be extremely secretive. I would have to do the asking on their behalf and begin that very afternoon.

I stood outside a four-storey building with cream-coloured bricks and tall windows. The number on the door matched the address on the card I held in my hand.

'Edith, it is good to see you,' Monsieur Legrand said, welcoming me into his office.

'I'm sorry to just show up like this,' I said, 'I hope I'm not interrupting.'

He waved away my apology and motioned for me to take a seat on the opposite side of his desk. I explained the situation with the bakery and showed him a copy of the bank's letter. His countenance altered as he read the words on the page.

'I had no idea,' he said, after a time, laying the letter on the desk in front of him.

'Madame Moreau is a very proud woman and honestly, she would probably kill me if she knew I was here, but we need help.'

'You have done the right thing, Edith. *Néanmoins*, I understand Madame Moreau's desire for privacy.' He stared into the middle distance and bit the inside of his cheek, an endearing habit of the overthinker.

'I will compose a letter to the bank on your behalf—'

'Oh, that would be wonderful, thank you!'

'And you will sign it? So Madame Moreau will never hear of our conversation?'

'Absolutely,' I said, grateful for his tact and willingness to help. Monsieur Legrand also gave me a template so I could create a business plan to show the bank that we were serious about increasing our turnover and, ultimately, our profits. He walked me to the door and as I waved goodbye, I spotted Nicole's mother, Jacqueline, across the street. She gave me one of her biggest smiles and I rushed over for one of her warm hugs.

'*Es-tu ami avec Monsieur Legrand*?' she asked, after some pleasantries.

'Oh, well, not *ami*, exactly,' I explained. 'He is a customer – *il est client de la boulangerie.*'

Her smile did not need any translation, as Monsieur Legrand waved across at us before closing the front door. Needless to say, I had no intention of interfering this time. Well, not right away.

It was a mild enough night for April, so I simply wore a black shrug over my dress. I knocked on Madame Moreau's door on my way out and her expression made me blush.

'*Très belle, Édith*, you are beautiful in that dress! It is good to see you having fun. I'm afraid I didn't give you such a warm welcome when you arrived, but I was glad to hear Nicole had taken you under her wing,' she said.

I realised nothing much could happen in Compiègne without Madame Moreau knowing about it. I remembered that Nicole's mother had only kind words for her, too. This gave me a little hope as I strutted down the street to meet Nicole at Nostalgie to watch Johnny and his band play. It was strange going back to the jazz club – I hadn't been there since the night I met Hugo and even though it had only been a few weeks, it felt like a lifetime ago. It was a bittersweet feeling and I found myself half hoping that he would be there, although if he had been, I wasn't sure if I would hit him or kiss him.

Nicole embraced me warmly as usual and oohed and aahed over my dress.

'How's little Max?' I asked, pulling out a chair for myself.

'Learning to play the guitar like his *papa*; it's quite the noise at 6am.' She grimaced.

I was practically bursting to tell her all about the goings-on at the bakery, so as soon as I'd ordered some drinks, I spilled the beans about Hugo, Chadwick Holdings and the bakery's financial problems. I was so tempted to paint the full picture, haunting and all, but I was sworn to secrecy.

'*Conard!*' she seethed.

'Duck?' I was confused, but I suppose calling him a duck was as good as any other barnyard animal.

'No, a duck is *canard*, not *conard!*' Nicole snorted. 'A bastard!' she translated.

I couldn't help laughing, too.

'I hate those corporate pigs, they don't care about the little people.'

I almost felt the need to defend Hugo then – it was awkward being so torn. I wanted to hate him, too, but I just couldn't. Instead I tried to steer the conversation towards what we could do to help save the bakery.

'We'll think of something, Edie, don't worry. We stick together in Compiègne.' She winked, full of fighting spirit.

After another night of jazz at the club, Johnny and Nicole walked me home. I invited them upstairs for a little brainstorming session and stuck on my Django playlist for inspiration. Just as we settled around the stove with a bottle of red wine and some snacks, a light knock at the door gave me a start. I was terrified that Monsieur Moreau would make some unplanned appearance and frighten them away. I walked hesitantly to the door and called out a tentative 'hello', but when I turned the knob, there stood Madame Moreau.

I was about to apologise for waking her or making too much noise, but she waved my apologies away. She asked if she might come in for a moment and of course we all welcomed her in.

'*C'est la musique,*' she said, 'I heard you playing it again and I had to come upstairs to be sure; it is Django, *non?*'

I remembered her displeasure the last time I played his music, but this time she seemed to be smiling. Johnny, being the expert among us in all things musical, confirmed that it was and this seemed to please her no end.

'I remember 'im as impulsive and wild, a bit of a gambler too!'

'You've met Django Reinhardt?' Johnny said, astounded.

'Met him? Why, he was my cousin,' she laughed.

While Nicole and I were surprised, I thought Johnny was about to experience heart failure. His mouth hung open for a very long time, and on seeing little or no response from us, Madame Moreau continued.

'He was a second cousin of my mother; he used to come and play in our camp sometimes. Everyone admired him, the way he learned to play the guitar again after that terrible fire in his caravan.'

'He's like, the king of gypsy music! He even invented his own style, after his hand was crippled in a fire. I mean, he's

the reason I wanted to come to France and play guitar!'
Johnny enthused, until a light cough from Nicole made him
rephrase his words. 'Well him and Nicole of course, I came
here for you, *chérie…*' He smiled meekly.

Madame Moreau leaned against the sideboard and
closed her eyes for a moment, lost in the music.

'He came to visit us here once, before my mother—' She
broke off.

I looked at her and tried to let her know with a slight
shake of my head that I hadn't told them the whole story.

'They've come to help,' I said, hoping that she would
trust them enough to tell them about her real parents. 'I'll
put on some coffee,' I added, guessing that this would be a
very long night.

Chapter Thirty-Two

'When the Second World War broke out, the original quintet was on tour in the United Kingdom,' Madame Moreau explained. 'Django returned to Paris at once, but Stéphane Grappelli, the violinist, remained in England. Django had word that my mother and I were living 'ere with Monsieur Moreau and so he came by one evening to visit us. Some friends of Monsieur Moreau's heard that he was staying with us and came by to 'ear him play. You understand, at that time, there was very little to celebrate, so that evening stands out in my memory like it was yesterday,' she said, with a fondness in her voice.

'I actually can't believe I'm hearing this!' said Johnny, for what seemed like the hundredth time. He was enthralled by Madame Moreau and her stories of 1940s France. But there was the harsh reality, too, that life for the Romani in Europe at that time was perilous, and while her story had a happy ending, there was no escaping the atrocities suffered by her parents and countless others.

'Still today the Romani are treated as outcasts. When the Industrial Revolution began, our way of life and our craftsmanship were belittled. Our nomadic lifestyle no longer fitted in with the rest of society and the struggle continues even now.'

And so it was once more, I thought to myself. They were being cast aside in the name of capitalism as a useless family bakery with an apartment overhead, not making enough money to be considered financially viable.

'There's got to be a way to save the bakery,' I said, turning off the music and bringing everyone's attention back to our true purpose.

'I remember Django complimenting Monsieur Moreau on his bakery, saying that you could taste his heart in every baguette! In fact, he joked that we should send deliveries of bread to Germany, that Moreau's bread would melt the stoniest of hearts.' Madame Moreau was still lost in her memories.

'Well, I think we have our answer right here,' Johnny said, looking at us all as though we were blind. 'Django Reinhardt, one of France's best loved musicians, came to his cousin's bakery during the Second World War to play an impromptu concert for the locals and declared Moreau's the best baguette in all of France. I mean, you couldn't make up a better marketing campaign!'

'Really?' asked Madame Moreau, looking doubtful.

'Of course! Do you have any idea what a big deal that is? Especially for musicians like me,' he said. 'It's easy, all we have to do is put some photos up, maybe display an old guitar and the story of the night he played here.'

'Actually, you might be onto something there,' I said, picking up the thread. 'Geoff, you know, the tour guide? He would love any story that connects to the war. He could bring all his expat tours here!' I was so pleased because, despite my misgivings, we actually had something of a plan. 'What do you think, Johnny?'

'Absolutely, I'll mention it to him tomorrow.'

'Unless you don't want us taking advantage of your connection to Django?' I said to Madame Moreau, just in case we were getting ahead of ourselves. I knew how much she guarded her privacy.

'*Tu plaisantes*? That cheeky musician won money from my father plenty of times playing billiards. I think he would be happy to 'elp his little cousin,' she smiled. 'It is a marvellous idea.'

'And if you like, I could play here at the weekend, create a bit of an atmosphere,' Johnny suggested. 'You'll sing, Edie, right?'

I audibly gulped.

'M-hmm,' I mumbled, a frozen smile plastered on my face.

What had I gotten myself into now?

We all had our jobs to do the following week and I started by revisiting the printers and designing new flyers to give to Geoff, the local hotels and the tourist office. I was able to find a black-and-white photograph online of Django Reinhardt, playing guitar with his crippled hand – which was quite remarkable. He sported a thin moustache and slicked-back hair. He had a mischievous look about him, just as Madame Moreau had said, and she was delighted to see her long-lost cousin helping to bring new customers to her bakery. I found a beautiful antique frame at the market and had another photo printed to hang in the shop, just beside the front door. Johnny sourced a very old-looking guitar that we hung behind the counter, and just below it I hung a poster detailing the events of the night Django Reinhardt played at La Boulangerie et Pâtisserie de Compiègne.

I felt such a renewed sense of optimism about our plan that I was sure the bank would change their minds about the bakery's future. Manu helped me to translate a cover letter into French and we polished up the business plan that Monsieur Legrand had given me. Despite my hopefulness, there was no way to predict what would happen or how the public would respond to our ideas. All I knew was, Madame Moreau could not be kicked out of her home – she could not leave her father, and Manu's future was riding on our plan's success.

Still, there was one issue I couldn't fix: Hugo. Seeing him in the bakery that day was so unexpected. I thought he had come to surprise me; take me out to lunch or ask me to dinner. I never imagined for a moment that he was part of the problem that was pushing Madame Moreau out of her home. Even though I didn't like admitting it to myself, I had quietly been building up my hopes and expectations around him. I had never felt that way about anyone before, and even though our time together had been short, I was able to open up to him in a way that came so natural to me. Now, that only felt like a betrayal. And that should have been enough for me to turn my back on him, but I couldn't.

I checked out Chadwick Holdings online and discovered that Hugo Chadwick had only held the position of COO for eighteen months. He had said that his brother had died five years before, so I started to wonder why he had only now taken over as second-in-command to the CEO, his father. Their website was a tribute to sterile buildings of glass and chrome, boasting high yields on investments with an international portfolio. It just didn't add up. The man I met and even sang to on a bench beside the river that night was deceptively shy and spoke at length about his love of photography. His boyish charm convinced me that he had the heart of a bohemian beating beneath his tailored suit.

Walking back to the bakery and armed with flyers, posters and little black-and-white postcards that Johnny thought might sell, I almost tripped over him as I turned the corner.

'Hugo, what are you doing here?' I said, trying my hardest to sound displeased at his presence.

'Can I help you with your things?' he asked politely but without smiling.

'No, thank you, I can manage fine on my own. Besides, I don't think you'd be welcome inside, do you?'

'Just give me the opportunity to explain, Edith. You can give me that much at least,' he said.

I considered it and figured there was nothing to lose by hearing him out.

'Just let me drop these inside,' I said rather coolly.

We walked to a café near the main square and sat at a table outside. The day was fine and bright, if a little chilly. When the waiter served us our coffees, I looked at Hugo expectantly.

'How are you?' he asked, again with a strained politeness.

'How am I? You asked me here so you could explain yourself. Explain!'

'Right, OK, straight to the point, then.'

'If it's not too much trouble.'

'Edith, like I told you, my brother passed away some years ago. My uncle took his place in the family business after that and grew it into the company it is today.'

'You must be so proud,' I said with a saccharine smile.

'I know what you must think, Edith, that we're the bad guys, but you're wrong.'

'Oh, I'm wrong now, am I?' I got up to leave, but he grabbed my hand.

'Please, just let me finish.'

I sat back down and nodded for him to continue.

'My uncle, he was taken ill some months ago, and my father decided that I must step into his role. I never wanted anything to do with the business. My father's original plan was that my brother should succeed him, not me. I was never the son he wanted me to be; I let him down. I ran away and, well, let's just say our differences were never resolved.' He had been stirring his coffee up to this point, but now he gulped it down as though it were brandy.

'Edith, if you only understood the responsibility that rests on my shoulders; I can't let my father down again.'

There were so many things I wanted to say, but the one thing that kept bugging me was why he'd concealed the truth in the first place.

'Why did you lie to me? What about your photography? All those pictures of the traditional shopfronts, the very thing you are trying to destroy… It just doesn't make any sense! You knew that I lived and worked at the bakery. Was it all some kind of joke? How could you have kept all this from me?' I suddenly realised that I was talking as if I was his girlfriend and felt my cheeks begin to burn. 'I mean, I know we don't owe each other anything, but the least I had hoped for was the truth.'

'I never meant to lie and I didn't lie about the photography. But it's not exactly a career, is it? This is real life and you have to make compromises.'

'Is that your father talking or you?' I asked. I got up to leave. 'You're a fraud, Hugo Chadwick.' His features changed dramatically and I suddenly wished I could take the words back.

'It's time to face reality, Edith, the bakery is going to default and Madame Moreau would be much better off accepting our offer and finding a nice little flat outside of town somewhere. Or perhaps you'd rather stay on your moral high ground and see her end up on the street when the bank forecloses, is that it?'

I was shocked into absolute silence. I couldn't believe he could be so hurtful and cruel and I could feel the tears start to sting my eyes as I got up to leave.

'Don't worry, I won't stop you this time,' he said, looking down at his feet.

'Well, thanks for explaining your motives, Hugo,' I said, my voice trembling, 'you've made things a lot clearer for me.'

I walked away and as soon as I turned a corner, the tears began to fall.

Chapter Thirty-Three

Nothing was really working out as it was supposed to. I lay in bed that night, thinking of all the expectations I'd had when setting off on that flight from Dublin to Paris. I had well and truly lost my way in life and that was long before my mother's passing. Although I was too ashamed to admit it to myself, I had used her illness as an excuse to avoid my own life. Every time someone suggested that I try something different or go somewhere new, I always had the excuse of caring for my mother. Not that I regretted that time, but I could have been there for her and lived my life at the same time. Cystic fibrosis had forced my mother to see life as one big opportunity that has to be grabbed and enjoyed before it's too late. I admired her for her courage and wanted so much to be like her. But life doesn't work that way.

Maybe Hugo was right. Maybe it was time I faced reality and took some responsibility for my role in how things had turned out. If my purpose in life was to look after my mother, then I didn't have to explain to anyone why my own life was so empty. Looking back, I could see that I never gave myself time to grieve, or acknowledge what was really going on. I distracted myself and everyone else with endless tasks and things to be done. The reality was just too difficult to accept. 'What will we do without her? How will we keep on living?' They were the kind of questions I couldn't ask my father at the time, and so instead, I either buried myself in the practicalities or escaped into a marathon of black-and-white films. The well of grief is deep, and I was afraid I would drown in sorrow if I ever acknowledged its presence. But just before her death, my mother sat me down and made me face the inevitable.

'I don't want to leave you and your father, Edie, we've had such a happy life together. But that's what I want you to focus on; how lucky we were to have had this wonderful time as a family. We've got to be grateful for that. Otherwise, you'll spend the rest of your life full of bitterness and resentment and I don't want that for you.' She smiled, brushing my hair from my face with her soft, porcelain-delicate hands.

'But I am bitter!' I said. 'It's not fair…' I said, then buried my head in her lap, crying all of the unshed tears that had stored up over the years. She had soothed me, then, like she had countless times before, saying that no, it wasn't fair, in a voice that made resignation seem like the right thing to do.

'I can't lose you,' I said finally.

'You'll never lose me, Edie,' she said, smiling. 'I'm in here,' she said, tapping my chest.

Her words gave me courage to carry on, but it didn't stop me missing her. I still wished I could be back there now, watching an old film with her and rhyming off the lines we knew by heart.

I needed a friend. Picking up my phone I texted Nicole and asked her if she had ever seen *The Wizard of Oz*. It was a bit late for such random questions, but she said she hadn't, so I suggested a DVD with Max the following evening and she enthusiastically agreed.

$$\sim$$

The next morning, I began baking macarons and frosting my cupcakes as usual and placed them on a tiered stand on the counter. They looked so bright and cheery and to my delight, sold out rather quickly. One remained when Manu came back from school for his lunch and he happily gobbled it down in three large bites.

'Is going well, no?' he asked, pointing to the empty cake stand.

'Yes,' I agreed, 'but it's still not enough to help our business proposal. I'm going to meet Geoff now and see if he can bring some tourists our way.' No sooner had I said the words when Geoff and Ruby arrived.

'Hello, cutie!' I greeted, fussing over Ruby, who rewarded my efforts with sloppy wet kisses on my cheek.

'For a moment there, I thought you were talking to me!' Geoff joked, and I laughed despite myself. 'Right, Johnny tells me you've got a business proposal,' he said.

I brought them inside and turned the 'closed' sign on the door for lunch. I made us all some coffee and served warm croissants with butter and jam.

'Only thing is,' Geoff mused after I'd suggested the

bakery as a stop on his tour, 'a lot of those history buffs might not be that interested in coming back into the town for coffee. Most of them just hop back on the motorway or the train and back to Paris.'

'Yes, but what if they were coming to visit the house where Django Reinhardt played during the war? The bakery where his cousin now lives and works?' I held my breath, hoping he would be interested.

'You don't mean here?'

'I do, indeed,' I said, rather smug.

Just then Madame Moreau appeared, as if on cue, and Ruby rushed to greet her.

'*Oh, bonjour, ma petite,*' she cooed, obviously a dog lover.

'Madame Moreau, you remember Geoff Harding?'

'*Ah, oui, Monsieur Éclair!*' she joked affably and shook his hands.

'Well, Geoff runs a tour-guide business,' I continued, 'and he might be interested in bringing his tours here.' I beamed with pride.

They embraced warmly and Madame Moreau sat down to discuss the details with him. She still wasn't comfortable talking about the loss of her parents to the camps in Germany, but Geoff was so experienced in the area that he made it a little easier for her. However, she became highly animated when talking about Django and his visit to the *boulangerie* that night.

'It was wartime and of course with the curfew, it was quite dangerous, so Monsieur Moreau was worried for our safety. But Django 'ad that charming way about him that seemed to make everyone forget about 'ze war, just for that night. Word spread quickly of our little soirée until all of the locals knew. 'Zey quickly shuffled through the side door that led down stairs and into our candlelit basement, where no light or sound could be seen or heard from 'ze street. I 'elped my mother set up some chairs and tables – old crates and flour sacks for tablecloths. I remember it so well, for it was the last time I saw my mother dance. I can hear it even now: her heels click-clacking on the flagstones, the laughter of our *voisins*, all enjoying themselves for that one, *joyeux* moment. Even Monsieur Moreau clapped along to the playful plucking of Django's guitar. Being young, I grew tired quickly, but I would not let myself fall asleep – even when my mother sat me on her lap. I let my head loll on her shoulder as we swayed along to the "Minor Swing".'

Geoff was enthralled. Ruby had lapsed into something of a coma at our feet and before I realised it, it was almost time to open up again and I had a batch of cake pops to prepare.

'So, what do you think?' I asked, abruptly breaking the spell Madame Moreau's story had cast. 'I've got some flyers printed up here that you could hand out to people.' I passed them to Geoff.

'What a story, eh?' he remarked, clicking his tongue against the roof of his mouth. 'I thought I knew all there was to know about this place in the Second World War, but this is a really interesting snapshot.'

I was delighted by Geoff's willingness to make the *boulangerie* one of his tour destinations. He reckoned Madame Moreau's story had something for everyone, although I couldn't help but think how he would react if I told him about Pierre Moreau's nightly presence in the basement. No matter how well-intentioned these people were, we couldn't risk telling anyone about the ghost in the basement. The only possible outcome of such a revelation would be mockery or worse, a downpour of ghost hunters landing on the doorstep, none of which would help Madame Moreau.

That evening I cycled over to Nicole's house with a copy of *The Wizard of Oz* I'd found on a market stall. I was glad to get away from the bakery for a while. I realised that I was doing the same thing I always did, burying my head in plans and schemes to avoid my true feelings, so I knew I needed time off to get some perspective. It was clear I had made the right call, when, snuggling up on the couch with an overexcited Max gnawing on my white-chocolate cake pops, my heart soared with joy. Seeing him experience the magic of the Emerald City, Dorothy and her faithful friends for the first time was extremely special. He didn't make it to the end of the film, which was just as well because I'd never liked the flying monkeys when I was a child and I wasn't sure how he would react. His heavy head slung over Johnny's shoulder as he put him to bed, no doubt dreaming of tin men and scarecrows and Toto the dog.

Nicole opened a bottle of wine and I let her pour me a very large glass.

'Now I know who you remind me of,' she said, out of the blue.

'Who?'

'Emma, from *le roman* by Jane Austen.'

I shook my head, mystified.

'Johnny is doing so well on the history tours, *Maman* has not stopped talking about Monsieur Legrand. It seems someone mixed their order up at the bakery the other day and he came to the salon to exchange pastries … would you know anything about that?'

'Just serendipity, I guess,' I replied, refusing to meet her gaze.

'Then there is *les Moreau*, they are happier than they have been in a long time. If it was not for your, how you say, meddling? None of this would've happened.'

'Oh, yes, I suppose,' I said, munching some pistachios she had placed in a bowl.

'Well, you are not excited,' she said, looking at me strangely.

'Sorry, Nicole. No, that's great, really. I just… Can I be honest?'

'I would be offended if you were not,' she said frankly.

'I just hadn't planned on taking on a cause, you know? That's not why I came here.'

'You're afraid of ending up like *Jeanne d'Arc*?'

'Joan of Arc? Hardly. Although remind me, what happened to her in the end?' I asked, slightly embarrassed at my lack of knowledge when it came to French history.

'She was captured in this very town.'

'You're kidding! Joan of Arc was in Compiègne? Is there anyone who hasn't been to this place?' I joked.

'You must have seen her statue in the main square?' She shook her head.

'Oh, *that's* who that is,' I said, sounding like the worst tourist in the world.

'Yes, she totally kicked ass and led France to victory in

many battles. However, she was captured by the Duke of Burgundy and the English army, right here, while she was attempting to save Compiègne from invasion. They burned her at the stake for heresy, but later she was made a martyr. Now she is a patron saint of France.'

'A martyr and a saint? Yeah, no. That's not exactly what I had in mind when I came here,' I replied.

'Do you mind me asking, why *did* you come here, Edie? I don't want to be nosy, but I didn't understand your story really,' she said in her candid way.

I took a large gulp of wine and tried to be brave enough to share my real story with Nicole.

'My mother died a year and a half ago, and after years of putting my own life on hold, I wanted to honour her memory by living the life she gave me.' Saying it quickly kept the tears at bay.

'Oh, Edie, I am so sorry – you poor thing,' she said, embracing me warmly.

'It's OK, we always knew her time was limited, so we just got on with it. But, ever since she … passed away, I've just been sort of lost … and drifting. So I did something completely out of character and I thought that by coming here, I would just shock myself into waking up and finding out who I am or what I want to do, I suppose. I think I used her illness as an excuse to avoid my own life. But now she's gone, and I don't know who I'm supposed to be.' I was slightly embarrassed at baring my soul like this, but the wine helped and there was something about Nicole that made it seem OK to not have things worked out.

'So now you find yourself trying to save a bakery and

take on a French bank, when all you wanted was a change of scenery?' she summed up.

'Yes, something like that. I mean, I really like Madame Moreau and I'd love to be able to help, but it's all starting to overwhelm me.'

'Hmm,' she nodded, pouring more wine. 'What about Hugo, have you heard from him?'

'I met him for coffee. He said he wanted to explain but...' The memory of it made me feel physically ill. 'We just ended up saying horrible things to each other.'

Nicole put her arm around me and gave me a squeeze.

'I thought I'd met my soulmate, but it turns out he doesn't even have a soul.'

'*Quelle pagaille*,' she said. 'What a mess. I thought you two were so good together.'

I shook my head. How had it all gone so wrong?

'I was sure I could convince him somehow; get him to see how important the bakery is to Madame Moreau, to the community.'

'*Attend, attend.* Forget about the damn bakery for a minute – what about you and him?' she questioned, putting her two forefingers together.

'There is no me and him, not now,' I said, feeling pretty glum. 'He crossed a line.'

'Ah, now I see why your spirits are so low.'

'He said some really nasty things; like how my life is just so boring that I had to come over here to try and "find myself", as he put it.' I was still fuming at the memory.

I noticed Nicole quietly smirking to herself, and, despite my reservations about her sometimes brutal honesty, I asked her why.

'This is just what you said to me, about why you came here. It sounds as if he read you like a book and you're upset because he said it.'

'That's not the point,' I argued, despite the fact that her argument made perfect sense. 'It's the way he said it.'

I was a little surprised; I just assumed that she would take my side, but as I was coming to learn, French people speak their minds no matter what. She was still smiling.

'Anyway, it doesn't matter. His company is still going to go ahead with the purchase, unless I can convince the bank not to foreclose,' I said.

'Maybe, but it's not over till *la grosse dame chante*, right?'

'Right,' I said, knocking back the rest of my wine.

'And remember, *ma belle*, you are not on your own. Just as *Jeanne d'Arc* had her army, you have friends here and we're going to fight with you to the end. *Jusqu'au bout!*' she shouted, raising her glass.

'*Jusqu'au bout!*' I echoed, as we clinked our glasses together.

Chapter Thirty-Four

Time had not made living in a haunted bakery any less unsettling. Every night before bed, I found myself wedging a chair against the door, despite the fact that everyone knows ghosts can quite easily pass through walls. Even the wine didn't help me to sleep that night, as I tossed and turned thinking about the presentation of our business plan to the bank the following day. Of course I couldn't go – partly because my limited French wouldn't lend itself to a financial meeting with the bank manager, but mostly because I wasn't a stakeholder, just an employee. Manu was too young, and so it was left to Madame Moreau to convince the bank that we had a plan to increase the bottom line and the means to service the loan. I despaired of our chances, because while Madame Moreau was very business-savvy in the bakery, her presentation skills were non-existent.

At some point during the night, I found myself on trial, surrounded by a lot of angry faces shouting at me in French.

They seemed to be blaming me for something, but I couldn't quite make out what. 'No, you've made a mistake – I'm not Joan of Arc!' I kept pleading, but it was no good. A line of red macarons with gargoyle faces led me to the stake, where the fiery flames licked the wooden logs and cake pops chanted 'burn her' in unison. I woke up from my confectionery nightmare, screaming my innocence. The dark, empty room just stared back at me, finally convinced of my lunacy. I refused point-blank to risk falling back into that weird dream, so I gave up on sleep and tottered downstairs for a hot chocolate, just as I had done all those weeks ago when I first 'met' Monsieur Moreau. I almost tripped over myself with fright when I saw Manu sitting at the counter.

'Good grief, you frightened the life out of me!' I cried.

'*Desolé* – sorry,' he said.

'What are you doing down here?'

'I couldn't sleep.'

'I know the feeling.' I ruffled his bed hair. 'Do you want a hot chocolate? We could use some of Pierre's secret ingredient,' I said, in a playful voice, as though we were two kids having a midnight feast.

He shrugged and decided it couldn't hurt. I put on some milk to boil and got out the packet of marshmallows from the cupboard. I had a feeling our chat would require marshmallows and cream. When I presented him with his drink, he smiled gratefully and bobbed the marshmallows into the cup with his finger.

'*Ça va?*' I asked.

'I don't know. If we are not successful tomorrow, maybe we lose the shop, our home, too,' he said, and sighed.

'Look, I'm worried, too, but we've got to be positive,' I said, more out of instinct than anything else. I didn't want to give him false hope, but what else can you say?

'*Merci, Édith*, for all your help,' he said, raising his cup to me.

'*De rien*,' I said, 'I'm hardly Joan of Arc, am I?' I joked, my psychedelic nightmare still fresh in my mind.

'You gave *Grandmère* hope again ... and me, too. Sometimes it was *difficile* to live with the secret – of Great-Grandpère. *Grandmère*, she does not trust many people, so when you came, well, *tu as tout changée*.'

'Well, I hope I've changed things for the better, but we won't be sure till tomorrow,' I said. 'But listen, Manu, no matter what happens, you are such a talented apprentice. Please promise me you will build on Monsieur Moreau's legacy?'

He nodded, quite satisfied with the compliment. He was looking better already and I felt much more at ease with everything. I looked down at the dark, chocolatey liquid in my cup and realised that I hadn't had any long-forgotten memory. I just felt better. I looked up at Manu and realised that he was thinking the same thing.

'The potion is losing its magic,' he said, in perfect English.

'Wait a second, have you read Proust? Because I could swear that's a quote from his book!'

He gave his usual shrug, which told me nothing at all, then checked the time and decided he should get downstairs and start the ovens.

'I'll come with you,' I said, somewhat hesitantly. 'We'll let your grandmother lie in – she has a big day today.'

Despite my own misgivings, working with the spirit of Monsieur Moreau was not the terrifying experience I feared it would be. In fact, there was something reassuring about his presence there – a timelessness that made you feel as though life could carry on, regardless of all the change in the world. Still, I did my best to tiptoe around the general area where he stood – although, to be exact, his feet never actually touched the ground. It was hard work, filling the mixing troughs with industrial amounts of flour, mixing the water and yeast at just the right temperatures. For a skinny teenager, Manu wrestled the dough like a prize-fighting champion, pounding it into submission. I floured all the tins and kept an eye on the fire, adding logs when necessary. It was quite moving to see the two bakers, Pierre and Manu, working side by side and it brought a tear to my eye to think that they had never met, not properly anyway, but still shared this family legacy.

If only I could have told people about *this*; they would have been queuing around the block. But it was impossible and, just as Madame Moreau had said, he would not be there for much longer. I noticed his light flicker and go out a little sooner than the last time I was there. I could sense Manu's disappointment when he turned to me and said, '*Il est parti*,' in a resigned tone.

We opened up the shop and after Manu left with the deliveries, I coped quite well with the morning's brisk trade. Madame Moreau came downstairs just before nine, wearing a dark navy skirt and jacket and a bright string of pearls at her neck.

'*Bonne chance*!' I shouted after her, as she made her way primly out the door. I knew she was anxious; their entire future rested upon this meeting, and I quietly prayed to God it would go her way. Still, there wasn't much time to brood. At around eleven, Geoff passed by the window with about a dozen tourists in tow. My heart soared, watching him gather them in, like wayward sheep.

'We've come for our packed lunches, Mademoiselle!' he called from the door. 'It's such a beautiful day, we've decided to have a good old-fashioned picnic in the woods.' He told me his group was more than happy to pay top dollar for our artisan bread. 'They want an authentic French picnic, so load her up!' he said, presenting me with a giant wicker basket.

I proceeded to cut thick slices of rustic baguette and stuff them with pâté or cheese as required. While I placed the tasty-looking sandwiches along with some patisseries in a picnic basket, Geoff held court in the middle of the floor and eloquently told the story of Django Reinhardt's visit to Compiègne and his connection to the proprietor, Geneviève Moreau. His group took photos to post on Instagram and gazed inquisitively at the large framed photo of the gypsy guitarist behind the counter. I mouthed a very big thank you to Geoff and was rewarded with that nonchalant wink of his that said, nothing is a problem.

'I'll be bringing another tour in the evening for coffee and a bun, so save some cupcakes for me, won't you?'

'I will be your own personal cupcake factory if you keep bringing in the punters like this!' I beamed. For the first time, I really believed we could make this work.

Then Madame Moreau returned.

'I can't believe it,' I repeated for the hundredth time. 'Did you show them our projections?' I could see that Madame Moreau was weary from answering my questions, but I did not cease asking them.

'I told you, *Édith*, it is just a drop in the ocean. I have been missing my payments for some time now, and these projections will only cover the interest on the loans. They want a lump sum now, before they will even consider a restructuring of the loans.'

It seemed unthinkable, but I felt that Madame Moreau was not as upset as I was about the news.

'You look like you're just giving up,' I said.

'And what would you have me do, *Édith*, chain myself to the door and refuse to sell?'

'Well, yes! Where is your fighting spirit?' I asked.

'I'm old, *Édith*, and I'm tired. I don't want to fight anymore. They are offering me a little apartment in the suburbs. At least Manu and I will have a home,' she said, slipping off her leather court shoes and climbing the stairs.

My heart sank and all of my hopes with it. The more I thought about it, the more I started to wonder if it wasn't the bakery I was trying to save, but myself. I just couldn't let it go. I texted Nicole with the news and she replied with a simple 'I'm on it'. I had no idea what she was on, but I hoped it would happen soon.

Chapter Thirty-Five

Saturday morning heralded another visit from Hugo. He wore a black suit with a black mac flying open behind him like a villain's cape. I was serving coffee to two elderly ladies who always stopped by with their teeny tiny dogs for some sweet treats and a gossip. Like a saloon in the wild west, the shop went deathly quiet when he entered, save for one of the little dogs who barked like a Rottweiler – clearly perturbed by the evictor's presence.

'Good morning, Edith,' he greeted me in that deep tone that made my skin prickle. But I was not going to be won around that easily – I was still smarting from his sharp tongue.

'Is it?' I replied.

'I wondered if I might speak to Madame Moreau,' he asked.

'I'm afraid she's taken to her bed with a headache, but then, being evicted from your home will do that to you.'

'I wish you wouldn't put it like that,' he muttered.

'Oh, really, well, how would you like me to put it, Mr Chadwick? Tell me, please, because I'd hate to offend your sensitive disposition.' My temper was rising and I no longer felt in control of what I would say to him.

'Well, it's not like we're putting her out on the street, is it? We are offering her perfectly adequate accommodation elsewhere,' he said.

'You're too kind.' I grimaced.

'Look, I came here to inform her that we have moved ahead with our purchase of the vacant premises next door.'

'What?' I was completely shocked at this revelation. 'Are you planning on buying up the whole street?'

'Not exactly, but we will be knocking through to next door and creating greater floor space for the bedrooms, with a larger reception area downstairs.' He seemed rather pleased with this summation of building works.

'How on earth did you get planning for that? This is a listed building,' I argued, even though I wasn't entirely sure what that meant.

'We're retaining the original exterior, I made that a red line,' he said. 'You have to give me some credit for that.'

'I don't have to give you anything.'

There was something about him that didn't ring true. He shifted uncomfortably and fidgeted with his tie.

'You don't really agree with this, do you?' I asked, trying to read his expression. After several moments of silence, during which the old ladies whispered something to each other in French, he erupted again.

'Look, this is happening whether you like it or not. Now, I know this bakery is your little "project", but my company is going to make a real success of this building and bring more tourism to the area. So just tell Madame Moreau, will you?'

'Don't you mean your father's company?'

He looked wrong-footed and I felt quite pleased with myself for catching him out.

'Is that how you usually get what you want, Mr Chadwick, by bullying people and shouting out orders? Because I can tell you right now, I'm not giving in without a fight,' I threatened.

He paused for a moment before speaking.

'Don't you mean "we"?' he said, with something approaching a grin on his face.

'Yes, that's what I said; we.' I was fuming with him and his know-it-all attitude. But most of all, it was the way he could read me like a book.

'Very well, Miss Lane. I look forward to our duel, but just to let you know, I usually win,' he concluded, looking intrigued at the idea of taking me on.

'Just so *you* know, I don't play fair,' I countered, determined to have the last word.

Hugo bowed theatrically and left the shop with a grin on his face.

'What the hell did I say that for?' I said to the ladies who, despite the language barrier, seemed to understand that our quarrel was not strictly business.

～

It was true. I read the letter Hugo had left for Madame Moreau and even with my limited French, I could understand that Chadwick Holdings had acquired the adjacent building, with plans to knock through and build a sizeable hotel. I gave the letter to her that evening, after we had closed the shop.

'Well, it is finished, then.' She rubbed her eyes and looked away from me.

'You can't give up, Madame Moreau, there must be some other way,' I pleaded, but I could see my supplications were falling on deaf ears.

'Édith, you are a kind girl, but I do not have the money; it is as simple as that.'

'I've heard that "kind girl" routine all my life – people almost always mean "weak" when they say "kind". But you know what? I might not look it, but I've got guts and I'm not afraid to use them! These faceless investors think they can just come along and buy their way into a piece of history, without a thought or care for the people they are trampling over, just to make a profit. And it seems to me as though the bank is in cahoots with them. I mean, they didn't even give our proposal a chance!' I ranted.

'Listen to me, I am just an old lady with an old bakery and a lot of debt. You cannot blame them for everything; I must take responsibility also.'

'But that's just it; you are taking responsibility and we can turn things around, if they'd just give us more time—' I broke off. I could see she was tired and that my ravings were only exhausting her even more, so I decided to head out for a walk in the cool night air to clear my head. I called my dad and explained the situation.

'I hate to say it, Edie, but it sounds like a fait accompli,' was his response.

'Fait accompli?' He'd picked a fine time to begin learning French.

'I'm practising for my trip.'

A moment or two passed before his words sunk in. 'You're coming here? That's brilliant news!' I said, realising how wonderful it would be to see a familiar face.

'So it's OK with you?' he said. 'Sure, I couldn't wait to see the bakery and meet all of the people you've told me about.'

'Of course it's OK with me! I'll find a nice hotel nearby,' I said. I figured he may as well visit sooner rather than later because as things stood, I mightn't have a reason to stay here much longer myself.'

I woke up to the sound of chanting and had to prop myself up on my elbows for a moment to try and remember where I was. I looked at the room, at my now familiar setting, and shook my head, but the chorus of voices was still there. I stepped onto the cold floor in my bare feet, tiptoed towards the window facing onto the street and drew back the curtains. When I opened the window, the wall of sound that hit me almost knocked me backwards.

'*Sauvez notre boulangerie! Sauvez notre boulangerie!*' The cacophony of voices rang out in the morning air, catching the bemused glances of passers-by. A gathering of about forty people stood outside the door to the *boulangerie* with placards of varying messages in French ranging from, '*A bas le capitalisme!*' – 'Down with capitalism' to '*Sauvons la baguette locale*' – 'Save the local baguette'. Leading the chants were Nicole and Johnny, equipped with tambourines and a large drum, beating out their message like a tattoo. I never felt so inspired in my life and ran to pull some clothes on.

'*Qu-est ce qui se passe?*' Manu asked what was happening, emerging bleary-eyed from the basement, his eyes adjusting to the bright lights.

Madame Moreau followed behind him, looking at the waiting crowd outside with some confusion.

'Who are these people, *Édith*? What are they doing here?' she asked.

'They're saving the bakery!' I cried happily.

I ran outside and into Johnny and Nicole's open arms.

'You two are completely nuts, you know that! Where did you find these people?'

'I told you I was on it,' said Nicole triumphantly. 'I put the call out on social media – told everyone that our local traditional bakery was being closed by the bank.'

Johnny butted in, 'Everyone's sick of being burned by the banks and if there's one thing the French are good at, it's protesting!'

'Exactly, so the whole thing, it snowballed,' Nicole continued. 'We're expecting a gang of students from the university in the afternoon.'

'I ... I'm speechless, Nicole. Thank you so much for doing this,' I said, kissing them both.

I wasn't sure what kind of effect this little protest would have on our banking friends, but at least it was going to raise awareness of Madame Moreau's plight. When I came back inside, I saw her looking rather stern.

'They've come to help,' I said.

But she simply turned around and went back upstairs.

'What's wrong with her?' I asked Manu.

'You can understand, she is ashamed that everyone will know about our problems,' he said quietly.

I bit my lip and turned again to see the small crowd chanting loudly and moving in a slow, circular procession. Maybe it was a tad over the top.

'You stay here and open up, I'll go and talk to her,' I said, as I ran up the stairs two at a time.

When I got to her apartment, I noticed that the door was left ajar. I stepped cautiously in and saw Madame Moreau clutching the photograph of herself and Monsieur Moreau, taken outside the shop.

'It was his ambition that I should take over from him,' she said gently. 'He never had any children of his own and he considered me like his own daughter.'

I edged close enough to see the smiles on their faces in the sepia-toned image.

'I didn't mean to upset you, Madame Moreau. To be honest, this wasn't even my idea, but people want to help.'

She looked at me then. 'I hardly know the people down there. Why are they here but out of pity?'

'It's not pity, I promise you. It's support. I know it's hard to accept help, especially from people you don't know, but they're doing this because they want to stand up for what's right. Just like Monsieur Moreau stood up for you and your mother that day at the train station.'

I hoped I wasn't crossing a line with her, but I desperately wanted her to understand how much the place meant to everybody around here.

'Besides, I think you'll find you know quite a few of these protesters. Just come to the window and have a look.'

We looked out onto the street below and saw Nicole's mother, Jacqueline, with Monsieur Legrand, the two old ladies with their dogs yapping, the couple who owned the crêperie, the Algerian man who ran the tabac and many of the *boulangerie*'s regulars – all of Madame Moreau's vintage, shouting and clapping and demanding justice.

'*Mon Dieu!*' she cried, clutching her hand to her heart.

'You see? People care about you and the bakery and they don't want you to leave. So what do you say – are you going to disappoint your customers?' I realised this was what I should have said at the start, for it was like a battle cry to her.

'*Les Moreau* never disappoint their customers!' she said, passionately.

I followed her down to the bakery, where she immediately set about handing out complimentary croissants, *pains au chocolat* and plastic shot glasses of hot chocolate to the crowd. This raised everyone's spirits and voices and even Manu took the day off school to keep the momentum going. It was like a party atmosphere outside the shop, which only served to drive more customers in, which in turn led to greater publicity about the foreclosure. I was so swept up in the euphoria that I hardly noticed Hugo weaving his way through the crowd.

'A protest, very original,' he said under his breath, but close enough for me to feel his breath on my cheek.

'Play it cool all you like, Chadwick, but I would chalk this up as a victory for the bakery,' I replied, rather smug.

'A handful of students with a drum? I'm literally quaking in my boots,' he said, deadpan.

But just then, I noticed a minibus pulling up at the end of the road, and out popped Geoff, with about twenty other people, who marched up towards us with more placards and whistles. Even Ruby tagged along.

'I think you may have underestimated us, Mr Chadwick.' I smiled, noticing the grimace on his face.

'Look, Edith, I really wish you would reconsider this whole thing. The truth is that you're only prolonging the agony for Madame Moreau and her grandson, because this deal is going through no matter what. I don't want to be the bad guy here, but if it wasn't our company taking over the property, someone else would. The bank doesn't care who they sell to.'

For a moment I saw a glimmer of the man I had first met, but it was too little too late. Battle lines had been drawn and he was on the wrong side.

'You don't get it, do you? The reason we're all standing out here freezing our bits off is because we're trying to show Madame Moreau how much the bakery means to us. These kinds of independent artisan bakeries are closing down every day. And pretty soon, there'll be no more left. You, of all people, should be trying to stop this. Or do you think that looking at these old shopfronts through your camera lens somehow keeps you detached from the reality? They make nice coffee-table books but to hell with the people who make their livelihoods in these places. I guess that wouldn't matter to people like you, though, who've had everything handed to them.'

'Now wait a minute—'

I was on a roll and wouldn't let him interrupt.

'These people,' I said, looking back at everyone who had gathered on the Rue de Paris, 'they value their heritage, and Manu – he is the future of this place. His skills have been handed down through generations…' I faltered, thinking of how present his ancestor really was.

'Fine, carry on. I can see you won't be reasoned with,' Hugo concluded.

'Wait,' I said, before he turned to leave. 'Take this.' I placed a cup of hot chocolate in his hand. 'It might help you remember a time when life was about more than business.'

He took a mouthful, but as always, his expression was unreadable and he turned away, disappearing into the crowd.

Chapter Thirty-Six

Hugo Chadwick

Hugo pulled the car door closed, hearing the familiar clunk of the Range Rover's framework. She'd done it again. Edith. Made him feel as though he were the devil incarnate. And the hot chocolate – what the hell was she putting in them, he wondered? Every sip he took felt like he was on the cusp of some great inner discovery, but whatever it was, it eluded him. Clearly it had been a mistake to give her his copy of Proust. But it didn't matter, he knew so many of the lines off by heart and couldn't deny the uncanny similarity. When Proust tastes the tea in which he'd soaked the madeleine, a memory evades him and with every subsequent sip becomes more obscure.

'The potion is losing its magic,' he said aloud, quoting the author.

He put the key in the ignition and drove off without any apparent destination in mind. Half an hour later he found himself pulling up at the gates of the cemetery. He hadn't visited in a long time and even then had made a point of never coming alone. The rain was falling more heavily now and his shoes crunched along the gravel pathway. He thought about returning to the car for the umbrella he kept in the boot. He stopped momentarily, looked back at the car park then returned his gaze to the path where his brother lay buried. Hugo knew that if he got back to the car he would get inside and drive away. On he walked, until he came to the headstone bearing Stéphane's name. His instinct was to harden himself to the reality of it. The cemetery was full of people who had once been brothers, fathers, sons, daughters, mothers. It was a fact of life and something you just had to get on with. And yet these thoughts did not sound like his own.

He crouched down and began to clear away the dead flowers that had probably been left by his father some time ago.

'You were always his favourite,' Hugo said, speaking to his brother for the first time since he'd died.

He could feel it happening again. A memory, just on the edge of his subconscious. Proust's illuminating words came back to him.

It is plain that the object of my quest, the truth, lies not in the cup but in myself.

Somewhere deep inside, Hugo understood that his survival this past few years had relied heavily on him keeping the truth from himself. It seemed preposterous now, here, at the graveside, that this had ever worked. But grief can do strange things to a person.

'I'm sorry,' he said, the words escaping his mouth like a

desperate prayer. His stomach began to quiver and he thought he would be sick, but all that came out were unshed tears. Tears he hadn't permitted himself to cry at the morgue, the funeral – not even when his mother had asked over and over what had happened that night. It was a stupid party that Hugo hadn't even wanted to go to in the first place. Stéphane had been seeing some model and was getting invited to all of these celebrity events. These kinds of things always had free champagne and free drugs. Hugo could see his brother was changing, getting wasted most nights, and had once even crashed his car.

'This is a wake-up call,' Stéphane assured Hugo at the time. But it wasn't long before he was partying again. Hugo trailed along, like some kind of useless bodyguard, trying to keep his brother out of trouble. But that night, they argued. Hugo stormed out and next thing he knew the police were at his door, saying Stéphane had been found dead at the scene.

'Scene? What scene?' he'd asked.

'On the bathroom floor in the nightclub. Asphyxiation,' the policewoman said.

Hugo shook his head. He didn't understand.

'He choked on his own vomit,' the other officer supplied.

Hugo had pulled in every favour he could to have the story changed in the media. 'A heart attack', the headlines read. Yes, Stéphane had been so young, yet of course these things happen. But the coroner's report didn't lie, so his parents knew the truth, and even though they never said it, Hugo knew they blamed him. Rightly or wrongly, they needed somewhere to vent their anger and Hugo was the only one left. Until they turned on each other and then Seraphine became ill. And Hugo had been trying to atone for it ever since.

'The stupid thing is,' he said, his tears subsiding, 'I must have thought that if I tried hard enough, it would make a difference. Like I could somehow change the outcome, bring you back.' He wiped his nose and pushed his soaking wet hair off his forehead before sitting down on the wet grass beside his brother. 'But you're not coming back, are you?'

Hugo wasn't sure how much time had passed, but the rain had eased off and the clouds were breaking to reveal patches of sky overhead.

'Maybe I can't change the past, Stéphane, but there's a chance I can change someone's future. And my own, too. There's a family, good people, you know? Our ancestor betrayed them in the past. *Papa* would have me betray them again, but...'

He looked to the sky and wondered if he had the nerve within him to turn all of this around.

'There's this girl, Edith. I think you'd like her. She lives with this family and – I don't know – there must be a reason we met on that very street. Like we were both drawn there.'

It felt so good talking to his brother again, like embracing a long-lost friend. He'd never really allowed himself to grieve. It was only now that he began to realise how much he missed his older brother's guidance.

'*Maman* was right. At first, I wasn't sure if she was just

imagining the whole thing, but I searched in the archives. There was an old article in the newspaper that spoke of the wife of Monsieur Moreau and how she was taken by the Nazis.'

Hugo had hardly believed his eyes when the local resident they quoted in the piece was Monsieur Arnaud Chauvel. Arnaud said it was a stain on the good people of Rue de Paris and that he was glad this woman's true identity had been revealed and that she had consequently been 'dealt with'. 'As for Monsieur Moreau,' Arnaud went on to say, 'his kind are not welcome on our street, either.' Hugo felt sickened that he could be remotely related to this person. For so long now, he'd worried that he had lost his soul, but he could see now what a soulless man truly looked like.

'All of these years I've been overcompensating – trying to be you! I haven't been doing such a good job of it, to be honest.' Hugo smiled. 'But if I don't stand up for what I believe in now, I may lose what little of myself I have left.'

He looked at the headstone, his brother's name engraved along with two dates like bookends. You were given a finite amount of time and whatever you didn't manage to accomplish within those dates would remain forever undone. Something within Hugo was galvanised. He knew what he had to do.

Chapter Thirty-Seven

B y the following week, Nicole's social media campaign to save the bakery had gone viral. Artisan bakeries from all over France pledged their support to Madame Moreau and it seemed that her individual story had sparked something of a national debate. Even celebrities were hopping on board, insisting that France needed to retain its cultural identity in the face of globalisation.

No one was more stunned by the response than I was. Frankly, I was a little out of my depth. All I wanted to do was help Madame Moreau to keep her home and her business for Manu, but now the protesters were talking about descending on Paris and the Minister for Food and Agriculture to demand more support for small businesses.

It was Friday night, and as planned, Johnny and his band came to the *boulangerie* to play some Django Reinhardt tributes. The floor space was impossibly small, but a nice crowd managed to cram their way in. I'd hoarded a box full of jam jars and lit candles in them and placed them all over the shop, which created a lovely atmosphere. As the music began to play, I could see Madame Moreau's face light up.

'He is good, this Johnny, *hein*?'

'He's passionate,' I replied, admiring his love of the gypsy style of playing.

'He has *duende*,' she remarked approvingly.

After every song, the crowd clapped and cheered for more, and I wondered if this is what it felt like on that night during the war. The music was hypnotic and defied anyone not to move or sway to its rhythmic beat. If only this place was bigger, I thought to myself, we could really make a go of this. We had no liquor licence, so everyone brought their own bottle of wine, but we served platters of bread, cheese and cold meats.

'There's a great atmosphere, isn't there?' I said to Nicole as I squeezed back behind the counter.

'That might be about to change,' she said, nodding towards the door.

I couldn't mistake his tall silhouette, his lean build or his piercing blue eyes.

'Shit,' was all I could say. Not because he was the enemy or that he might be bringing us more bad news, but because I hadn't done my hair in ages and at that moment it was scraped back into an unflattering ponytail. Why wasn't I wearing my new red dress? Instead I was in my usual black blouse and skirt with my pink polka-dot apron. It wasn't exactly a power suit or an outfit to stop traffic in.

'You're blushing, Edie!' Nicole whispered.

'It's just hot in here,' I assured her, trying to hide behind the counter. Johnny and his boys wrapped up another swinging number by Django Reinhardt – 'I'll See You in My

Dreams' – and the small audience clapped their appreciation. I could hear a voice shouting something beyond the hubbub and everyone else stopped their cheering in order to hear.

'Let's hear Miss Lane sing a song,' came the taunting words from the door, then repeated in French for everyone else's benefit. Heads turned in search of this elusive Miss Lane and people asked each other if anyone knew of her.

'Eh, that's you Edie,' Nicole pointed out needlessly.

Johnny, in his enthusiasm, shouted at me to join him on the imaginary stage.

'Come on, Edie, give us a song!'

My head now resembled a well-roasted beetroot. 'No, no,' I replied. 'I'm not a singer,' I assured everyone, while my nails dug into the counter.

'*Au contraire*,' the goading voice came again, 'you told me you were a singer – and I'm sure the lovely lady wouldn't tell a lie.' He smiled mischievously, like the villain in a pantomime, entertaining the crowd. It had the desired effect, for the audience assumed that this was an act, that I would feign reluctance only to turn around and belt out a heartwarming number like Edith Piaf. They all clapped, including Madame Moreau, Manu and Nicole. There was no way of backing out and he knew it.

I smiled graciously at the audience and took my apron off. They all cheered supportively and I made my way, jelly legs and all, over to Johnny and his band.

'You can do this,' he said with an encouraging nod.

'You haven't heard me sing yet,' I whispered out of the corner of my mouth.

'So, what will it be, Miss Lane?' Johnny asked, returning his guitar.

The first song that came to mind was 'Cry Me a River', but I didn't want to give Hugo the satisfaction of thinking I had shed any tears over him. 'I'm a Fool to Want You,' I said, with my tongue firmly in my cheek.

'Oh, I love Billie Holiday's version of that,' said Johnny, as he began discussing keys and arrangements with the guys, while I stood looking out at the expectant crowd.

It was one of those moments when you think to yourself, *How the hell did I end up here?* I could feel Hugo's eyes upon me and saw his Cheshire grin from across the room. He was calling my bluff and was probably going to make a fool of me in front of all these people. Correction, I was going to make a fool of myself; he had just instigated it. Once again I found myself in a moment of intense fear, and once again I prayed to my mother for help.

'One, two, three, four…' counted Johnny and I took a deep breath.

Think Billie Holiday, I whispered to myself; slow, relaxed and sultry. I opened my mouth and began to sing, but all that came out was a whisper. I missed my cue. The band kept playing but I looked at Johnny with terror in my eyes.

'I can't do this,' I whispered.

'*Tiens.*' Madame Moreau appeared with a glass of water. 'Take a sip, clear your throat and let the world hear you.'

I had not been expecting a pep talk, but it seemed to do the trick. I did exactly as she said, took a sip of water, cleared my throat and waited for the band to play the melody again. I took a deep breath and tried to remember what Johnny had said before. I didn't have to perform. I just had to let people see the real me. I closed my eyes and let the words flow out.

I'm a fool to want you; I'm a fool to want you
To want a love that can't be true
A love that's there for others too
I'm a fool to hold you, such a fool to hold you
To seek a kiss not mine alone
To share a kiss the devil has known...

I lost myself in the song and the words and by the last verse, I was actually enjoying myself. Despite my complete lack of confidence, I knew that I was somehow captivating the audience. Perhaps it was the song, or the story I was telling, but I believed it and I knew they did too. It was my first time singing with a live band and I relished every second of it. Instead of hearing myself a capella, my voice was supported by a soft snare drum, a deep resonating bass and a rhythmic guitar. When I sang the last line, I finally dared to look over where Hugo had been standing. He was leaning against the door, his head cocked to one side and a sly grin on his face. Our little gathering of people erupted into wild applause when I stopped singing and I was showered with kisses and shouts for an encore. For the first time in my life, I felt as though I was doing what I was always meant to do. It felt natural and just ... right. I'd found the same flow I'd experienced when doing my TikTok videos. Something magical happened when I stopped putting pressure on myself to be someone – the person I thought people wanted me to be. I discovered an inner self, someone who'd been there all along, just waiting for me to stop getting in my own way.

I saw the door opening and Hugo's tall frame exiting and it was only then that I realised he had done me a favour. Perhaps he wasn't trying to humiliate me, after all. Maybe he was giving me a shot at my dreams. I extricated myself from the embraces of my newfound fans and ran after him out onto the street.

'Why did you do that?' I shouted.

He turned around in that insouciant way he had that meant he never looked as though he was in a rush.

'I wanted to hear you sing.'

'No, you wanted to prove your point; that I had lied about being a singer just as you lied about being a photographer,' I panted, out of breath after my impromptu performance.

'Now why would I do that?' he said, leading me.

'To prove we're both as gutless as each other when it comes to living our dreams,' I replied.

He smiled at me in a way that made it difficult to stay angry with him.

'The only difference is, I'm not a very good photographer, while you…' he trailed off.

'I'm assuming that's meant to be a compliment.'

We were smiling at each other, which made a nice change to our recent encounters.

'Why are you being kind to me now?'

'I never wanted to be unkind, Edith. It's this place that came between us,' he said, gesturing to the bakery.

'Well, I still can't see a way around it,' I said and we both fell silent for a time.

'I see your protests have reached Paris,' he said, 'I saw an article in *Le Monde*. You're really not going to give up, are you?' He looked at me thoughtfully, as though he begrudgingly admired my tenacity.

'If you knew what this place meant to Madame Moreau, Hugo, you wouldn't give up either. If I could only tell you…'

'*Édith!*' came Manu's voice, just in time. '*Ils veulent un encore,*' he shouted.

At this, Hugo bowed slightly and said, 'Your audience awaits, Mademoiselle.' With that, he took his leave and it took all of my willpower not to call after him.

The cheer that welcomed me as I came back in almost floored me. It couldn't all be pity, I told myself. They really wanted to hear me sing again.

'Why didn't you tell me you had those pipes?' Johnny said, as I rejoined him and the guys.

'I wasn't sure they'd work outside of the shower!' I shouted over the noise.

'Fancy giving it another go?'

I nodded, almost afraid to voice my overwhelming desire to sing all night. Like a latecomer who's hidden their light under a bushel for too long, I wanted to shine. I sang a little French song by Melody Gardot, aptly called 'Les Étoiles' – 'The Stars'.

Finally, it was time to call it a night and after we'd thanked our patrons and sent them home, I began cleaning up. I felt a little like Cinderella after midnight, returning to her day job. I stacked the chairs up onto the tables and mopped the floor, while Madame Moreau totted up the receipts at the cash register.

'Why do you think Mr Chadwick stopped by this evening?' she said after a time.

'I've no idea,' I replied, applying myself to an imaginary stain on the floor.

'He seemed to know that you had a beautiful voice,' she remarked casually.

I couldn't think of a reply, so I just kept my mouth shut and hoped she'd forget about this line of inquiry.

'I think he likes you.'

'What? Don't be ridiculous,' I blustered.

'I think you like him, too,' she continued, sounding not altogether displeased with her revelations.

'Well, it wouldn't matter, anyway. I mean, it's not like anything can happen between us.' I kept mopping and she kept prodding.

'Why not? You're both young, single…'

'Eh, hello? I said, leaning the mop against the counter. 'He is our nemesis, remember? He's shutting down the bakery? How could I possibly love a man like that?'

'Love, eh?'

'Oh, you know what I mean,' I said exasperated.

'*Édith*, how many times must I remind you, it is the bank that is closing us down. Mr Chadwick, 'e is just a businessman hoping to buy a premises at a good price.'

'Or a vulture picking at a carcass,' I said under my breath.

'Is that what you truly believe? Or is that what you're

telling yourself, so you can avoid the feelings that are obviously shared between the two of you?'

If it had been a game of chess we were playing, she would have declared checkmate. I then confided in her about how Hugo and I had met, that magical night, and then the terrible arguments we had about the bakery. Not to mention the hurtful things he had said about my life here.

'It's natural, *ma belle*, you care about what he thinks of you,' she said gently. 'But just think; maybe he cares about your opinion of 'im also…'

I remembered then how I had accused him of bowing down to his father's expectations. Perhaps I had touched a raw nerve. It was obvious he felt guilty about letting his father down.

'And if you ask me, I think he went out of his way to put things right tonight, *n'est ce pas*?'

Chapter Thirty-Eight

On Sunday, I cycled all the way to Château Compiègne for some headspace. A fresh breeze set the grass swaying like a Van Gogh painting, making everything feel alive and full of energy. Once again, I found myself in awe of its grandeur and wondered what life must have been like for its occupants. I walked the long avenues that led to the forest; the perfect place for reflection and contemplation. So much had happened since my arrival in France, not least my singing debut the night before. I felt like I really needed to process everything, including whether there would be any point in staying on if and when the bakery closed. Despite all our efforts and the public goodwill, the final say still rested with the bank and they didn't have any emotional attachments to the building – only the desire to balance their books.

Hugo had touched a nerve that day when he said I had come to France to find myself. It was such a cliché, but clichés are only so because they are true. I had never had the courage to put myself out there and find out what my dreams were, until last night when I'd sung for that little gathering in the bakery. I could feel an unfamiliar sensation running through my veins and all I knew was that I didn't want it to stop. Still, I knew nothing about the music scene here, or back home in Ireland for that matter. Could I make a living out of it? Or even a hobby? Was I good enough? These were all questions I couldn't answer, but it felt like a huge step forward, finally knowing the right questions to ask. It felt as though I was getting to know myself a little better. Which made me wonder: what would my mother make of this new career choice? That was still the hardest part about missing her. I wished I could just ask her things like I used to; run my ideas by her. I wondered if her spirit was out there somewhere, conscious and able to hear my thoughts. Before I knew it, I found myself talking to her out loud. I chatted as though she were right there with me, like we used to do at the kitchen table back home over a cup of tea. I told her all about the bakery, Madame Moreau and my conflicting feelings towards Hugo.

By the time I got back to Rue de Paris I felt lighter and happier. I'd picked up some groceries on the way at the *supermarché*, and texted my friend Gemma, from home, some photos from the night before. Her response pinged back.

I always knew you'd find yourself over there!

I smiled to myself and hopped up the stairs to my apartment, just as evening was setting in and turning the sky from pale blue to a soft amber glow. I opened my attic window to let the air in and changed out of my clothes before turning on the water for a shower. The sensation of warm water hitting my skin sent a subtle message to my brain – I could relax. I scrunched up my shoulder and could feel the muscles easing. I hadn't realised how much stress I'd been carrying around all of this time, and even though there were no certainties about my future in this place, I knew one thing. I'd handle it. Whatever came my way. Maybe it took coming all the way to France to learn this one, irrefutable fact about myself. I dipped my head under the spout and let the water rinse my head clean.

Wrapped in a towel and sorting through my laundry for a clean T-shirt, I thought I could hear voices outside. I leaned out the window and saw two figures standing in the lamplight. I could hardly believe my eyes – it was Manu and Hugo. Their voices were hushed, so I tried to judge what was going on by their body language. It didn't seem as though they were arguing. That was good. If Hugo said anything to upset Manu I would have been down there like a shot, towel or no towel. Well, preferably with my towel. Then I caught a few words on the breeze.

'How much do you need?' Hugo asked.

I saw Manu run his hand through his hair and then explain something that resulted in Hugo nodding his head.

Then they shook hands. What was going on? Was Hugo bribing Manu? It seemed just like the kind of tactics a soulless corporation would use to get what they wanted. But did he really think he could turn Manu against his own grandmother?

Chapter Thirty-Nine

Pierre Moreau

1945

It was clear that Arnaud from *le tabac* had betrayed their secret. Not only was he an informant for the Boche, but he was a bitter man who saw the happiness and joy Mirela and Geneviève had found in the bakery and wanted to destroy it. Pierre was not a violent man, but he imagined going into Arnaud's shop and breaking every bone in his body. But he had to think of the little girl's future. If anything happened to him, who would look after her then? He had to keep quiet in order to protect her and so he kept Geneviève hidden in the atelier after that. He told everyone that she had run away, probably back to her own village. In the misty blue hours of the early morning, while everyone on the Rue de Paris was still asleep, she would tiptoe down the stairs and join Pierre in the bakery.

'When *Maman* returns, I will bake her a beautiful cake,' she would say, listing all of the magical ingredients she would use.

Pierre wasn't sure whether to indulge her fantasies or prepare her for the worst. He had never heard of anyone returning from the camps. What was a greater cruelty – a harsh truth or a kind lie? Being a thoughtful and methodical man, he considered it for some time. In his new role as sole guardian, it was up to him now. The responsibility might have overwhelmed him if it weren't for the fact that his love for this little girl was stronger than anything he'd ever known. He would give his life for her and would never, ever abandon her. She needed him, it was clear. But he needed her even more.

One day, not long after the war was over and Geneviève no longer needed to hide, Pierre made them their favourite breakfast – crêpes with blackberry jam, made from berries they had foraged along the hedgerows.

'Do you like living with me at the bakery?' he asked.

She nodded her head, her mouth smeared with purple streaks of jam.

'Good.'

He took a sip of his coffee, then began biting the inside of his lip. How could he tell her that her mother might never return? That they would have to live with not knowing what happened?

'We are a family now, you and I. You know, for years, I never thought it would be possible for me to have a family of my own. And now, if you will allow it, I would love nothing more than to call you my daughter.'

Geneviève put her crêpe down on the plate and looked up at him. Her eyes were overflowing with bright, happy tears. She didn't need to say anything, he knew in that instant that these were the words she had been waiting to hear, and the words that he had so desperately wanted to say. She jumped up from her chair and flung herself into his arms, weeping with relief, joy and woeful sadness.

'*Maman*,' she kept saying. '*Maman*.'

'I know, I know,' he soothed, rocking her slowly.

She knew. Of course she did. She was the brightest child he had ever laid eyes on. The war had forced everyone to grow up too quickly.

'I can stay with you … for ever?'

Pierre Moreau thought his heart would burst.

'Of course, *ma petite*. For ever and ever.'

But there are some promises, no matter how much we wish it were otherwise, that are impossible to honour. When Pierre Moreau's heart began to weaken at the age of sixty-eight, it was Geneviève who took over the running of the bakery and nursed him on his deathbed.

'I will always be here,' he said with his last breath. And with every particle of stardust and bone that made up his spirit, he stayed true to his word.

Chapter Forty

As I turned the key in the lock, I noticed a red envelope tucked under my door. Bending to pick it up, I saw that it was addressed to Miss Lane in a familiar script. Inside was an invitation.

You are cordially invited to dine at
No. 20 Rue de Paris
This evening at 7.30pm

I flipped the card over, but no more information was forthcoming. I leaned against the doorjamb for a moment, trying to figure out what was going on. That was the vacant building next door to the *boulangerie*, the one Hugo's company owned and planned to convert, along with the bakery building, to create a larger hotel. I couldn't understand what it was all about.

I jerked myself out of my thoughts when I realised that it

was nearly six o'clock. I was still standing in the doorway dressed in jogging pants and sporting four-day-old hair. Obviously I wasn't going. Well, maybe I would show up but I wouldn't stay long. I'd just dress up so he'd know I had other plans. I rushed into my little apartment, switched on the immersion for a hot shower and hung Nicole's red dress in the bathroom to get the creases out.

By 7.15pm, I had finished drying my hair and was brushing the side parting to the left like Nicole had shown me. I put on some red lipstick and pressed powder on my face with a puff. A little dab of Chanel behind my ears and I was ready to go. One last look in the mirror showed me a shapely woman with something approaching *joie de vivre*. I was no longer a waitress watching the world go by – I was a waitress living her life and it felt good. I realised I didn't need to be like everybody else, I just needed to be me.

Madame Moreau was out at Sunday evening mass and Manu was over at a friend's, so all was quiet as I stepped carefully down the stairs in my high heels. I had wrapped a shawl around my shoulders, but I still had goosebumps, either from the chill or the anticipation. I walked out of our door, locking it behind me, and took three steps to the left. Number 20 was also a timber-framed building, and while I had passed the burgundy wooden door plenty of times, I'd never really noticed it before. Now, the door was open, with a dark velvet curtain obscuring my view. I pulled the curtain aside and peered into the dimly lit room. Once my eyes adjusted, I could see a table at the far end of the room with a candelabrum lighting the corner. Then I saw him, sitting patiently, wearing a suit and waiting for me to come in.

'What are you doing here?' I asked. 'What's all this about?'

'Good evening to you, too,' was the reply. 'Would Mademoiselle care for a glass of champagne?' He got up to pull out the other chair. 'That is some dress,' he added admiringly.

I felt slightly hypnotised by the whole thing. It was ridiculously romantic and he looked simply ravishing in a black dinner jacket and white shirt. I felt so flattered, but my integrity tugged at me like a persistent child. I couldn't let myself be swayed so easily. A sweet female voice sang in hushed tones from a stereo in the corner, creating a seductive atmosphere.

'You're not going to change my mind with all of this, you know,' I said, taking my seat.

'I don't doubt that.'

Something tugged at the back of mind and then I realised what it was.

'I didn't see your car outside.'

'The Range Rover? No, I sold it,' he said as he poured the champagne.

'Oh.' That was a bit weird. But then, the whole set-up was a bit weird and Hugo's demeanour was at odds with the man I'd been fighting with. I noticed a silver cloche on the table and when he lifted it, I was surprised to see a pepperoni pizza.

'Pizza?'

'*Bon appétit*,' he said.

'Are you having some sort of episode?'

He laughed out loud at that and the sound made my

defences crumble. It was like we were back at the vineyard, two people falling in love with each other.

'Why do you say that?'

'I don't know, you just seem really calm and happy.'

He looked down at the table and for a moment it seemed as though he was full of regret. But for what, exactly?

'Why am I here, anyway? Do you want to rub my nose in it or something?'

'Rub your nose in what?'

'Ooh, I don't know, the fact that you're so rich you can just snap these kinds of places up and eradicate years of history so you can turn them into some sterile, money-making investment?' I couldn't believe I was arguing with him again. It seemed to happen on the turn of a sixpence.

'Actually, if you'd let me explain…' he began, but I was already getting up from my seat.

'Hugo, I don't want to argue with you, but this is hopeless. We're never going to agree and seeing you, like this, it's just too hard. We may as well cut our losses,' I told him straight. 'Thank you for dinner, though.' I walked towards the door, but in the gloom, tripped over something hard and ended up splayed out on the floor.

'Edith? Edith, are you OK?' Hugo called out.

'Oww!' I groaned, as I held my arm up to assess the damage.

'Hang on, I'm coming… Woah!' Hugo shouted, as he landed in a rather ungainly fashion on top of me.

'Oh, God, I'm so sorry,' he began. 'Are you hurt?'

'It's OK, I don't think I quite broke all my bones with the first impact, so thanks for that,' I said, panting under his weight. I could barely make out his features in the gloom, but I could feel his warm breath on my skin.

'Are you OK?' he asked, in a deep voice.

I lifted my arm and reached up to touch his face. We were both breathing heavily. Before I knew what was happening, my lips had betrayed me and met his, hungrily. It was as though I had forgotten everything that had just happened and my mind was clear. Everything was Hugo. His taste, his touch, the warmth of his body. He began kissing my collarbone and as my head lay back against the cold cement floor, I eventually came to my senses.

'Wait, sorry, I can't,' was all I could manage, as I broke away from him and scrambled to my feet.

'No, I shouldn't have— Hang on, I haven't had a chance to tell you!' he pleaded, but I was already out on the street and opening the door to the bakery. I ran up the stairs and let myself into my apartment, leaning against the door behind me as I tried to catch my breath. My lips curled into a smile despite my best efforts to resist the attraction between us. I simply couldn't trust myself around him anymore. I was already making great plans to avoid him in future, when I heard him calling my name out on the street.

'Edith, please, we need to talk!' he shouted.

I stood motionless for a moment. I realised that Madame Moreau was right. I was afraid. My feelings for him were overwhelming and it frightened me to death.

'Will you come down, please?' he asked again

I moved towards the window, which I opened wide.

'You'll have to speak to me from there,' I said, trying to arrange my features into that of a mature woman in control of her senses.

'And have the whole street listen in?'

I just shrugged.

'Fine, have it your way, Miss Lane. What I was trying to tell you, if you had given me half a chance, is that Madame Moreau will not lose the bakery.'

He stood awaiting my response, but I just leaned on the window frame, staring at him agape.

'You'll catch flies doing that, you know.'

'I'm coming down,' I called, and almost did myself another injury taking the stairs at speed. I ran out into the lamplit street and saw him there, casual as anything, leaning against a lamppost.

'What did you say?' I panted.

'I said, the bakery will not close. I've cleared Madame Moreau's debts with the bank so she won't have to sell.'

'You've cleared her debts. You personally?'

He nodded.

'But how?'

'I sold my apartment in Paris.'

'I don't understand. Why would you do that?' The enormity of what he was saying was almost too much to take in.

'To settle an old family debt,' he said, looking up at the building as though it held some kind of personal resonance.

I was still confused and my expression confirmed it.

'It was something my mother said,' he began to explain. 'At first I wasn't sure – her memory is … she suffers from Alzheimer's.'

'Oh, Hugo, I'm so sorry,' I said, my hand instinctively reaching for his and gripping it tight. I had some idea of what he must be going through.

'But I did some research,' he went on, 'and I found some old archives of newspapers, and it turns out she was right. Madame Moreau's mother was sheltering with the baker who lived here, Pierre Moreau. She was discovered by the Nazis and taken—'

'Yes, I know, Madame Moreau told me.'

'Well, what she doesn't know is that it was my great-great uncle who betrayed them.'

I shook my head in disbelief.

'No one in the family had ever spoken about it before now. I think the shame and the guilt they felt must have kept them silent. I don't know how or why my mother remembered, but I knew I had an opportunity to put the ghosts of the past to rest.'

My whole body shivered. Little did he realise the significance of what he was saying.

'The hotel group pulled out when they couldn't get the bakery, so I've taken ownership of Number 20. Or rather, I've inherited it from my mother. I'll run through the details with Madame Moreau tomorrow, but I wanted to tell you tonight.'

I struggled to take it all in.

'Look, I know it's a lot, but I realised that we only get a short amount of time in this life and I don't want to spend another second of it in Paris working for my father. I want to live closer to my mother and spend as much time as I can with her now.'

I reached up and ran my fingers through his hair at the back of his neck.

'You're mad, you know that?'

'Takes one to know one, I suppose,' he smiled.

I was still holding his hand and now he reached for my other one.

'So, that just leaves the small matter of where you and I stand, now.' He took a step closer.

I held my breath for a moment, before easing my hands out of his.

'Nothing would make me happier than to fall into your arms and let myself go, but I can't, Hugo.' I began to walk away.

'Why not?'

I hesitated before turning back to face him.

'Because I'm better on my own. I know how to do this life – the one where dreams don't come true and love isn't some kind of fairy-tale ending.' I was angry, I was upset, I was on the verge of tears. I wasn't sure if saving the bakery could just magically save us. Or me.

'I understand,' he said, nodding. 'If we both keep toughing out our way through life, maybe we can avoid getting hurt.'

'That's not what I'm saying.'

'Is it not?' he asked.

For one terrifying yet longed-for moment, it felt as though he could see right through me, past the mask I wore to protect myself and maintain some kind of composure. I was so scared of letting myself love again. What if my heart was too broken?

'Look, Hugo, what you're offering … hang on, I don't even know what you're offering!'

'Honestly, I don't have much to offer anymore. Just myself. And this old building, I suppose,' he said, looking back at Number 20. 'But that's not the point. The point is, I know that love means risking your heart, but it's not a risk if the guy standing in front of you feels how I feel.'

Something gave way inside my heart and like a wave rushing to shore, I rushed into his arms. I kissed him without holding anything back. All of the fear and doubt that had made a home in my heart released as I felt his strong arms pull me closer.

Chapter Forty-One

I woke up in the middle of the night, wrapped in Hugo's arms. Tempted as I was to stay there and fall asleep, I could see from the alarm clock in his hotel room that it was almost four o'clock, and I knew Manu and Madame Moreau would be up soon. He woke up just as I was pulling on my shoes.

'Where in God's name are you going at this hour?' he asked, with one eye barely open.

'I just have to tell Madame Moreau the good news,' I whispered.

'Why are you whispering? There's no one else to wake up,' he pointed out.

'Ah, yes, I see you're just as pedantic in the morning,' I said, kissing him on the cheek.

'But it's not morning,' he groaned, trying to pull me back into bed.

'I can't, I have to tell her, you've no idea what it means,' I said excitedly.

'I think I do.'

I zipped up my dress and sat back down on the bed, taking his hand in mine.

'What made you change your mind about everything? I know you've told me the story about Arnaud, but selling your apartment, going against your father's wishes... Why did you do it?'

'Seriously? You've been harassing me for weeks now about being a vulture capitalist!' he joked.

I gave him a stern look.

'Many things. In the end I think it was coming to terms with my brother's death. It's like I've been trapped in someone else's life since he died. One day something just finally clicked. It felt like my chance to break free.'

'So what are you going to do with the building now?'

'Well, I spoke to Manu about it—'

'Manu?'

'He gave me the idea, actually. We got to talking about his great-grandfather, Pierre Moreau, and his legacy of giving shelter to people who needed it.'

Ah, I thought to myself, so that's what they were whispering about.

'Manu introduced me to Father Bernard and showed me how they are trying to help the homeless and the immigrant population here. He is hoping to set them up with accommodation but what they really need are jobs. So, I started looking into it and I've applied for funding to set up a restaurant as a social enterprise. That way, people get the training they need and patrons on low incomes have a low-cost place to eat.'

'Hugo Chadwick, a social entrepreneur,' I said.

He shook his head, but I knew he was pleased with his decision.

'My mother says you're a good influence on me.'

I had to stop myself from saying 'yikes'. He'd told his mother about me?

'Is that so? She sounds like a wise woman,' I said, smiling.

'She said that I could choose between being an unsuccessful imitation of my father, or a successful expression of who I was born to be.'

She definitely sounded like someone I'd like to meet.

'But I think I'd made up my mind long before that,' he said.

'Oh, really?' I wrapped my arms around his neck and felt the warmth of his chest against mine.

He began kissing my earlobe and I almost forgot what we were talking about.

'When was that, then?'

'You really need to ask?' He kissed me softly on my neck. 'It was the day you made me that hot chocolate, the best one I've tasted in years,' he said, smiling.

'*C'est un miracle!*' Madame Moreau kept saying, while she hugged Manu and myself until we could hardly breathe. As the elation began to die down, I noticed something.

'Wait a minute,' I said, sensing that there was something amiss. 'Where is Monsieur Moreau?'

They both exchanged regretful looks, then Madame Moreau turned away.

'He only appeared for a few seconds,' Manu explained. 'It was different this time. His light burned so brightly, like a kind of golden glow, like never before. Then … nothing.' He glanced over to where Madame Moreau was standing, arranging some bread pans.

I walked over and put my hand on her shoulder.

'He's gone,' she said in a very small voice.

'How do you know?' I asked.

'I felt a kind of peace. It was as though his promise to me all of those years ago was discharged.'

The basement suddenly felt very empty.

'But why now?' Manu asked.

Madame Moreau wiped some tears from her eyes. 'Perhaps he knew that the bakery will be saved?' she pondered. 'Maybe he didn't need to stay anymore.'

I searched desperately for some words of comfort, but what could you say to someone who was mourning the loss of a ghost? Then I remembered something I'd read online about souls not being able or willing to move on.

'I think you're right,' I said, linking arms with both of them. 'I think Monsieur Moreau's instinct to protect you was so strong in life that he could not let go of his role in death. But now the future of the bakery is safe, he can finally let go of you, Geneviève.'

It was the first time I had used her first name, because it seemed a bit too formal at this stage to be calling her Madame Moreau.

'There's something else,' Manu said, his eyes lighting up

as he reached up to the long wooden shelf that held all of the spices. He took down a rectangular tin canister and placed it on the work bench.

'What is it?' I asked.

'Open it,' he replied, a mischievous look on his face.

I prised open the lid and immediately the scent filled my nostrils. I knew what it was before I saw them. Rows and rows of long black vanilla pods.

'These aren't…' I looked to Manu for confirmation.

He nodded.

'*Vanillao!*'

'I knew it! That cocoa flavour mixed with the vanilla, it's Pierre's secret ingredient.' There was something so intoxicating and comforting about that scent, it was unparalleled. 'But where did you get it?'

'When Hugo and I were speaking, he asked me about the magic hot chocolate you had made for him.'

I blushed on hearing Hugo's name and hid my face behind the lid of the canister, which Madame Moreau duly shut, almost catching my nose.

'It will lose its potency,' she said, carefully placing it back on the shelf.

'Anyway,' Manu continued, 'I told him about the vanillao beans and how we had no more left. So, he made contact with his friend at the vineyard…'

'Jean!' I said.

'*Oui, exactement ça, Jean*. He made some research and found a small grower in Argentina.'

'Argentina,' Madame Moreau repeated, suitably impressed.

'So we can make Moreau's bakery just as it was before,' I said, imagining all of the lives that might change course thanks to Monsieur Moreau's secret ingredient. And then it struck me –the real secret ingredient was the love he'd had for this place, these people. That was what had made it so special and that was the legacy they would all carry on.

Chapter Forty-Two

After several months of banging, drilling and general construction noise, Number 20 opened its doors as Compiègne's newest restaurant. I helped Hugo with a lot of the interior design, choosing colours and accessories. We painted the walls a clean baker's-hat white, and hung large photographic prints of all the Parisian shop fronts he had snapped over the years. It was an eclectic mix of reclaimed tables and wooden chairs painted in bright colours. Although done on a budget, it had a welcoming, modern atmosphere. Hugo received a social innovation grant, so he could hire a full-time chef and manager, then, with Father Bernard's help, they found their first batch of recruits to train as waiting staff and commis chefs, who could gain work experience in a safe environment.

On opening night, we all gathered outside for the unveiling of Number 20's new name. Madame Moreau was chosen for the task, and as she pulled the material from the sign above the door, the name appeared: 'Chez Stéphane'.

'It's beautiful,' I mouthed to Hugo, as the crowd clapped and our eyes locked. It was the perfect tribute to his brother.

'I would like to thank you all for coming here this evening,' Hugo began, standing at the entrance where I had tied a red ribbon for him to cut. Manu had his camera out to film the occasion and I stood, arms linked, with my father, who had travelled over for the occasion. On Dad's other arm was Seraphine Chadwick, smiling proudly at her son.

'Chez Stéphane, as some of you may know, will be a training restaurant for students from all backgrounds. It will be a welcoming space for customers and, I hope, an inclusive space for people to learn, to integrate with the community and, above all, to eat good food!'

We all gave him a large round of applause and cameras flashed as the local media snapped Hugo cutting the ribbon.

'I am so pleased for you both,' Seraphine said, kissing my cheek.

'Oh, this is all Hugo's work,' I said, wondering if perhaps she had forgotten that I worked in the bakery next door.

'Perhaps, but it is you who inspired him and made him believe he could.'

'I think you did that a long time before I came along,' I said, truthfully.

'Maybe, but sometimes you need to throw a pebble into a tranquil pond to make some ripples,' she said rather cryptically, implying that I was the pebble in this scenario.

'Make sure you hang on to this one, *hein*? Hugo?'

Hugo shook off the fact that he was being embarrassed by his mother.

'That's the intention,' he said, linking arms with both of us as we crossed the threshold.

There was a party atmosphere inside and the tables were already dressed, displaying platters of delicate appetisers and glasses of sparkling wine.

In the far left corner, where I had sat with Hugo for dinner all those months ago, was a small plinth doubling as a stage for Johnny's band, who were playing an upbeat version of Glenn Miller's 'In the Mood'. The staff moved efficiently between tables, wearing monogrammed shirts and navy aprons. I could hardly believe that the empty old building had been transformed into something so vibrant and welcoming.

'Where is Hugo, anyway?' Nicole asked, looking hot as ever in a sprayed-on dress in canary yellow.

'I'm not sure, he might be up in his apartment,' I shouted over the music. 'I'll go have a look.' I climbed the back stairs to the top floor where Hugo had converted the attic space into a small apartment. We had joked about knocking through a door to our adjoining ateliers, but Madame Moreau was having none of it. The door was unlocked and when I walked in, I saw him splashing water on his face in the bathroom.

'What are you doing? The party is downstairs, you know,' I said.

'Oh, just taking a moment. It went OK, didn't it?'

I wrapped my arms around his waist and he kissed me, a little longer than was entirely necessary.

'Hugo, you were amazing! Everyone's enjoying themselves, the restaurant looks fantastic and the staff seem really excited. You should be really proud of yourself.'

He smiled that crooked smile I'd fallen in love with all those months ago.

'Not sure if your father likes me,' he said, tucking a stray tendril behind my ear.

'He's my dad, he's not supposed to like you,' I joked.

'I'll get Manu to give him one of your special hot chocolates,' he said, nuzzling my neck.

'Ahem, ahem.'

We both turned to see who it was audibly clearing their throat and saw Dad standing in the open doorway. Hugo instinctively shoved his hands in his pockets, as though we were two teenagers caught kissing behind the bike sheds.

'Eh, you're needed downstairs, lad,' he said and Hugo, glad to have an excuse to leave, practically launched himself out of the doorway.

'You're making him nervous, you know,' I said, giving Dad a scolding look.

'Sure, isn't that my job?' he winked.

'Seriously though, do you like him?' I asked.

'You know, your granddad tried to talk your mother out of marrying me,' he said, linking my arm and walking out into the hallway. 'But you know your mother, once she'd made her mind up about something, there was no changing it.'

I smiled at the memory of her. And just like that, I realised that it was the first time I'd been able to do that. The pain was still there, but it had softened somehow. Just like she said it would.

'What do you think she'd make of all this?' I asked.

'I think you know she'd be the proudest mother in the world, Edie. Just like I'm the proudest dad.'

I gave him a bear hug, the way he used to hug me when I was younger.

'Easy now, I'll need a defibrillator!'

'And to think,' I said to him, as we descended the stairs and saw all of my new friends waiting for us in the restaurant, 'if I'd gone to Paris, I would have missed all of this.'

~

Later that night, I walked with Madame Moreau back to the bakery. Although she leaned heavily on a walking stick, she seemed so much lighter in herself. I took the keys from her and began unlocking the door. I held it open for her, but she didn't move. She looked at me with an unreadable smile on her face.

'What is it?'

'As I said before, I underestimated you, *Édith*.'

I returned her smile.

'I think I underestimated myself!' I leaned against the door for a moment and looked up at the old bakery sign, swaying in the breeze. 'You know, I think we have a lot more in common than I first realised. I think we both needed to put the past to rest before we could move on with our lives. And I think you were stuck, every bit as much as I was.'

Madame Moreau nodded, and at last I realised that just because you get older, it doesn't mean you get wiser. If anything, you become more protective of what little you can control in this life, shutting out all of the possibilities that require you to trust, have faith and let go.

She reached into her pocket and held in her arthritic hands some dried grains of wheat.

'I keep these, always,' she said. 'After my mother was taken, I did not know how to live. Who was I to become, now? Pierre explained to me, holding this grain of wheat between his fingers. "Inside," he said, "it holds the potential to become any number of things." "Like a croissant?" I asked, in my childish voice. "Yes, like a croissant, or a baguette, or an entire meal if you were a little field mouse!"' She smiled. '"Remember," he told me, "you have that same life force inside of you to become anything you want."'

'That's so beautiful,' I said.

'So you see, no matter what happens in life, given the right environment to prove, your life force will rise, *ma chérie*.'

We walked inside and the thought struck me: all along I had believed that I hadn't found the right bakery in Paris, when, in truth, the bakery on Rue de Paris had found me.

Epilogue

And so it was that La Boulangerie et Pâtisserie de Compiègne once again became a place of nourishment, belonging and a certain *je ne sais quoi*. Pierre Moreau felt a gentle sense of pride in what he had created all of those years ago and was now at peace. He knew that his legacy was safe in the hands of Manu, Edith and Hugo.

The cobbled streets now whisper with a new story, a romantic story of a young man who found the courage to embrace the life he truly wanted and a young woman who followed the impulse of her heart and filled the bakery not only with hope, but with friendships that blossomed from the seeds she'd sown.

Life on Rue de Paris had changed for everyone who opened their hearts just wide enough to let it. Mysteries, it would seem, are not so complicated, in the end. The magic ingredient was the enduring power of love all along.

And vanillao beans, of course!

Acknowledgments

In writing *The Mysterious Bakery on Rue de Paris*, I finally married my two great loves: France and pastries!

I owe the genesis of this story to the Irish food writer, Trish Deseine. Years ago, she had a TV series set in France and in one episode, she visited the lesser known areas of culinary Paris. There was a very ordinary looking bakery that produced some of the finest pastries in Paris and for some reason that is now lost to time, no one was ever seen going in or coming out! The idea stayed with me and so the mystery began.

As ever, I want to take the opportunity to thank all of my readers for taking my magical stories into your heart. You've made my dreams come true because now I can write about mysterious bakeries, lost bookshops and missing notes, knowing that I have an audience eager to travel on these journeys with me. To the entire team at One More Chapter and HarperCollins and specifically my editor, Charlotte Ledger – publishing books with you has been one of the best experiences in my life! It's such an exciting imprint to be a part of, where anything feels possible and I'm so fortunate to be working with such talented individuals.

Finally, to my parents, Maureen and PJ, my sister Tracy,

my brother Paul, Siobhan, Dannan, Eabha and Charlotte, thank you all for your love and encouragement. I'll always treasure that time we shared together in Toulouse, many years ago – *formidable!*

**Read on for an extract from Evie Wood's
forthcoming novel, *The Missing Notes*.**

∽

Prelude

♪

London, 2025

On any given day, there are thousands of items slowly
gathering dust in the Lost and Found of Heathrow Airport. A bag
stuffed with £50,000 in five pound notes, a diamond encrusted
Rolex watch, the keys to a Porsche, and two wedding dresses, to
name but a few. The more bizarre include a set of false teeth,
several crutches, and an artificial skull. After 90 days, if the items
are not reclaimed by their owners, they are auctioned off for
charity.

Unbeknownst to anyone, there is one very special box that
holds an item with an ancient provenance. This object can change
the fortunes of those who possess it – sometimes for good,
sometimes for ill, but all on the whims of a young woman whose
heart was betrayed. The object is a violin, one of rare beauty.
Awakening desire in the hearts of musicians for almost 200 years,
her sound is pure and true. All are helpless in their yearning to
possess her, for she imbues a strange and intoxicating power.

Now, as if by chance, she has fallen into the hands of three
unlikely guardians, hopelessly lost and yet connected by a melody
only the violin (or fate?) can unlock. However, just as there are
four strings on a violin, there is a fourth stranger, waiting in the
shadows for their chance to reclaim what once belonged to them.

But we are all bound by the same laws and like the leaf that has fallen from the tree, there are some things you can never get back.

Chapter One

♪

The day had started off so well. Another busy morning at Heathrow, with the sun shining high in the bluest of skies, criss-crossed by the white trails of jetliners carving their way through the atmosphere. Devlin worked as a baggage handler in Terminal 2. He was the right build, or so the interviewer had told him and he took that as a positive. It was around the same time he had met Melissa, who didn't always see his build as a positive. She introduced him to juicing.

When most people thought about airports, they thought about leaving. But Devlin always thought about the people coming home; reuniting with loved ones and feeling that sense of familiarity. He liked working there. It was as far away as he could get from his old life. It was steady, reliable. Like the scheduled flights that arrived and departed on time (for the most part) his days had the kind of boring structure that he could carry out with his eyes closed.

And yet a confluence of two significant events was about to change the course of Devlin's life. Namely his girlfriend's birthday and a recent arrival at the Lost and Found department. Devlin had always thought that there was something a bit lonely about the Lost and Found, a room for unclaimed treasures that washed up like flotsam from discarded lives. He could imagine the passengers setting off with their prized possessions and then for some reason, along the way, being parted from them. Were they forgotten or simply abandoned?

On his morning break with Karim he spotted it. It looked rather inconspicuous in its black case, battered by age and rough handling. The shape was unmistakable however; the gentle curves betraying the contents.

'That's it, it's perfect,' he said, running his hands along the edges of the case.

'Eh, am I missing something here? You planning on a career change, Devlin?'

'Nah mate, it's for Mel.'

'Does she… play the fiddle? She doesn't seem like the musical type.' Karim's wonderfully full eyebrows formed an apex shape, giving him a perplexed look.

'It's a violin, Karim.'

'There's a difference?'

Devlin wasn't entirely sure what the difference was, so he said nothing.

'I thought you got her some perfume from the duty free?'

'Yeah, but this is THE gift. She mentioned it years ago; how she always wanted to play the violin but her parents couldn't afford the classes.'

Judging by the case, this one probably needed a bit of tender loving care, but if he could get it at the right price, he could take it to a repair shop. Or a music store. He really knew very little about violins.

After some lengthy negotiations with Pete, the guy in charge, who insisted that every item had to be kept for three months before it could be sold - 'in case the owner comes back,' he'd explained – Devlin had bought himself a violin. And somehow he just knew it would change everything.

~

The evening took a turn for the worse when the paramedics arrived. After that, the guests had made a hasty escape from the party and Melissa opened a bottle of champagne that Devlin could not recall having bought. In fact, he couldn't remember ever having bought an ice bucket either, but there it sat, on the kitchen counter, floral bouquets reflecting in the gleam. Now *those* he could explain. The multi-coloured arrangement that resembled cuttings from an exotic forest were from James at the salon. The plant was from her mother, practical as ever. The dozen red roses were his own contribution. He had planned on getting thirty; one for every year of her life, but they were all under strict orders to avoid any reference to numerology.

'Do you think we should have brought your Mum to the emergency room?'

'She'll be fine, you know what she's like,' Mel answered dismissively.

He did know. Melissa's mother was often prone to heart palpitations at moments of high drama. *Fit of passion*, her father would say, with a tone of admiration for his wife's Italian roots.

Melissa sat rigidly on the bespoke window seat she and Devlin had built together the summer before. She'd watched a couple build something similar on Instagram and insisted on filming it for her socials. In the end, she had to cut most of it out, as they'd spent the entire time swearing at each other. The whole apartment was an instagrammer's dream: white walls, clean lines and countless framed prints of botanical drawings and motivational quotes. Devlin was surrounded by other peoples' words: *Let your smile change the world, but don't let the world change your smile.* At least that made more sense than the nonsensical advice of *Follow Your Karma!* Surely it was karma's job to follow you?

He liked it though, even if nothing in it belonged to him. The last of his possessions to go was the wicker coffee table he had brought from his old bedsit, replaced by a glass table that always threatened to bruise a leg if approached from the wrong angle. He missed the way his table tended to sag in the middle, as though the wicker was forming a protective hug around whatever items he put on it, including his feet.

Plus, second-hand stuff felt like less of a commitment. *Easy come, easy go* it seemed to say. There was no point clinging on to things. Or people. Melissa called him a drifter and saw it as her personal project to de-drift him. Or un-drift him. They lived in the flat above Melissa's hair salon, Haute Cuture. It had all been part of her master plan since she got her first summer job as a hairdresser. As Francesca's catchphrase went, 'People will always need their hâir cut!' Based on this sound business advice, Melissa built up her empire. He admired her vision, her determination. Everyone did. Her life worked like a well-oiled machine and Devlin understood, not for the first time, that he was the spanner causing the whole thing to malfunction.

'I've never been so embarrassed,' she said, swallowing half a glass of champagne and filling it up again.

'What do you mean?' The violin lay quietly in its case on the gleaming coffee table. She hadn't looked at it since she'd opened it in front of all of their friends and family, letting out a high-pitched shriek.

'Are you really that clueless?'

There were tears now, which she immediately wiped away roughly with the back of her hand. Devlin ran his hands through his hair, as though he might find the answers there. He couldn't understand it; he thought he had outdone himself this time. Really listened to her. He stood halfway between the kitchen and the living room. He knew this because there were different coloured rugs marking out the areas.

'What's wrong, Mel?' He tried to strike a tone somewhere between concern and mystification.

'Look around you; look at what I'm wearing.'

Devlin blinked. He was never any good at cryptic clues. Just as he raised his shoulders helplessly, she got up and waved the back of her hand in his face.

'The manicure? Surely that gives it away.'

He noticed that one of her fingernails was a slightly different colour to the rest and had some sparkly stuff on it.

'Oh for God's sake Devlin, I thought you were going to propose. We all did. It's my 30th!' Her voice cracked when she said her age, the disappointment plainly evident and the blame laid squarely at his feet.

'Mel, I... I...' The words wouldn't come. Because the truth was, he had known. Deep down. He had thought about it every year. Every Valentine's Day, Christmas Day, birthday, equinox. As time marched on, the inevitability of it was beginning to choke him. He challenged himself to come up with ever increasingly thoughtful gifts, over-compensating for the lack of a marriage proposal. He spoke to Karim about it at work. Younger than Devlin, he had been married for five years already. With two kids.

'Do you love her?' he asked during one of their shifts, taking off his protective headphones.

'Of course I love her!' Devlin responded, throwing a bulky suitcase into a luggage bin.

'Then what's the problem? Afraid she'll say no?'

That wasn't it. He'd even got as far as the jewellers on the high street once, spoke to the assistant. But his mouth started to go dry and his heart suddenly started hammering, as if he'd been running a marathon. He began feeling dizzy and when the assistant went to get him a glass of water, he ran out of the shop. It took a good ten minutes for his breathing to return to normal. He wanted to move on with his life. He wanted to settle down; he wanted stability. He wanted kids and he knew that Mel wanted them sooner rather than later. And he wanted to be the one to give her all of that. Yet when the moment came, he bottled it.

His awareness returned to the present, where Melissa was now shouting and gesticulating. Words like 'mortified', 'marriage material' and 'not getting any younger' snagged on his conscience. It was all his fault. He had caused all the upset; or at least that's what she was telling him and he had no defence. How many more times would they go through this routine before she dumped him for good and found someone who *would* marry her? Without breaking her flow, she reached down and took the violin out of its case, shoving it into Devlin's arms.

'I don't even play the bloody violin!'

He held the instrument tentatively, with arms outstretched. For reasons he couldn't quite explain, it felt like he was holding a living, breathing thing. He had only peeked at it earlier, making sure it was actually a violin he had bought and not an empty case. But now he brought it closer to him. It had the deepest amber hue that looked as though you could dive into it and lose yourself forever. It seemed both powerful and yet strangely fragile. Without thinking, he held it protectively to his chest. A peculiar feeling rose from within him, a strange sense of certainty. With this, his mind began to clear. His shoulders straightened. Suddenly, he found the words.

'Last Christmas, we had coffee in that place in Covent Garden, and there were those buskers, remember? And you said you'd always wanted to play the violin.'

Silence descended. A brief respite.

'What?' she asked, cocking her head to the side.

Just as Devlin was about to add more details to the memory – it had been snowing, it was the day before Christmas Eve, they'd gone in to see the lights – Melissa threw her hands up and left the room. The echo of the front door banging confirmed that she had gone out.

Devlin sat down on the sofa and held the violin in front of him, turning it this way and that. It had been a long time since he'd held a musical instrument in his hands. Nine years, four months and seven days, to be precise. It was a day in his life that he couldn't permit himself to think about. Yet now, he felt oddly calm. Relaxed even. The opposite to how he should have felt, given the fact that Mel had just walked out on him.

He let his thumb pluck the first string. The sound it made was unexpectedly rich and golden. It resonated around him like a forcefield. He plucked it again and without thinking, he hummed the note. G. The vibration of sound in his throat was both familiar and strange, opening up a chasm inside of him. The before and after; two parts of him that never communicated. Until now. It felt as though, after years of travelling further and further away from himself and everything he knew to be true, he was finally returning home. A place that had been inside of him all along.

Don't miss the *Sunday Times* bestseller, *The Lost Bookshop!*

On a quiet street in Dublin, a lost bookshop is waiting to be found...

For too long, Opaline, Martha and Henry have been the side characters in their own lives.

But when a vanishing bookshop casts its spell, these three unsuspecting strangers will discover that their own stories are every bit as extraordinary as the ones found in the pages of their beloved books. And by unlocking the secrets of the shelves, they find themselves transported to a world of wonder... where nothing is as it seems.

Available in paperback, eBook and audio!

You may also love *The Story Collector*, an evocative and charming novel full of secrets and mystery!

In a quiet village in Ireland, a mysterious local myth is about to change everything...

One hundred years ago, Anna, a young farm girl, volunteers to help an intriguing American visitor translate fairy stories from Irish to English. But all is not as it seems and Anna soon finds herself at the heart of a mystery that threatens her very way of life.

In New York in the present day, Sarah Harper boards a plane bound for the West Coast of Ireland. But once there, she finds she has unearthed dark secrets – secrets that tread the line between the everyday and the otherworldly, the seen and the unseen.

Available in paperback, eBook and audio!

YOUR NUMBER ONE STOP

ONE MORE CHAPTER

FOR PAGETURNING BOOKS

The author and One More Chapter would like to thank everyone
who contributed to the publication of this story...

Analytics
James Brackin
Abigail Fryer

Audio
Fionnuala Barrett
Ciara Briggs

Contracts
Laura Amos
Laura Evans

Design
Lucy Bennett
Fiona Greenway
Liane Payne
Dean Russell

Digital Sales
Lydia Grainge
Hannah Lismore
Emily Scorer

Editorial
Janet Marie Adkins
Kara Daniel
Charlotte Ledger
Ajebowale Roberts
Jennie Rothwell
Tony Russell
Emily Thomas
Helen Williams

Harper360
Emily Gerbner
Jean Marie Kelly
emma sullivan
Sophia Wilhelm

International Sales
Peter Borcsok
Ruth Burrow
Colleen Simpson

Inventory
Sarah Callaghan
Kirsty Norman

Marketing & Publicity
Chloe Cummings
Grace Edwards
Emma Petfield

Operations
Melissa Okusanya
Hannah Stamp

Production
Denis Manson
Simon Moore
Francesca Tuzzeo

Rights
Helena Font Brillas
Ashton Mucha
Zoe Shine
Aisling Smythe

Trade Marketing
Ben Hurd
Eleanor Slater

**The HarperCollins
Distribution Team**

**The HarperCollins
Finance & Royalties
Team**

**The HarperCollins
Legal Team**

**The HarperCollins
Technology Team**

UK Sales
Isabel Coburn
Jay Cochrane
Sabina Lewis
Holly Martin
Harriet Williams
Leah Woods

eCommerce
Laura Carpenter
Madeline ODonovan
Charlotte Stevens
Christina Storey
Jo Surman
Rachel Ward

**And every other
essential link in the
chain from delivery
drivers to booksellers
to librarians and
beyond!**

ONE MORE CHAPTER

One More Chapter is an
award-winning global
division of HarperCollins.

Subscribe to our newsletter to get our
latest eBook deals and stay up to date
with all our new releases!

<u>signup.harpercollins.co.uk/
join/signup-omc</u>

Meet the team at
<u>www.onemorechapter.com</u>

Follow us!
 @OneMoreChapter_
@onemorechapterhc
@onemorechapterhc
@onemorechapterhc

Do you write unputdownable fiction?
We love to hear from new voices.
Find out how to submit your novel at
<u>www.onemorechapter.com/submissions</u>